APR 2 2 2019

W9-ACO-502

Beware the Court of Owls, that watches all the time.
Ruling Gotham from a shadowed perch, behind granite and lime.
They watch you at your hearth, they watch you at your bed.
Speak not a whispered word of them, or they'll send the Talon for your head!

BATMAN

THE COURT OF OWLS

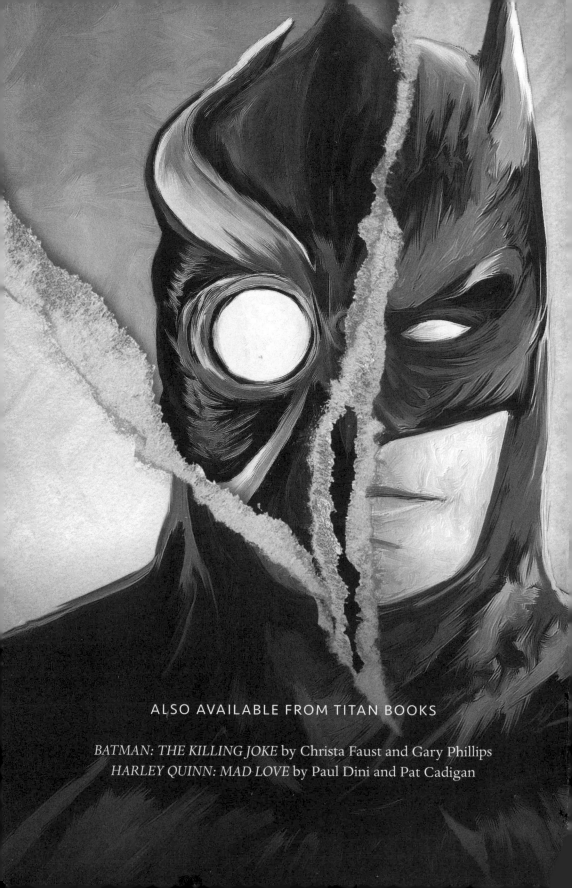

ALSO AVAILABLE FROM TITAN BOOKS

BATMAN: THE KILLING JOKE by Christa Faust and Gary Phillips
HARLEY QUINN: MAD LOVE by Paul Dini and Pat Cadigan

BATMAN

THE COURT OF OWLS

AN ORIGINAL NOVEL BY GREG COX

Batman created by Bob Kane with Bill Finger

TITAN BOOKS

BATMAN: THE COURT OF OWLS
Hardback ISBN: 9781785658167
Ebook ISBN: 9781785658174

Published by Titan Books
A division of Titan Publishing Group Ltd
144 Southwark Street, London SE1 0UP
www.titanbooks.com

First edition: February 2019
10 9 8 7 6 5 4 3 2 1

This is a work of fiction. Names, characters, places, and incidents either are the product of the author's imagination or are used fictitiously, and any resemblance to actual persons, living or dead, business establishments, events, or locales is entirely coincidental. The publisher does not have any control over and does not assume any responsibility for author or third-party websites or their content.

Copyright © 2019 DC Comics.
BATMAN and all related characters and elements © & ™ DC Comics.
WB SHIELD: ™ & © Warner Bros. Entertainment Inc. (s19)

TIBO41795

No part of this publication may be reproduced, stored in a retrieval system, or transmitted, in any form or by any means without the prior written permission of the publisher, nor be otherwise circulated in any form of binding or cover other than that in which it is published and without a similar condition being imposed on the subsequent purchaser.

A CIP catalogue record for this title is available from the British Library.

Designed by Crow Books.

Printed and bound in the United States.

In memory of Audrey Munson
and Evelyn Nesbit

PROLOGUE

Publish or perish.

That harsh imperative brought Professor Herbert Morse back to his book-lined office at Gotham University. After a long day of lectures and meetings, and a quick supper at a campus salad bar, he was hoping to get some serious work done on his upcoming article for the *International Journal of Art History Studies*.

It was, he reflected wryly, one of the paradoxes of his profession that the day-to-day business of teaching often got in the way of serious scholarship. He sighed as he flicked on the lights and shut the office door behind him to guarantee his privacy, even though it was unlikely that anyone would disturb him at this hour.

"Don't move, Professor," an icy voice whispered behind him. "Don't say a word."

Morse froze. All thought of academic pursuits fled his brain, replaced by sheer primal terror. Whatever gray matter remained capable of rational thought raced through various alarming scenarios. A disgruntled student, out to settle a score? A burglar, surprised in the act? The latter struck Morse as unlikely, given the contents of his office—which consisted mostly of books, journals, papers, a beaten-up old desk, and an overworked laptop badly in need of an upgrade.

His office wasn't worth burgling.

Yet this was Gotham, so anything was possible: killer clowns,

1

man-bats, clayfaces, mobsters, serial killers, masked vigilantes. For a moment, Morse allowed himself to hope that it was Batman standing behind him, wanting to question him for some bizarre reason.

I'm no criminal, Morse thought. *Batman poses no danger to me. Does he?*

"Turn around," the voice ordered.

Morse did as instructed. His heart sank as he spied the ominous figure standing between him and the door.

It wasn't Batman.

Black body armor protected the tall, imposing intruder, while an equally dark hood concealed his features. Metal-rimmed goggles with wide, circular lenses and a jagged beak for a nose gave the stranger an eerie, owl-like visage, but even more disturbing was the way he was armed to the hilt. A black-leather bandolier slung diagonally across his chest held at least a half-dozen gleaming metal throwing knives, and another blade was sheathed at his hip. Two scabbards crossed each other atop his back, forming an X with the hilts of twin swords visible above his shoulders. Steel gauntlets ended in threatening steel claws that resembled the talons of a predatory bird.

Who? Morse wondered. He didn't recognize the intruder from the nightly news or the city papers. Like many Gothamites, he preferred not to dwell on the various homicidal maniacs who seemed to escape from Arkham Asylum on a regular basis, but one couldn't live in Gotham for as long as Morse had without acquiring a working knowledge of the city's most infamous public menaces. Morse could tell the Joker from the Riddler—although he'd been lucky enough to keep that knowledge, well, academic up until the present.

He had no idea who this particular costumed grotesque was, or what he wanted. Just that the armed stranger radiated menace.

"Sit," the intruder said, indicating the chair that faced the desk.

Instantly Morse dropped into the chair, which was customarily occupied by his visitors during office hours.

Sitting in the wrong chair only added to his unease, as though his own sanctuary no longer belonged to him. He contemplated the looming stranger, and began to tremble. His mouth felt as dry as a dusty Grecian urn. His limbs were rubbery. He was acutely aware of just how empty the building was at this time of night and yet how unlikely it was that campus security would take note of his office lights burning after hours.

"Please," he whimpered. "Just tell me what you want."

"Answers." The avian mask concealed the man's expression, but not his sardonic tone. "We're going to have a conversation... about art and history."

Morse blinked in surprise. "This is about my work?"

A dry chuckle escaped the mask.

"*Your* work? Not exactly."

Morse didn't understand. The intruder's cryptic responses scraped away at what was left of his nerves.

"Please, no games." Tears streaked the professor's cheeks. A framed photo of his family, resting on his desk, reminded Morse just how much he had to lose. "Ask me anything. I'll tell you whatever you want to know."

"Yes, you will." The intruder drew one of the knives from his bandolier. "Eventually."

1

"You can come in now," Commissioner James Gordon said to the seemingly empty office. "The coast is clear."

Batman entered the professor's office through an open fourth-story window. His matte-black suit, cape, and cowl blended with the night outside, much as the winged sigil emblazoned on his chest matched the Bat-Signal currently shining above Gotham, summoning him from his nightly patrol. A soaked carpet squelched beneath his boots as he joined Gordon in the office—which appeared to be a crime scene, as well. He scanned the room.

A fluorescent light flickered overhead.

The charred remains of what was presumably Professor Herbert Morse slumped in a fire-damaged wooden chair facing his desk. The ceiling was blackened directly above the corpse, while scorch marks spread outward from the body. The building's sprinkler system had drenched the room, leaving water pooling on every surface. Any lingering smoke had dispersed, but a disturbing odor hung in the air.

Batman scowled. The smell of burnt human flesh was, unfortunately, all too familiar to him.

"The fire department completed their preliminary inspection and pronounced the scene safe to enter," Gordon said. His rumpled trench coat was buckled against the brisk autumn breeze blowing in through the window. His weathered features bore a stoic expression. A pair of glasses reflected the overhead lights as he took in the grisly tableau. Like Batman, the veteran cop had seen more than his share of horrors. "I have a full forensics team waiting for me to give them the green light, but I assumed you'd want to look things over first." He glanced at his wristwatch. "I can give you ten minutes, more if absolutely necessary."

"Thanks," Batman replied. "I came as soon as I saw the signal." He had been patrolling the Narrows when he'd spotted the beacon in the sky. A quick scan of police communications had let him know where to find Gordon.

Surveying the office, he regretted that the firefighters had intruded upon the scene before he could examine it thoroughly, but he understood the protocol. The fire marshal had to verify that the flames were out and deem the premises structurally secure before the GCPD could get to work. At least the sprinklers had been turned off, Batman noted—hopefully before the spray washed away too much valuable evidence.

He tilted his head back to inspect the blackened portion of the ceiling directly above the dead man's head. The sprinklers had put out the blaze before it could spread too far from the burning body.

Completing his initial scan of the office, he turned his full attention to the body in the chair. The head appeared more badly burned than the rest of the body, leaving the face a blackened ruin so that the victim's features resisted easy identification. Dental records likely would be required to confirm that the dead man was indeed Herbert Morse.

"He wasn't caught in the fire," Batman said. "The fire started with him."

Gordon nodded in agreement. "That's why I fired up the Signal. This was no accident."

Leaning in, Batman sniffed the remains. "No obvious smell of accelerant." Pulling a portable vapor trace analyzer from his belt, he confirmed that no suspicious fumes lingered in the air. Melted glass on the man's wristwatch indicated that the fire had reached a temperature of at least 1,500 degrees Fahrenheit. Not enough to reduce the body to ash in the time that had elapsed, but hot enough to burn off most of the victim's clothing and blacken the remains from head to toe.

What could cause the fire to burn so hot and so fast? he wondered. *And…*

"The question is," Gordon said, "was he dead before or after he was set on fire?" The detective contemplated the corpse while keeping out of Batman's way. "Can't imagine he'd just sit still while he was burning alive."

"Unless he was restrained." Batman inspected the dead man's hands and wrists, which were still resting on the chair's armrests. Ordinarily a burning body would curl into a fetal position as the cooked muscles contracted, so the fact that Morse remained seated in his chair merited a closer look. A low grunt escaped Batman's lips as he made a gruesome discovery, which the charred flesh had obscured until now. He crouched lower to examine the man's feet, then straightened again.

"Look here, Jim," he said, pointing. "Morse's hands were nailed to the chair and his feet were nailed to the legs. He wasn't going anywhere, no matter how much pain he was in."

"Good Lord," Gordon said, shaking his head. He came forward to see the charred nail heads. They were driven deep into the tops of Morse's bare hands and what was left of his shoes. Fragments of burnt flesh made them difficult to spot. "The poor bastard. That's an ugly way to go, even by Gotham standards."

"Yes," Batman agreed. He studied the surface of the wooden chair, noting that it had blistered in a pattern resembling alligator scales—another indicator of the extreme heat coming from the burning body. It would take an autopsy to tell for certain whether Morse had died before or after going up in flames, but Batman feared that the professor had suffered badly either way.

Closer inspection revealed what appeared to be dozens of small incisions and puncture wounds in the carbonized epidermis, indicating that the victim had been stabbed repeatedly before burning. It was difficult to determine without a full medical examination, but Batman estimated that there were at least fifty such wounds. Despite that fact, there was no indication that blood had sprayed in the area around the victim.

"From what I can tell, Morse was tortured first, then set ablaze."

"Jesus," Gordon murmured. "Who would do that—and to a college professor, of all people?"

Good question, Batman thought. There was something about the killing that bothered him for reasons beyond the obvious. Something both familiar and troubling. *More than fifty knife wounds...*

"The door was locked from the inside," Gordon said. "The firefighters had to break it down to gain access."

Batman moved to the entrance. The splintered remains of the door were propped up against the frame. Continuing a circuit of the room, he began a more focused examination of the surroundings. Waterlogged books and papers rested atop the professor's desk, too heavy to be blown about by the breeze coming in through the window.

"Was the window open when the firefighters arrived?" Batman asked.

Gordon consulted his notepad. "I believe so. Why?"

"Maybe I'm not the only one who preferred the window to the door." He crossed to the sill and activated the UV lenses in his cowl. They detected minute traces of blood on the outside of the window. Heedless of the drop, he climbed out onto the ledge and scanned the red-brick exterior. Additional splotches of blood—most likely belonging to Morse—could be spotted between the top of the window and the roof. Batman also spied what appeared to be fresh gouges in the brickwork, as though somebody had clawed their way up the side of the building after dealing with Morse. Somebody with blood on their hands.

Or claws.

"Morse's visitor left this way," Batman said, rejoining Gordon in the office. "Escaping via the roof, probably while Morse was still burning."

"But after he was tortured," Gordon said.

Batman nodded, and a theory began to take shape. Morse had been stabbed repeatedly by somebody who knew what they were doing, and the lack of blood splatter suggested that the assailant had carefully avoided any major arteries while torturing— interrogating?—Morse. The fire was new, but Batman had seen this technique before. Indeed, his own great-great-grandfather had endured a very similar ordeal, nearly a century ago…

Careful, he warned himself. *Don't jump to conclusions.*

"What is it?" Gordon asked.

"Too soon to say," Batman said. *But I hope to God I'm wrong.* The key lay in determining the killer's motive. Had Morse been tortured for information?

Stepping over to the desk, Batman conducted a quick sweep of Morse's papers and files. The soaked documents on the desk seemed innocuous enough: print-outs of administrative memos and announcements, class calendars, lesson plans, and such. Inked notes bled onto a soggy yellow legal pad, but held nothing that would warrant burning someone alive. The contents of the desk drawers were unremarkable, as well, and there weren't any conspicuous gaps in Morse's library, which held the sort of volumes appropriate to an art historian's bookshelves.

One thing was missing, however.

There was a printer, but no computer in sight. Nor was there the distinctive smell of burnt circuitry.

"Did Morse have a laptop?" he asked.

Gordon checked his notes again. "Nothing reported found by

the firefighters. You think the intruder made off with it?"

"Possibly." If Morse had planned to work late, he would have needed something on which to do so.

A row of low wooden file cabinets lined an interior wall. Each drawer had a lock on it, but they pulled open easily enough, exposing hanging files crammed with overstuffed folders. Switching the lenses in his cowl to magnify, Batman knelt to examine the locks. Almost invisible scratch marks indicated that the locks might have been picked by an expert looking for... what?

Most of the drawers were crammed to capacity, but one of them showed some extra space between two hanging files, as though a folder or two had gone missing. Leafing through the surrounding files, Batman quickly determined that they contained work by and evaluations of various graduate students being mentored by Morse. The files were in alphabetical order by the students' names.

The gap occurred somewhere between "K" and "N."

"Find anything?" Gordon peered over his shoulder.

"I can't be sure, but it looks as if the intruder may have rifled through Morse's student files—and absconded with some of them."

"You think this might have something to do with one of his students?"

"I'm not ruling anything out," Batman replied. "But the torture, the missing laptop, the files... everything indicates that the intruder was after information."

"From an art history professor?" Gordon scratched his head. "I still don't get it."

Gordon's confusion was well-founded. Although no place in Gotham was truly safe from crime, the university wasn't one of Batman's usual hunting grounds. The science labs occasionally attracted burglars intent on taking valuable equipment, but in his experience there had never before been a murder in the Arts Buildings. Academia was seldom cutthroat enough to warrant his attention.

What had Morse known—or been suspected to know—that had cost him his life? Batman made a mental note to thoroughly review Morse's publications, classes, syllabi, and curriculums. The more he knew about the professor's work, the more likely he could deduce why Morse had been targeted.

"How much more time to do you need?" Gordon shifted his weight restlessly. "Not to rush you, but…"

"I'm almost done here." Batman's cape swept the floor as he turned away from the file cabinets to take one last look at the baked corpse on the chair. Not for the first time, he wished he could conduct the autopsy himself, but he knew Gordon would provide him with the medical examiner's report before long. There was just one more thing he had to do, to address the dreadful suspicion lurking at the back of his mind.

"I'm going to need a tissue sample," he said. "I wouldn't ask if it wasn't important."

"Do what you have to."

Gordon turned his back for the sake of plausible deniability. Batman removed a razor-sharp scalpel from his belt. Carefully scraping a few centimeters of burned tissue from Morse's unnaturally flexed forearm, he deposited the sample in a compartment in his left gauntlet. There was a test he urgently needed to conduct, if only for his own peace of mind.

"Done."

Gordon turned to face him. His shrewd eyes narrowed behind his glasses.

"You look to me like a man with a theory," he said. "You have any idea who's behind this?"

Batman couldn't voice his concerns—not just yet.

"I hope not, Jim," he replied. "I really do."

2

The Batcave had undergone numerous expansions and renovations since he had first selected it as his base of operations. State-of-the-art computers, a garage of specialized vehicles, a machine shop, crime lab, and trophy room occupied several levels of the vast cavern, all connected by sturdy ramps, stairs, and walkways. A sleek black hydrofoil was docked at the shore of a subterranean lake in one of the lower grottos, while hanging stalactites preserved some of the primeval ambience of the natural cavern onto which young Bruce Wayne had first stumbled as a child.

Bats skittered as they returned to their roosts in the upper reaches of the cave, carefully segregated from the more delicate electronics. Despite Alfred Pennyworth's occasional complaints about the unruly wildlife, Batman was determined not to evict them from their home. They'd been here first, after all, and had served as his inspiration from the very beginning of his crusade. He owed them too much to displace them.

Owls, on the other hand…

"It's nearly dawn, sir," Alfred observed. He was tall and lean, impeccable in both his dress and manners. A pencil mustache complimented his apparently timeless features, and he often seemed as much a fixture as the very walls of the manor house above. "Your winged namesakes are retiring for the day. Perhaps you should consider doing the same?"

The butler looked on as Batman sat before an array of sophisticated monitors in the cave's nerve center. Holographic screens responded to his touch, allowing him to manipulate data more efficiently than a physical keyboard would. Although there was no present need to conceal his identity, Batman kept his cowl on. In the back of his mind, he couldn't truly let his guard down until he confirmed or debunked the dire suspicions preying on his mind. There could be no sleep until he knew the truth, one way or another.

They watch you at your hearth,
They watch you at your bed...

Batman checked on the status of the tissue sample he'd procured at Morse's office. The sample was undergoing a comprehensive spectrographic analysis—one that he had customized to search for a very specific substance. The time-consuming procedure tried his patience; there were quicker tests, but they were less reliable, and he had to be *certain* of the results.

The progress bar on the screen crept forward at a steady, methodical pace that chafed at his usual stoicism. He wanted answers and he wanted them now.

An electronic chime signaled that Gordon had news.

"Finally." Batman reached out to tap the screen.

In the early days of his crusade he'd had to sneak through air ducts to visit the city morgue, but that was before he'd wired the morgue for remote surveillance. He opened a new window on the central monitor and Jim Gordon peered at him with a slightly quizzical expression on his face. The sterile interior of the facility could be seen behind the commissioner.

Morse's carbonized remains were stretched out on a stainless-steel examination table beneath the harsh illumination. Sutures sealed the Y-shaped incision on the body's torso. His blackened skullcap had been put back into place, although it was doubtful that there would be any public viewing of the remains. A closed-casket funeral—or possibly cremation—awaited the deceased.

"Are you there?" the cop asked. The visual transmission was strictly one-way. "Are you reading me?"

"Loud and clear." Gordon appeared to have the morgue to himself. They had this drill down to a science by now, although Batman winced as he recalled the very first homicide on which he had tested the remote-viewing system. He prayed that history wasn't repeating itself. "What do you have for me?"

"As we expected, dental records confirm the victim is Herbert Morse," Gordon reported. "His family has already been notified of the discovery, of course, but I'll need to call them back just to eliminate any doubt… or false hope."

Batman didn't envy Gordon that sad duty, but trusted him to treat Morse's loved ones with compassion and empathy—just as a much younger Lieutenant Gordon had attempted to console Bruce Wayne on the worst night of the young boy's life. There hadn't been many decent cops in Gotham back in those days, but Jim Gordon had been one of them.

"I spared Morse's wife all the grisly details, at least for now," Gordon added. "She had no idea why anyone would want to hurt her husband, not that wives always know everything."

Batman doubted this case involved anything as prosaic as a cheating husband.

"What else did the medical examiner turn up?"

"That Morse was indeed alive when he burned to death. His white blood cell count and the quantity of proteins in the blisters indicate that his flesh and blood were attempting to combat the damage, as opposed to already being inert." Gordon grimaced at the picture that data painted. "But here's where it gets weird. According to the ME, Morse was burned from the *inside, out*. His internal organs were baked much more severely than the outer skin and tissues."

"I see."

Batman raised an eyebrow. What Gordon was describing was far from ordinary. Most often, even the most badly charred bodies were comparatively undamaged internally. He had no reason to doubt the ME's findings, but wanted to verify them.

"Spontaneous combustion?" Gordon suggested.

"Possibly." Batman's brain raced. Some kind of exotic microwave weapon, perhaps, or a chemical compound that triggered an exothermic reaction when taken internally. Any number of theories came to mind, demanding further investigation. He recalled that Morse's head had appeared more badly burned than the rest of the body. "What about his brain?"

"You're getting warmer, no pun intended." Gordon grimaced at his own remark. "The brain was charcoal—almost incinerated, as though the fire started inside the victim's skull, then spread through his body like a fever. The examiner said she'd never seen anything like it. If it wasn't for the nails and the knife wounds, she'd have been tempted to notify the CDC."

Like a fever, Batman thought. He filed the observation away in case it proved relevant later. "What *about* the knife wounds?"

"You called it," Gordon said. "Despite the fire damage, the skin and bones were still relatively intact. The ME located at least fifty-three separate stab wounds, none of which would have been immediately fatal. He was tortured, all right... in a way we've seen before."

So Gordon recognized the MO too. No surprise there. Gordon was Police Commissioner for a reason. He was a good detective— with a good memory.

"You think it's them?" Gordon asked. "The Owls?"

"Just a theory," Batman said, as much to himself as to his ally. It pained him to even concede the possibility. *If only I could dismiss it out of hand.*

It had begun months ago, with the mutilated body of a John Doe who had been crucified against the wall of his dingy apartment.

He, too, had been repeatedly and expertly stabbed by someone skilled enough to avoid any arteries or major organs. The killer had turned out to be a "Talon," a master assassin employed by the Court of Owls, an insidious secret society that Batman had once regarded as nothing more than an urban legend—until he was forced to accept the fact that the Court had lurked in Gotham's shadows even longer than he had.

His own family had been touched by their covert machinations. Nearly a hundred years ago his great-great-grandfather had died at the hands of a Talon. His bones, exhumed at Bruce Wayne's request, were found to have been punctured almost fifty times.

Not unlike what was done to Herbert Morse.

"Let's not get ahead of ourselves," he told Gordon. His gaze darted to the progress bar that was charting the tissue analysis. A flashing icon informed him that the results were ready for his inspection. Batman decided he'd learned all he could from Gordon for the moment. There would be time enough later to download and review the full autopsy report. "Thanks for the information," he said. "I'll be in touch."

Cutting off the transmission, he knew Gordon wouldn't take offense at his abrupt exit. Small talk had never been essential to their partnership, and beyond that, he wasn't ready to talk about the Court of Owls. Not just yet, not before he saw the test results.

The test was for electrum, a highly conductive alloy composed of silver and copper. It had been prized for its unique qualities as far back as ancient Egyptian times. Electrum was also favored by the Court of Owls, who employed it in their weapons as well as their arcane elixirs, their emblems, and tokens. Because of this predilection, Batman had developed a means to test for even the tiniest traces of electrum in organic and inorganic samples, no matter how damaged or degraded. If electrum played any part in Morse's mysterious incineration, the test would tell him.

The answer was only a command away, yet he paused before

17

calling up the results. Such hesitation was uncharacteristic of him. He believed in facing facts head on, not indulging in denial. Yet this hypothesis was… different. More personal.

"Master Bruce?" Alfred prompted him. Engrossed in the details of Morse's death, and fearful of their implications, Batman had almost forgotten the butler's presence.

"Just taking a moment, Alfred."

"I quite understand, sir."

But stalling wasn't going to solve Morse's murder, or allay Batman's fears. Overcoming his reluctance, he called up the results. The answer appeared on the screen in glowing green letters.

PRESENCE OF ELECTRUM:
CONFIRMED

The temperature in the cave seemed to drop abruptly. There was no denying it anymore.

It's them, Batman realized, and on instinct the rhyme leapt to mind.

> Beware the Court of Owls
> That watches all the time.
> Ruling Gotham from a shadowed perch
> Behind granite and lime.
> They watch you at your hearth,
> They watch you at your bed;
> Speak not a whispered word of them,
> Or they'll send the Talon for your head!

The anonymous sing-song had been part of Gotham's lore for as long as anybody could remember, sending shivers of delicious fear through generations of the city's children. But the reality behind the rhyme was even more sinister.

The Court of Owls was a ruthless conspiracy of the rich and powerful, which had long operated from the shadows to shape Gotham's very structure, accruing ever more wealth and influence with each passing decade. The Court had eyes and ears everywhere, as Batman had discovered the hard way, and highly trained Talons to dispose of their enemies. Herbert Morse hadn't literally lost his head, as in the rhyme, but there could be no doubt who was responsible for the professor's ghastly demise.

Batman recalled the claw marks on the outside of the Arts Building, leading up to the roof.

No, he corrected himself. *Not claws.*

Talons.

He took no satisfaction in his discovery. To the contrary, his heart sank at the damning test results. His history with the Court was more than just personal—they troubled him in a way few of his other foes could manage.

As both Batman *and* Bruce Wayne, he had always thought of Gotham as "his" city. His family's long tradition of civic duty meant that the history of Gotham and the Wayne bloodline were inextricably bound together, for better or for worse. Gotham was his legacy, its welfare his responsibility, so discovering that the Court of Owls had been pulling the strings all along, right beneath his nose, had shaken him deeply, particularly after he had uncovered the Owls' ancient vendetta against the Wayne family.

The Waynes had been among the founders of Gotham. They had made their fortune and had always given back to the city as philanthropists, reformers, and patrons of the arts. Seeking to improve the lives of everyone, both rich and poor, their efforts had been tireless. Gotham's very skyline had been crafted by the late Alan Wayne, one of the foremost architects of his day, before the Court of Owls sentenced him to death back in 1922.

Batman had only recently discovered the long-buried truth behind his great-great-grandfather's "accidental" death. Not only had Alan been killed by a Talon, he'd been kidnapped and driven to the point of madness in an underground labyrinth hidden within Gotham's very foundations.

He suppressed a shudder. He knew exactly what Alan Wayne had endured decades ago. Like his doomed ancestor, Batman had spent more than a week trapped in the same labyrinth. He had been starved, drugged, and physically and psychologically abused before he had finally done what no other man or woman had done before—found a way out of the maze. Yet he had not escaped unscathed.

That had been months ago, but he would be lying to himself if he pretended that he had put the ordeal entirely behind him. Owls were the natural predators of bats, and the Court had come closer to breaking him than any maniac or mobster. They had even launched a direct assault on Wayne Manor and the Batcave, although Batman and his allies had managed to repel it. They took the fight back to the Court, thwarting their attempt to seize total control of the city.

The Owls had been laying low ever since, but he had always known that they would creep from their hidden nests once more. They had been the secret lords and ladies of Gotham for generations. They weren't going to surrender their grip on the city after just a few temporary reverses.

"Damn it," Batman muttered. "Damn *them*."

"If only it were that easy." Alfred peered over his shoulder. He knew full well what the test results signified. "But true justice seldom is."

Batman turned and found the butler's expression notably somber. The two men shared a common antipathy toward the Court of Owls. Although they had never confirmed it, there was good reason to suspect that the Court had been behind the death of Alfred's father, Jarvis Pennyworth, as well. Batman's frown deepened. At times it seemed as if the Owls had infested every part of their lives, past and present, without him ever knowing.

"If I may ask, sir," Alfred said gravely, "what are you going to do now?"

Batman already knew the answer to that question, owls or no owls.

"My job."

3

After a few hours of restless sleep, interrupted by nightmares that could not be dispelled by even the most reliable lucid-dreaming techniques, Bruce Wayne got down to work, making a determined effort to push his personal apprehensions aside.

Bruce was dressed casually in everyday attire as he resumed his place at the cave's nerve center. He sipped absent-mindedly at a high-energy protein drink Alfred had pressed upon him, his face lit by the glow of the computer screens and the floating holographic control panels. Even without a cowl, his celebrated good looks wore a mask of intense concentration.

Approach this like any other homicide, he thought. *Who, what, why, and how.*

He already had a pretty good idea who had sentenced Herbert Morse to death, and who had carried out the killing, but what about the "why?" The Court of Owls was relentless when it came to guarding their secrets. Had Morse stumbled onto something the Court did not want unearthed?

An advanced search engine of his own design turned up links to Morse's most recent publications and lectures, most of which reflected a focus on the influence of Themiscyrian iconography on post-War depictions of classical themes. A quick review of the material found nothing the Court of Owls might want to keep under wraps. At first glance, Morse's work hardly warranted a visit from a Talon.

But what about his students' work?

Bruce recalled the files in Morse's office. Fortunately, the Wayne Foundation had paid to upgrade the university's computer servers and networks, which meant he had a private backdoor into the systems.

Always suspected that would come in handy, he thought. "Computer, call up all Gotham University students currently enrolled in classes taught by Professor Herbert Morse, deceased."

The computer responded to his voiced command. "Running..."

It was possible, of course, that the murder involved a former student, but Bruce had to start somewhere. He could always expand the search later, if necessary. As it was, a daunting list of names scrolled down the central screen. Running a cross-reference, he didn't identify any names known to be associated with the Court of Owls, either as victims or heirs to the Court's sinister legacy. He looked for a way to narrow the parameters.

"Highlight surnames beginning with letters K through N."

"Running."

The list shortened to a more workable number.

"That's more like it," he said. "Cross-reference selected names against campus security and medical records for the last six months."

"Running."

Bruce wasn't aware of any recent suspicious deaths at the university, let alone any art history majors who had spontaneously combusted, but perhaps some warning signs had been overlooked. The Court of Owls and their assassins were nothing if not devious. Alan Wayne's death had been considered "accidental" for generations, while the increasingly paranoid behavior he had exhibited in the weeks leading up to his demise had been chalked up to encroaching senility.

Perhaps something had foreshadowed Morse's assassination.

The requested data scrolled before his eyes. Reports of drunk and disorderly behavior by hard-partying college students, an ugly hazing incident at a fraternity house, a restraining order taken out by a student against an obsessed ex-boyfriend, an apparently well-founded accusation of plagiarism, and... a missing-person report filed only two days ago by the student's roommate.

The missing student's name popped out at him.

LEE, JOANNA

It took him only a moment to recognize the name. "Joanna?"

Several Years Ago

The First Friday Community Street Fair was supposed to be a festive event drawing crowds to the shops and galleries and restaurants in Old Gotham. Fourth Avenue had been closed to traffic for six blocks so that pedestrians could stroll freely down the street, which was lined with food carts, street vendors, arts and crafts booths, and tables promoting various civic organizations and charities. Live music was provided by local bands performing on temporary stages at opposite ends of the blocked-off stretch, while the weather had cooperated by providing a warm summer evening without a cloud in the sky. Throngs had flocked to the fair in search of fun, food, and excitement, which Gotham was serving up in spades.

Until two rival street gangs—the Deacons and the Speed Demonz—decided to settle some old scores, turning the fair into a battlefield and potential bloodbath. Pandemonium erupted as terrified citizens fled for their lives, practically trampling over each other in the desperate rush to flee the gunfire. Cops on hand to maintain order at the fair suddenly found themselves in the middle of a full-fledged firefight and outnumbered two to one.

Music was replaced by the blaring guns, screams, shouting, and the frantic cries of the wounded. The Bat-Signal appeared in the night sky, calling out for assistance.

Soon the Batwing jetted over the city, its stealth-black wings slicing through the muggy air as Batman monitored the ongoing emergency by means of live TV coverage and police radio transmissions. SWAT teams and riot police were en route to the scene, under the direction of Gotham's Major Crimes Unit, but the Batwing was way ahead of them. Every minute counted when innocent lives were at stake.

The sleek customized aircraft came in low over the avenue, which was wide enough to allow the plane to cruise down the middle of the street. The firefight was still going strong. Shooters fired from behind food trucks, hot-dog stands, and doorways. Stray bullets perforated a dunk tank, spilling gallons of tepid water onto the pavement. Bodies—some moving, some not—littered the street. Gang members made up the majority of the casualties, but there were innocent civilians among them, collateral damage.

Bad blood had been building between the Deacons and the Demonz for weeks, Batman knew. It was just Gotham's luck that all-out warfare had broken out at the worst possible time and place.

The Batwing's arrival drew heavy fire from both sides. Ammo bounced off the plane's reinforced armor plating and bulletproof windshield. Cameras and sensors supplied Batman with a variety of views and tactical displays. Although he growled at every bleeding body sprawled upon the pavement, he was relieved to see that street and sidewalks were clearing out as the panicked innocents sought safety elsewhere but Fourth Avenue.

Aside from the dead and injured, the crowds were dispersing rapidly, abandoning the street fair to the armed combatants who had callously turned it into a killing field. Batman gladly drew the shooters' fire. With any luck, the surviving fairgoers would be well clear of the scene before Gordon's soldiers arrived to engage with the feuding gangbangers.

That's it! Run! he silently urged the frightened masses. *This is no place for civilians—not tonight, at least.*

Then he spotted her: a teenage girl kneeling beside the apparently lifeless bodies of an adult man and woman who Batman assumed to be her parents. Telescopic lenses zoomed in on her, magnifying her image on a monitor in the cockpit of the Batwing. She sobbed convulsively, heedless of the overlapping pools of blood spreading from the unmoving fatalities. She held tightly to her mother's hand, unable or unwilling to leave. Unlike the other fairgoers, she appeared too shell-shocked to seek safety for herself.

The tragic tableau, painfully reminiscent of a long-ago night in Crime Alley, jabbed Batman in the heart, but he couldn't afford to relive his own past sorrows. Not while the teen remained oblivious to the danger. It was a miracle she hadn't yet been caught in the crossfire, and she needed to be extracted from the kill zone immediately. He couldn't even take the time to land the Batwing.

Scanning the area, he spotted an old-fashioned carnival photo booth across the street from her, tucked between a cotton candy stand and a voter registration table. Sudden inspiration hit him.

That could work.

The Batwing executed an aerial loop that brought it back and over the imperiled teen. Batman switched the plane to VTOL mode so it hovered in place above the photo booth. Its exterior walls were already riddled with bullet holes, stressing the urgency of the situation. The plane's dramatic entrance penetrated the fog of grief enveloping the girl. She looked up in surprise. Dyed purple hair framed her ashen face. In a bitter irony a helium balloon, tied to her wrist, had survived the gunfire that had claimed the teen's parents.

A loudspeaker amplified Batman's voice.

"**Girl with the balloon, get to the photo booth!**"

A random bullet hit the balloon, which popped loudly a few inches from her face. She jumped, suddenly grasping the jeopardy she was in. Then she hunkered down, as though afraid to move. Looking across the street she saw the booth, only a few yards away, but she hesitated, frozen in fear.

"**Go! I'll cover you!**"

The Batwing rotated above the booth. As promised, Batman opened fire with a hail of rubber bullets that would discourage any shooters in the vicinity. The protective fusillade spurred the teen to action. Jumping to her feet, she dashed for the questionable shelter, diving into the compartment.

Good girl.

The flimsy portable structure offered little or no protection from gunfire, but that wasn't the idea. Keeping up the barrage of rubber bullets, Batman released a grapnel hook and cable from the rear of the Batwing. The magnetic hook latched onto the framework of the booth's ceiling.

"**Hang on for your life!**"

An infrared scan confirmed that the parents' bodies were cooling too fast to have any life left in them. Sadly convinced that they were past saving, Batman opened the throttle on the Batwing, which moved vertically into the sky, taking the booth with it. Even with the enclosed teen, the weight of the booth posed no difficulty for the aircraft's powerful turbine engines or the sturdy metal cable, which had in the past proved capable of transporting everything from the Batmobile to a parade float packed with plastic explosives, courtesy of the Joker.

"**Hold on,**" Batman assured his passenger. "**We're getting out of here.**"

From dozens of feet above ground level, he saw Gordon's forces closing in on Fourth Avenue. Realizing they were under siege, the gangbangers began to disperse, heading straight into the waiting arms of the GCPD. Batman fired a volley of tear-gas grenades after them, just to make Gordon's job easier, before departing with the rescued teen literally in tow.

If any shooters eluded Gordon's net… well, Batman would see that they didn't stay at large for long. Those guilty of tonight's massacre could expect a late-night visit in the near future, followed by a long stint in Blackgate Penitentiary.

Minutes later, blocks away from the carnage, he carefully lowered the captured booth into the middle of a rooftop restaurant in a classy part of town. He watched with grim satisfaction as the girl stumbled unsteadily out of the booth and onto the roof. Startled patrons and servers hurried to help her.

Good, Batman thought. *I may have been too late to save the parents, but at least their child is safe.*

Her name, he would later learn, was Joanna Lee.

•

"Joanna Lee," Alfred said. The butler retrieved the empty shake container as he appeared at Bruce's side in the cave. He was almost as good as his employer at slipping quietly in and out of places. "I remember her."

"I'm not surprised," Bruce replied. In the years since her parents' death, the Wayne Foundation had quietly looked after her, along with many other crime victims. "I met her again not too long ago, when the Foundation awarded her a full scholarship. It was at a ceremony at the Manor. I was impressed by her passion for Gotham's architecture and history, despite what the city had taken from her."

"A very bright and resilient young woman, as I recall." Alfred lingered within the nerve center. "You fear something has become of her?"

"I hope not." Bruce's expression darkened. Guilt heightened his concern for Joanna's safety. "Damn it, why am I just now discovering that she's missing?"

"You mustn't castigate yourself, Master Bruce. You're not omniscient."

"That's not good enough." Bruce shook his head. "I should have known."

"Need I remind you, sir, that you have been occupied with matters most urgent? You only just returned from that hostage crisis in Corto Maltese, and then there are your duties to the League. With all due respect, even Batman cannot be everywhere at once."

As much as he appreciated the butler's attempts to ease his conscience, Bruce still held himself responsible. He called up an image of Joanna—the one that appeared on her student ID card. Henna-colored red hair, bobbed and banged, gave her a chic, bohemian look, as did a U-shaped metal nose ring. Chestnut eyes, alive with intelligence, peered out from behind a pair of black cat's-eye glasses. It was, indeed, the promising young student he had honored at the mansion not long ago.

Now she was missing—had been since *before* the professor's murder.

But *why*?

"A lovely young lady," Alfred observed. "There's something strangely familiar about her features, almost as though I've known her for decades."

"I know what you mean," Bruce said. "She reminds me of someone, as well, although I can't quite place it. I remember thinking as much the last time we met." More than that, however, he was troubled by the idea that the dark skeleton in Gotham's closet—the Court of Owls—had claimed Joanna when he wasn't looking. He had saved her once. He wasn't about to let anything happen to her now.

Unless he was already too late.

4

Joanna and her roommate, Claire Nesko, shared a top-floor apartment in the University District. A block of red-brick row houses, converted into off-campus student housing, faced a tree-lined avenue that was far too public. He intended to question Nesko about Joanna's disappearance, but preferred to do so discreetly, out of the glare of public scrutiny. Bats hunted best under the cover of night.

As do Owls…

The sun had long since set as Batman approached the house via an unlit back alley. The Batmobile was parked nearby in one of many hidden garages Bruce Wayne had bought or installed throughout the city via a variety of shell companies and cut-outs. Loud music blared from the ground-floor apartment, making him sympathize with the other tenants and neighbors. Lights in the top-floor apartment indicated that someone was home. It was possible that Joanna had found her way back to her apartment by now, but he knew better than to hope for the best in Gotham, where missing persons often stayed missing for good.

Cloaked in darkness, he silently climbed a rear fire escape to the back door of the apartment. A light bulb over the doorway was out, adding to the shadows. Batman frowned. That was almost too convenient. He checked the bulb and discovered that it had been unscrewed just enough to cause it to go dark. He couldn't think of a good reason for anyone to do that.

Bad reasons, on the other hand…

He paused before the back door. As a rule, Batman didn't knock before entering, the better to preserve his mystique, but Claire Nesko wasn't a criminal, nor even a suspect to be intimidated. He had no desire to terrify an innocent by invading her home without warning. Considering his options, he tried the doorknob—and was troubled to find it unlocked. The University District was hardly Crime Alley, but no one in Gotham left their back door unlocked, particularly after dark. Apprehensive, he pushed open the door, entering a hallway.

That he *didn't* smell burnt flesh only slightly eased his mind.

"Claire?" he said. "Claire Nesko?"

Nothing. He raised his voice.

"Claire? Can you hear me?"

The ominous silence spurred him to action.

Trusting his instincts, he swept through the apparently empty two-bedroom apartment, spotting everywhere the signs of *very* recent occupation. The television set in the living room was on pause, as though Claire had just stepped away for a moment. A plate of dinner sat uneaten on a low coffee table in front of a worn thrift-stone couch. An enticing aroma arose from the abandoned meal, which was still warm to the touch.

A microwave oven in the adjoining kitchenette beeped incessantly. Investigating, Batman found a mug of hot water awaiting a teabag. The front door of the apartment was chained and bolted from the inside. A breeze rustled the curtains in a kitchen window, which was open despite the chill of night.

Just as in Professor Morse's violated office…

Batman sprang to the window, fearful that he was already too late. There was no time to investigate further, not if his suspicions were correct. Flinging himself out through the opening, which overlooked a side alley below, he drew his grapnel gun from his belt and fired it in the direction of a chimney he had clocked earlier. A titanium hook, complete with a motorized microdiamond drill head, dug into the structure and the cable went taut. Tugging once on the cable to make sure it was secure, he rapidly scaled the side of the building to reach the shingled roof.

A Talon, distinguishable by his ebony body armor and gleaming blades, had Claire Nesko. She was a petite Caucasian woman, college-age, casually dressed in a school sweater and jeans. Zip-ties bound Claire's wrists and ankles. A gag muffled her cries. The Court's malignant agent had her slung over his shoulder as he nimbly crossed the pitched slope of the rooftop toward an adjacent building.

To Batman's relief, the Talon appeared to be intent on abduction, not assassination, which meant there was still a chance to save Claire from whatever ordeal the Owls had in store for her.

He knew too well how they treated their prisoners...

Batman's arrival didn't escape the Talon's notice, who peered over his shoulder and across the length of the rooftop. Despite himself, Batman felt an uncharacteristic chill at the sight of those round owl-like goggles. For a moment, even high above the city streets beneath the open sky, he felt as if he was back in the underground labyrinth again, desperate and driven to the edge...

Shake it off, Batman thought. *A life is in danger.* The smell of Herbert Morse's corpse haunted his memory as he confronted the hooded kidnapper. He had beaten Talons before. He could do it again.

"Talon!" he barked. "That's far enough. Put her down."

Even as he braced for battle, the detective in Batman wondered what the Owls wanted with Claire. The Talon's attack had to be connected with Joanna's disappearance, as well as Morse's immolation. Yet the big picture remained obscure.

"I don't answer to you, Batman," the assassin replied. "The Court of Owls has need of this woman. This is none of your affair."

The hood and goggles concealed his true face, but Batman felt certain this wasn't a Talon he'd faced before. Was this a fledgling assassin, newly activated, or an experienced one brought out of hibernation? Perhaps he'd been imported from one of the Owls' more distant nests. Although the Court had deep roots in Gotham, their reach was global—with secret branches and operations all over the planet.

"You're in my city," he said. "That makes it my business."

"Your city?" the Talon scoffed. "You have no idea what secrets have been hiding right in front of you all this time."

"Enlighten me."

"You are the great detective," the Talon said. "You figure it out." With that, the kidnapper took off with his captive. Getting a running start, he leapt from one roof to another, moving briskly despite the weight of his squirming burden.

Batman chased after him, his scalloped cape spreading out behind him like the leathery wings of his nocturnal namesake. He landed nimbly on the mansard roof of the adjacent row house. Chimneys, satellite dishes, and dormers sprouted from the urban rooftop as he gained on his foe. The Talon had speed and stamina to spare, but he had no chance of eluding Batman while carrying his hostage. Choosing fight over flight, he plucked a gleaming throwing knife from his bandolier and hurled it at his pursuer's face.

The blade sliced through the air, its grooves filled with mercury for steadier flight. Electrum glinted like polished moonlight.

But Batman's billowing cape was more than just decorative. Composed of a Nomex fire-resistant fabric, it also boasted a Kevlar bi-weave to repel everything from bullets to napalm without losing flexibility. With split-second timing and reflexes, Batman deflected the knife and the blade struck an undeserving satellite dish before skittering harmlessly across the tiled roof. The Talon was going to have to do better than that if he wanted to get away with his captive.

My turn, Batman thought.

Selecting a Batarang from his belt, he flung it at the Talon, who deftly evaded the weapon. It missed him by inches as it spun off into the night. A mocking laugh escaped the assassin's hood.

"You're slipping, Dark Knight," the Talon said. Batman could practically hear the sneer, despite the other man's hood. His tone and body language conveyed the arrogance of youth. A new Talon, eager to prove himself against the Owls' greatest foe? The Talon spun around to face his pursuer, shifting Claire in front of him to serve as a human shield. The razor-sharp metal talons on his gauntlet grazed her neck. "Now go back to your cave before I'm forced to cut this young lady's throat."

Was he bluffing? Batman wasn't sure. If the Owls wanted Claire dead, the Talon could have killed her back in the apartment. He wouldn't have abducted her unless they needed her alive for some reason. Yet did he dare call the bluff?

"What do you want with her anyway?" he challenged, buying time. "And what you done with Joanna Lee?"

"Nothing… yet," the Talon said. "Rest assured, however, she will not escape the judgment of the Court. She may run, she may hide, but none can escape—"

His words were cut off as the Batarang circled around to strike him in the back, slicing through his body armor to embed itself deeply in his flesh. More than an ordinary throwing weapon, this boomerang also delivered a powerful electric jolt. The startled Talon stiffened in shock, his limbs jerking spasmodically.

"There's a reason I call it a Batarang," Batman taunted. "Should have watched your back."

The jolt was strong enough to bring down Killer Croc, but it only staggered the Talon. Batman had been afraid of that, having dealt with his ilk before. Talons used a serum that relied heavily on the unique properties of electrum. It heightened natural healing abilities to a preternatural degree. The electrum suffused every cell of his body, meaning a Talon could be hurt, even killed, but seldom stayed that way for long. Despite the high-voltage shock to his system, this Talon was healing almost as fast as the built-in taser was frying his nerve endings.

Convulsing but still not falling, the Talon nevertheless lost his grip on Claire, throwing her forcefully to one side. She hit the roof hard, grunted, and began rolling down the slope toward the edge—and the forty-foot drop beyond. Panic showed in her eyes as her bound hands and feet kicked and scratched at the old-fashioned slate shingles in a frantic attempt to slow her descent. A muffled scream slipped past her gag as she hit the gutter at the bottom of the slope—and went flying over the edge toward the sidewalk below.

Batman dove after her without hesitation. Forgetting the Talon for the moment, he propelled himself off the roof, counting on his momentum to intercept the falling woman as she arced over the front steps of the building. Their bodies collided and he grabbed onto her waist with one arm while firing his grapnel gun at the upper reaches of a sturdy maple tree.

"I've got you," Batman said. "Hang tight."

A mechanized winch yanked them upward and out over the street. Horns honked and brakes squealed as they swung across two lanes of traffic before touching down on the sidewalk opposite the multi-story building they had just departed so precipitously. He held Claire upright, feeling her tremble, as his eyes sought out the Talon, employing telescopic lenses to find their enemy gazing down on them from several stories above.

His body still jerking erratically, the Talon nonetheless managed to reach behind him and wrench the sparking Batarang from his back. He flung the missile back at Batman—or perhaps Claire—with astonishing force and speed. Batman barely had time to thrust his right fist in front of Claire's throat, blocking the weapon with the protective steel scallops on his glove. It slammed into his gauntlet with considerable impact. Fresh blood—the Talon's blood—wetted the sharpened tip.

Better his than hers, he thought. *Seems he wasn't bluffing after all.* Or perhaps the Talon preferred Claire dead than in Batman's custody. Because he feared what she might reveal?

Police sirens wailed in the distance, drawing closer. A news chopper approached the neighborhood, the whirr of its rotors competing with the blaring sirens. His rescue mission had not gone unnoticed. Already a crowd was gathering on the sidewalk to see what was happening. Gawking bystanders whipped out their phones to capture the scene for posterity and social media.

This was apparently too public for the Talon, who retreated from sight, vanishing from the edge of the rooftop. Batman frowned at his escape, wishing he could pursue the assassin, but he couldn't abandon Claire. Justice for Morse, and who knew how many others, would have to wait.

Later, Batman promised himself. *That Talon hasn't seen the last of me.*

He used the sharpened tip of the Batarang to slice through the zip-ties that bound her. For Claire's sake, it was probably just as well that the Talon had retreated, instead of prolonging the conflict. He deftly removed the gag, and she gasped as the cloth came away. Propping her up as she tottered unsteadily, he eyed the growing crowd of bystanders as well as the copter that hovered above the neighborhood. A police blimp was also gliding toward the scene.

"We need to talk," he said. "Away from here."

5

The vehicle sped through the city, its camouflage mode engaged as it headed north toward Midtown, away from the University District. A holographic projection concealed the vehicle's true nature, the better to evade the eyes of the Owls or anyone else. With the Talon still at large, it was better not to take any chances with his precious cargo.

"Oh, God," Claire said from the passenger seat. "I still can't believe this is happening."

Her apartment no longer safe, and their presence on the street attracting too much attention, Batman had opted to hustle Claire to the most immediate refuge—the Batmobile. The customized vehicle had been built to repel or evade most any attack. It was sturdier than an armored truck and considerably faster and more versatile. It was a tank that handled like a sports car, and just the place for Claire at the moment.

"How are you holding up?" he asked. He was anxious to question her, but understood that she had just endured a frightening, potentially traumatic ordeal. Unlike Batman, she'd be unaccustomed to encountering master assassins or flying off rooftops.

"Honestly?" she replied. "I'm not sure why I'm *not* in hysterics, or curled up in a fetal position." She shuddered at the memory of her narrow escape, tugging fitfully on the seatbelt that buckled her in. "Maybe it's still sinking in... or maybe I'm distracted by the fact that I'm riding through town with the freaking Batman... no offense."

"None taken."

As he expertly navigated the late-night traffic, he inspected his passenger. Claire Nesko was noticeably less hip and artsy in appearance than her missing roommate, with light-brown hair cut in a simple, low-maintenance do. Dressed for comfort, rather than style, she didn't have any obvious makeup, jewelry, or body art.

In advance of their meeting, Batman had learned that Claire was a twenty-four-year-old anthropology student with family in Coast City. She had no criminal record, aside from a few traffic tickets, and blogged occasionally on the subject of classic screwball comedies. Apart from her connection to Joanna Lee, there was no obvious reason for the Talon to target her. He was impressed by how well she was holding it together, all things considered.

"Who... who was that man?" she demanded. "The one who attacked me?"

He debated how much to tell her at this juncture, and decided that she didn't need just yet to hear about Morse's grisly incineration, let alone the Court's long history of covert killings, kidnappings, and extortion. She had enough to process at present.

"He calls himself a Talon."

"Like in the old nursery rhyme?"

Batman nodded. "But he's no boogeyman. Trust me on that."

"You'd know, I guess." Her hand went to her neck, as if to assure herself that it was still in one piece. "I suppose I'm lucky I still have my head."

And that you haven't been crucified or reduced to ash, Batman thought, but he didn't say it. "I suspect he was after what's inside your head. He wanted information from you, one way or another."

"About what," she asked, then it seemed to dawn on her. "About Joanna? And her disappearance?"

don't claim to know everything there is to know about what Joanna was studying. Art history isn't my field, and I have my own classes, so I wasn't paying a whole lot of attention to her research. I like to think I got the gist of it, though."

"Which was?"

"Joanna was writing her thesis about some old-time sculptor named Percy Wright, who was supposed to have been quite the big deal back in the day."

Batman recognized the name. Wright had, indeed, been a notable sculptor in the early part of the twentieth century, and a celebrated son of Gotham City. His work could still be found in various public and private collections throughout the city, including a few endowed by the Wayne Foundation.

"I've heard of him," Batman said. As far as he knew, Wright's life and work had been well documented and extensively critiqued over the years. "I assume Joanna had some new approach to the topic?"

"Yep," Claire said. "She was focused on this one particular model, Lydia somebody, that Wright used over and over again. She was his 'muse' or something and, according to Joanna, you can still find her face and body immortalized all over Gotham— on monuments, fountains, old buildings, you name it. Joanna used to point her out to me sometimes, when we were out and about downtown, not that I was always listening. Did I mention that art isn't really my thing?

"Anyway, get this—apparently the *real* Lydia vanished at some point. It was a whole big mystery way back when, and Joanna believed that Percy Wright never got over her. In fact, she had this theory that Wright hid clues about what happened to her in lots of his statues." Claire shrugged. "Sounded kind of far-fetched to me, but Joanna was convinced that she was onto something."

"Before she disappeared too," Batman observed.

Claire's face fell. "Funny. I never made that connection before."

"That's what we need to talk to about."

Pulling into a Midtown parking garage not far from Wayne Tower, he drove to an upper level where an inconspicuous spot was permanently marked "RESERVED." A blind spot, as far as the garage's security cameras were concerned, which offered a strategic view of both the entrance and exit to this level. Batman backed the car into the spot, positioning it to peel out in a hurry if necessary. Polarized windows kept any light from escaping the interior, so the car would appear dark and empty from the outside. The doors and windows were soundproof, as well, guaranteeing their privacy.

"We can speak safely here," Batman said, "then we'll find a more secure location for you elsewhere." He couldn't take her back to the cave or the manor, for obvious reasons, so he would have to arrange with Gordon to place her in a GCPD safe house. "I apologize for questioning you so soon after your ordeal, but time may be of the essence... especially where Joanna is concerned."

"I understand." Claire wasted no time unbuckling her seatbelt, perhaps in reaction to having been restrained by the Talon. "What do you need to know?"

"Tell me about Joanna, and as much as you can about her disappearance." He had reviewed the official reports, skimpy as they were, but wanted to hear from Claire directly.

"All right." She settled back into the car seat and took a deep breath before answering. "Two nights ago, Joanna never came home, which wasn't like her. She'd been putting in long hours at the campus library, working on her thesis—but she wasn't responding to my calls and texts, and nobody seemed to have seen her for a while. So I started getting seriously worried.

"I tried contacting campus security, then the regular police, but they pretty much blew me off." Her tone turned sarcastic. "College girl doesn't come home for a couple days? Big deal. She was probably just off with some guy, right?"

She looked anxiously at him. "But that's gotta to be a coincidence, right? All that stuff with Percy Wright and Lydia was like a hundred years ago. It can't have anything to do with today."

"I wouldn't be so sure of that," Batman said. The Talon's words came back to him again, about secrets hidden right in front of Batman's eyes.

The Court of Owls dated back to Percy Wright's time and then some. Could they have been responsible for this Lydia's disappearance, long ago? Certainly she wouldn't have been the first person to be erased by the Owls for their own enigmatic reasons. Perhaps Joanna had unearthed some long-forgotten secret that the Court preferred to keep buried.

As a working theory, it seemed to fit the facts of the case. Presumably the Talon had interrogated Morse and searched his office to find just how much the unlucky professor already knew about Joanna's discoveries. Likewise with Claire's abduction, although the Talon may have also hoped that Claire could help him track down her roommate.

So much for that plan, Batman thought. It was unlikely, however, that the Talon would give up after one try. As long as the Owls suspected that she knew too much about Joanna's work and location, Claire was in danger. He feared they would not stop until they silenced anyone with whom Joanna might have shared her work, which meant that anyone close to Joanna might be in mortal jeopardy.

"The boyfriend," he said. "Do you have his contact information?"

"Not to hand," Claire said. "Believe it or not, that 'Talon' didn't let me get my phone before tying me up and dragging me out the window." She eyed Batman quizzically. "Why do you ask?"

"Just playing it safe." The wireless headset in his cowl allowed him to subvocally access the computer mainframe back at the cave. Within moments, he had located an address and phone number for a Dennis Lewton who was roughly the right age to be Joanna's boyfriend. He called up the man's driver's license photo on a monitor built into the vehicle's dashboard. The photo depicted a good-looking young man of Eurasian descent.

"Is this him?"

"How… how did you just do that?" she sputtered. "Find him so quickly, I mean?"

"Never mind that. This is the right Dennis Lewton?"

"Yes, that's him."

"Good." He tried to call via the headset, but got a recorded message instead:

"Yo, Dennis here. If you're looking for me, leave a message. If you're not looking for me, what are you doing with my digits anyway? And if this is a solicitation call, go drink a gallon of Joker Juice, loser!"

Batman frowned, for more reasons than one. He switched to a private line.

"Gordon, I'm sending you the address for a Dennis Lewton, who may have been targeted by the Court of Owls. Recommend dispatching a unit to take him into protective custody. Will explain later."

Claire stared at him. "You think Dennis is in trouble, too?"

"Better safe than sorry." He needed to stow Claire somewhere safe before looking for Dennis—or Joanna. "That's my problem, not yours."

It was time to call in another favor.

6

MacDougal Lane, Gotham City, 1918

"Remarkable," Percy Wright said. "Just remarkable."

Clad only in sunlight, Lydia Doyle reclined on her side atop a velvet-covered platform at the center of his airy, well-lit studio as he sculpted in clay a preliminary maquette of his next major work. As so often before, he was struck by what a superlative model she was. Not only were her face and form sublime—the very epitome of feminine perfection—but her ability to maintain a pose for long, grueling periods of time was, in his experience, unparalleled.

Many an artist's model was willing to pose in the altogether for fifty cents an hour, but few possessed Lydia's singular ability to enter into the spirit of a piece and embody the desired mood and emotion—in this case a languorous moment of peace and relaxation. One hand hung below the edge of the platform, while she peered down at it with an expression of utter tranquility.

Perfect.

He blessed the propitious day she had first presented herself at the door of his downtown studio, seeking modeling work. In the months since she had become his muse, his collaborator, and more.

Much more.

"You're welcome," she replied, and she broke the pose long enough to cast a coquettish grin. "Your appreciation is duly noted, sir." Flaxen blonde braids fell to her shoulders. Her porcelain skin and rosy complexion pleased the eye and exceeded the ability of his hands to capture her true radiance. Striking blue eyes made him long to paint her portrait as well.

"Please curb your mirth, my dear," the sculptor chided her gently. "If only for just a little longer." He was some years older than she, going grey at the temples, but still lean and fit for a man of his years. A rumpled apron shielded his attire as he worked. A walrus mustache added character to his face, or so he flattered himself. His gaze, as ever, was fixed on Lydia.

"Yes, yes, I know," she teased. "A nude with a serene expression is fine art and suitable for public display, but a girl grinning without any clothes on is simply lewd. Or so I have been told."

"It is simply a matter of aesthetics... and propriety," he replied. "Not that I am immune to your smile, as you well know." He extracted his pocket watch from his trousers and discovered, with a twinge of remorse, that Lydia had in fact been holding her pose for more than thirty-five minutes without pause. "Then again, it is past time that I allow you a rest period. You must forgive me, dearest. You make it rather too easy for me to become lost in the work."

"No need to apologize." She rose from the velvet stand and stretched her limbs before donning a robe that hung from a hook nearby. "Far be it from me to object to your rapt attention."

Percy's studio was located in the attic of a row house he had acquired in one of Gotham's more "bohemian" neighborhoods. Skylights provided ample sunlight by day, while gaslights allowed him to work well into the night when time and stamina allowed. Stands, easels, and workbenches cluttered the space, which was entirely devoted to serving his craft. Sketches and studies of various works-in-progress were strewn about, along with a handful of chiseled stone sculptures in various stages of completion, awaiting further inspiration.

Wherever the eye might fall, Lydia's exquisite form was on

display—captured on paper and in clay, plaster, bronze, and stone. Her ubiquity testified to her astounding versatility, as well as to his increasing inability to perform without her. A fire blazing in a brick hearth kept the room warm enough for her comfort, even when she was posing *au naturel*. A well-cushioned couch was available for catnaps on long nights—and for more passionate pursuits.

Drawing the robe about her, she joined him by the movable stand on which her miniature replica resided. The final sculpture was to be life-sized, but the maquette allowed him to work out the details of the project on a smaller and more convenient scale. A turntable gave him the ability to rotate it as needed.

Percy stepped back to inspect his progress thus far. There was still work to be done, refining the lines of the piece, but he was pleased with how it was coming along, in no small part due to his subject's uncommon grace and intuitive knack for posing. It was always a pleasure to sculpt her. She brought out the best in him.

"Don't forget," she reminded him, "you promised to pose for me sometime." Among her other gifts, Lydia had a talent for illustration. Her sketchbooks were filled with line drawings of considerable quality, which she often produced during times of leisure. It was one of her favorite pastimes.

He raised an eyebrow. "In the altogether?"

"Of course," she replied. "Fair's fair."

There was that grin again, so vivacious and beguiling. He took her in his arms and drew her close. That she was years his junior hardly seemed to matter when they were alone together, making him profoundly grateful for the privacy afforded them by his lodgings in the city, so far from the cares and obligations of his unhappy home life.

A sigh escaped him.

"Is something amiss?" she inquired.

"I simply regret that idyllic afternoons such as these cannot last forever," he confessed. "It pains me to recall that all too soon

I must catch the six o'clock train back to that drafty old house outside town."

"And back to Mrs. Wright," she added for him. There was no bitterness or jealousy in her voice, only a rueful acceptance of things as they were. She nestled against him, resting her head against his shoulder. "Does she suspect... about us?"

"I don't believe so," he replied. "She understands that artists employ models. Truth to tell, however, I'm not certain she would care overmuch, even if she did know—provided we remained sufficiently discreet. Her foremost concern would be social embarrassment, as opposed to the loss of my affections."

"How terribly sad for you," Lydia said, sounding sincerely sympathetic, "and for her."

If only she knew Margaret as I do, Percy thought.

"Your generous heart makes me adore you all the more," he said aloud, "but let us not waste these precious hours dwelling on such dismal matters." He glanced at the unfinished maquette, which called out for further refinement. "I hope to make further progress on the piece before the day is out."

"You artists!" She laughed, and the merry sound lifted the pall that had briefly fallen over their embrace. "Always obsessed with your work. If I didn't know better, I would swear that you care more for my effigies than you do for me."

"Not possible," he insisted. "But perhaps you can resume the pose for just one more brief interval? I'm not entirely satisfied with how I've rendered the elegant flow of your neck into your shoulder." He cast a beseeching look in her direction. "Indulge me, please?"

"Of course, my love, if you insist." She turned her head to contemplate her miniature reflection. "But might I ask where my charms are next to be displayed?"

"In a lovely garden," he informed her, "on the Wayne family estate."

7

The safe house was a former boarding house in Lower Gotham that the GCPD had quietly commandeered after its previous owner pled guilty to a shocking number of safety violations. Having turned Claire over to Gordon and his people, Batman crouched atop the building.

The neighborhood was a quiet one, consisting of assorted small shops and businesses that mostly shut down after dark. Railroad tracks ran directly across the street from the safe house, rendering the location less than desirable to tourists, developers, or organized crime. He hoped Claire would be secure here, even if her missing roommate was still unaccounted for.

According to Gordon, police officers dispatched to Dennis Lewton's apartment had found no one at home. The address remained under observation, but for the time being Lewton's whereabouts remained unknown. It might be that Joanna's boyfriend was simply difficult to contact, but they had to consider more ominous possibilities, as well. Chances were he was in hiding with Joanna, or the Talon had found him already. The lack of a body was promising, for sure, but the remains—charred or otherwise—might still turn up.

"You called?"

The voice came from behind. Nightwing joined him on the rooftop, appearing seemingly out of nowhere. Batman had been aware of his protégé's approach, but was impressed by the newcomer's effortless stealth nonetheless.

I trained him well.

The young hero's garb was less ornate than his mentor's. Minus a cape and cowl, he wore a streamlined black uniform that suited his acrobatic fighting style. The red-winged insignia on his chest declared both his individuality and his affiliation with Batman, while the black adhesive mask over his eyes echoed the domino disguise he'd once worn as Robin. The former Boy Wonder had grown into a crusading adventurer in his own right, but Dick Grayson could always be counted upon to lend a hand.

"Thanks for coming," he said, then he briefed Dick on the case at hand.

"The Owls again," Nightwing replied. "And a new Talon?"

Batman nodded. "I'm afraid so."

"Great, just great." Nightwing scowled at the news, and ran a gloved hand through his tousled black hair. "I suppose we always knew they'd be back."

"It's more like they never truly went away."

"That's one way to look at it, I guess."

Dick Grayson had his own troubling history with the Court and their handpicked assassins. For generations they had recruited Talons from circuses and carnivals, procuring the most promising young acrobats, aerialists, and escape artists. They trained them to become assassins instead of performers, while indoctrinating them in the lore and traditions of the Court—essentially brainwashing them so as to ensure their absolute loyalty.

William Cobb, Nightwing's great-grandfather, had been such a Talon and it had been intended that Dick would follow in his footsteps—until the unanticipated death of his parents had led Dick to be raised by Bruce Wayne, thus placing him out of reach of the Owls.

Had fate proceeded differently, the son of the Flying Graysons might well have become a Talon himself. Perhaps the deadliest of them all.

We got off lucky there, Batman mused. *Better a Robin than an Owl.*

"The Talon has already come after Claire Nesko once," he said to his former partner. "I trust Gordon's people, but the Owls have eyes and ears everywhere. I'd appreciate it if you keep an eye on her, while I search for Joanna Lee and find out what they're trying to accomplish here." Batman peered into the night, as if searching for answers. "The Court wouldn't be going to such lengths just to cover up a scandal from generations ago."

"Torture, murder, kidnapping, arson." Nightwing ticked them off on his fingers. "That does seem like overkill."

"Yes," Batman agreed. "There has to be more to it." He gazed out over the sleeping city, wondering what new nightmares were brewing even as they spoke. Like bats, Owls were more active after dark, and showed no mercy to their prey.

"What about you?" Nightwing asked.

Batman kept looking out at his city. "What *about* me?"

"The stoic act might work on everyone else, but not with me," the younger man replied. "Your history with the Owls runs deep. Where does that put you?"

Batman's first instinct was to shrug off the question—to shut it down. He had work to do, and the Talon was still out there. Talking about his feelings wouldn't help save Joanna, or stop the Court from getting whatever it was they were after—regardless of the body count.

Yet this was Dick. He deserved an honest answer.

"It's difficult to parse," he replied. "Not just these new attacks, but the fact that they seem to relate back to something that occurred more than a century ago. It drives home the point that Gotham may *always* have been a city of Owls. What if they're rooted so deeply in the city's history that they can never truly be eradicated? What if, despite everything we've done, Gotham's future belongs to them, as well?"

There was a moment of silence between them.

"I like to think we make our own futures." Nightwing clapped his hand on Batman's shoulder. "You taught me that. And remember, you're not in this fight alone."

It was true. The Court might have its minions, but Batman had allies, too.

They would have to be enough.

8

Wayne Manor, Gotham City, 1918

The unveiling of Percy Wright's latest work was the occasion for a lavish garden party on the grounds of Wayne Manor. Champagne flowed like water, while liveried servers provided delicious *hors d'œuvres* for Gotham's upper crust, who were taking advantage of the sunny spring afternoon to mix and mingle at the exclusive event. Blooming rose bushes perfumed the air, as though Nature herself had been enlisted to set the atmosphere. In a gazebo on the expansive lawn, a band played ragtime.

Standing off by himself, Percy studied the immaculately contained garden and judged it to be an ideal setting for his latest sculpture, which was the centerpiece of a marble fountain, newly installed on the grounds. Carved from pristine white stone, the graceful nymph relaxed by the water's edge, her fingers dipping beneath the surface as though trailing through a stream, her polished limbs stretched out to enjoy the sunlight. Her hair was braided, her expression one of utter peace and tranquility.

A pity, he thought, *that Lydia herself cannot be here, to see how her beauty provides the crowning glory to this Arcadian garden spot.*

"Admiring your work, Mr. Wright?"

The host of the party, Alan Wayne, approached, bearing a flute of champagne in each hand. Expanding on the work begun by his father, the noted architect was celebrated as the creator of Gotham's modern skyline. He was advancing in years, but appeared in good health and spirits. He cut a distinguished figure with silvered hair, neatly trimmed mustache, and confident bearing, looking not too far removed from the bold young visionary who had proposed a city of soaring stone and steel, of towering suspension bridges and skyscrapers, all in place of the brick and wooden Gotham into which he had been born.

For Percy, Wayne was a long-time friend and patron who had done much over the years to promote his career and reputation. The fashionable Beaux Arts movement sought to beautify America's great cities by filling them with decorations in the classical tradition, the better to rival the historic grandeur of the Old World. Properly trained sculptors were needed to fulfill such ambitions, so Percy found himself much in demand—due in no small part to the patronage of movers and shakers like his sponsor.

"Merely appreciating the exquisite setting," Percy responded cheerfully. "I could ask for no better home for my sweet, recumbent nymph. I hope your family enjoys her for generations to come."

"I'm quite certain they will." Alan foisted his spare flute of champagne on Percy. "Now drink up, man, before those blasted Temperance crusaders make it illegal." Percy accepted the drink. He'd already enjoyed one dose of the bubbly, but assumed that another would do him no harm.

"You don't truly suppose that Prohibition will be enacted into law, do you?"

"Who knows?" Alan said with a shrug. "I'm old enough to have learned that most anything is possible. Why, I remember when the tallest building in Gotham was only fifteen stories high, and sheep still grazed in the parks.

"In the meantime"—he raised his glass in a toast—"here's to another masterwork from my favorite artist. You did a fine job, Percy. Some of your best work, without a doubt."

Percy joined him in the toast. The champagne, which was of

the finest quality, went well with the praise from his old friend. He savored both.

"You're too kind," he said. Turning then, Percy regarded the statue once more, smiling as he recalled its creation. "I was... inspired."

"By my money," Alan quipped, "or by the model?" He joined his chum in admiring the marble nymph in her repose. "A vision of loveliness, truly. Were I a younger man, and less concerned with my reputation, I would be buttonholing you for the particulars."

"You have no idea," Percy replied. "Cold marble can only approximate the sublime charms of the genuine article. She is positively incandescent, setting the world aglow by her very presence... as an artist's model, of course."

Suddenly he feared that he might have rhapsodized overmuch, and blamed the champagne for his lapse in judgment. One drink too many had loosened his tongue, perhaps to a reckless degree. He glanced anxiously at Alan, and found the older man eyeing him knowingly.

"Of course." Alan glanced around to make certain no curious ears were listening in on their conversation. Then he leaned in and lowered his voice. "A word to the wise, Percy—take it from one who has learned better regarding such matters. Don't be drawn in by this particular flame, no matter how 'incandescent' she may be. Your wife is a formidable woman and—if I may be so bold as to say so—not someone to be crossed, if you value your hide."

Percy had to agree, not that he was in any position to admit this to Alan. To the contrary, he was strictly bound on the topic. His wife had secret affiliations—and ambitions—that could never come to light.

"Oh dear!" he said instead, feigning bemused innocence. "I hope I haven't given you the wrong impression. I spoke only of the model's talent for posing, which is indeed exceptional. Certainly I appreciate your sage and well-intentioned advice, but I assure you that my relations with the young lady are strictly professional. She is but a tool of my trade, not unlike my chisel or sandpaper.

"I see only the work, not the woman," he concluded.

Was he protesting too much?

"Say no more." Alan held up his hand to curb Percy's strenuous denials. "It's none of my affair. Forget I said anything." He contemplated the empty flute in his hand. "I suspect we've both partaken more than was entirely prudent." His eyes widened as he looked past Percy. Chagrin flickered briefly across his wizened features. "Speak of the devil," he muttered, then added, "No offense."

Percy turned to see his wife making her way toward them. She was a handsome woman, sturdy and statuesque, whose patrician features were too often—in Percy's opinion—marred by a severe expression that betrayed her harsh, unyielding nature. A silk gown, imported from Paris, flattered her figure while her auburn hair was neatly contained in a stylish chignon. She moved imperiously through the garden, fully expecting the other guests to make way for her, as indeed they did.

She was accustomed to getting her way.

"There you are!" she said to him. "I was wondering where you'd wandered off to this time." She politely acknowledged their host. "A lovely party, Alan. I must thank you again for the invitation."

"You're quite welcome," he replied. "One can hardly unveil the art without artist… and his enchanting better half, of course." Wayne glanced around. "Now if you'll excuse me, I must check with the caterers to see about another round of *hors d'œuvres*. A host's duties are never done, don't you know." Deftly making his escape, he left Percy with Margaret.

Her courteous façade fell away.

"Seriously, Percy, is it too much to ask for my husband not to slip away from me every chance he gets? Must I place a leash on you, simply to keep you at my side?" Percy knew she would do so, too, if she thought she could get away with it.

"My apologies, Margaret," he replied. "You appeared happily engaged with the other guests, so I assumed you would not mind my absence—in fact, I did not expect you to even notice. I wished only to remove myself from the hubbub for a spell."

"Appearances concern me," she said tersely. "A husband escorts his wife at public functions. It is the expected thing." She turned a scornful eye toward the sculpture in the fountain. "I should have known I'd find you here, captivated by your own creation. One would think you would have seen enough of this marble strumpet, after all those days toiling away at your squalid little studio."

Alan's warning echoed in Percy's ears.

He had to choose his words carefully.

"You must forgive me, my dear," he answered. "An artist's vanity."

"Which you have indulged quite enough today." She took him firmly by the arm. "Now then, the Elliots are dying to speak with you, as are the Cobblepots. Speaking of which, the latter have invited us to bridge on Thursday. I told them *we* would be delighted."

Percy groaned inwardly at the prospect of another tiresome evening playing cards with Margaret's society friends. He pined for his studio… and Lydia.

"Must we? Can't we get out of it, somehow?"

"Really, Percy." She gave him a withering look. "You could at least pretend to be sociable."

"You know how little patience I have for idle hobnobbing," he protested. "Left to my own devices, I prefer to occupy myself with my work."

"And your muse?"

He froze, caught off guard by the insinuation.

"I… I'm sure I don't know what you mean."

"Oh, please, Percy," she said. "Do you think me a fool? At least do me the courtesy of not insulting my intelligence." She led him toward a secluded arbor.

The jig is up, he realized. There was no point in denying it.

"I don't know what to say, Margaret."

"Then hold your tongue before you embarrass yourself further." Stopping out of sight of the rest of the crowd, she fixed him with a basilisk stare. "Let me make myself perfectly clear. I have no inclination to play the wounded spouse. If you *must* dally with some immodest odalisque—if she satisfies your animal urges, clearing your mind to focus on more vital tasks—please don't refrain on my account. Far be it from me to come between an artist and his *muse*." Her voice was cold as ice as she released his arm. "But for God's sake, Percy, be discreet about it… and don't abandon me in public to go mooning over her likeness. I expect you at least to *play* the dutiful husband. I have my pride."

Chastened, he tried to offer an explanation. "Margaret, you must understand. It was never my habit to 'dally' with my models—"

"Spare me your feeble excuses," she said. "It serves me right for marrying an artist, albeit one of suitable pedigree. The union of our families has benefited us both, even if you fail to appreciate it."

It was true that their marriage had been more of a merger than a love match. They had made a good fit on paper, if not in practice. He sighed wearily.

"What do you want from me, Margaret?"

"At present?" she responded. "You are going to take my arm, we are going to socialize with our peers, and you are going to do your level best to appear as though you couldn't be happier spending time in my company. Then, come Thursday, we *will* join the Cobblepots for bridge."

"Very well, my dear. If you insist." Under the circumstances, Percy judged that a small price to pay.

"I do insist," she stated. "And lest you forget, we have a rather more important engagement the following Monday."

Percy felt a chill come over him. "To be honest," he said, "I was thinking of perhaps skipping that meeting. I'm not certain my presence is truly required."

"Don't be ridiculous," she said coldly. "The Court of Owls demands your attendance."

9

It was a bad day for busking.

Strumming his guitar outside the downtown farmer's market, Zeke glanced at the cloudy gray sky, which was threatening rain. A fair number of people still came and went, milling in the public square at the south end of the market, but the chilly, overcast afternoon had definitely cut into the turnout. Even the folks who were out and about seemed disinclined to pause to listen to him play, let alone pay for the privilege.

Zeke had snagged a prime spot at the base of a large marble statue of Abundance, depicted as a graceful maiden wearing Grecian robes, bearing a cornucopia that overflowed with fruit and grains. He had done well in this spot before, but today the overturned hat lying at his feet held only a handful of singles and some loose change. When a raindrop bounced off his cheek and a light drizzle began to fall, Zeke considered calling it a day.

"Help me somebody, please! I'm burning up!"

What appeared to be a distraught homeless man staggered into the plaza, shouting wildly. He tore at his rumpled, threadbare clothing as anxious shoppers and pedestrians scurried out of his way. His frantic cries were hoarse and barely coherent.

"Oh my lord, it feels like fire! Fire in my head!"

Zeke's first response was to roll his eyes. This was hardly the first time he'd found himself competing with the mentally damaged, vying for the crowd's attention. Just the other day, a crazed doomsday preacher had shouted himself silly for hours while jaded Gothamites did their best to ignore him. Another day, another crazy.

"Please, somebody, please!"

Hang on, Zeke thought, growing concerned. Looking closer, the young musician saw that the homeless stranger looked to be in pretty bad shape. Bloodshot eyes bulged from their sockets. A grizzled face was flushed and slick with perspiration. Despite the damp autumn air, the man was sweating as if it was ninety-plus degrees out. His lips were cracked. He reeled unsteadily.

"Fire in my brain, in my blood—!"

The man lunged at a wary onlooker, snatching a plastic water bottle from her grip. Zeke expected him to gulp the water down, but instead he poured the contents of the bottle over his head, dousing himself. Zeke gaped in shock as *steam* rose from the homeless man's head and shoulders.

How was that even possible?

Bulging veins throbbed beneath flesh the color of a boiling lobster. An agonized shriek erupted from the man's throat.

Screams erupted from the crowd as he burst into flames.

•

"Joseph—'Joe'—Bava." Gordon identified the latest victim, addressing Batman via the morgue camera. "A few arrests for vagrancy. In and out of various mental-health facilities. A history of substance abuse. A sad story, but not an unusual one… until he spontaneously combusted in front of dozens of eyewitnesses at…" He checked the report. "Two-seventeen this afternoon in the farmer's market."

Day two, and the body count had doubled. Frustrated, Bruce pressed weights in the cave as they conferred. Working out did little to relieve the sense that he wasn't solving this case fast enough.

"Same autopsy results as before?"

"Aside from no punctures this time?" Gordon said. "Pretty much. The poor bastard was baked from the inside out."

Behind him, the charred remains of the newest victim were visible on the autopsy table. The blackened cadaver was almost indistinguishable from the professor's, including the severe damage to the cranium. Bruce would need to test a tissue sample to confirm the presence of electrum, but he already knew what the result of that analysis would be. Bava had suffered the same fate as Morse.

But why?

What connection did a homeless street person have to Morse or Joanna Lee or the Court of Owls? Or, for that matter, to the disappearance of a model named Lydia, decades ago? In his mind Bruce was assembling a puzzle, and Bava's fiery demise didn't fit into it, which could only mean he still wasn't seeing the whole picture.

"Anything to connect Bava with the Court's other targets?"

"Not that we've been able to determine," the cop replied. "You?"

Bruce put down the weights. "Let me work on that."

Fortunately, he knew just who to ask.

10

"This is fascinating," Barbara Gordon said.

The police commissioner's daughter operated out of the Watchtower, a penthouse looming over the Old Gotham historic district. Covert contributions from the Wayne family fortune had equipped the facility with a state-of-the-art security system, as well as an advanced computer station that rivaled the nerve center back at the Batcave.

The backside of a gargantuan clock face, built into the ancient red-brick walls of the tower, contrasted with the high-tech gear that filled the space. Century-old newspaper clippings, sepia-toned photographs, and archival legal records filled an array of screens and monitors. Barbara's fingers worked a keyboard as confidently as her costumed alter ego, Batgirl, traversed the rooftops of Gotham and matched blows with some of the city's deadliest criminals.

"I thought you'd be intrigued," Bruce said. Dressed for daylight in civilian attire, he was impressed by the vast array of information Barbara had already managed to excavate from the dustier corners of cyberspace. He stood behind her, preferring to remain on his feet. "And that it would be right up your alley."

As Batgirl, Barbara was a first-rate crime-fighter, easily as good in the field as Nightwing, but for the moment he didn't require another masked vigilante. He needed one of the best researchers on the planet, the slender redhead who sometimes prowled the digital realm under the code name "Oracle."

"Hush. You could dig up this info yourself," she protested. Stylish eyeglasses flattered her lightly freckled features, in lieu of the computer-enhanced contact lenses she wore as Batgirl. "What with being the world's greatest detective and all." There was a hint of mischief in her voice.

"If I had the time and didn't have an escalating situation on my hands."

Here in the twenty-first century lives were at stake and the clock was ticking. With Barbara's help, he could ferret out the connections that hadn't made it into the "official" history of Gotham.

"In other words," she said, "you want me working the past while Batman addresses the present."

And while Dick keeps an eye on Claire Nesko, he thought.

"Exactly." Bruce judged it a sound division of labor. "Plus, it can't hurt to have another pair of eyes searching the historical record."

"Happy to oblige," she said with a smirk. "And to give Alfred a break from being your only sounding board."

Bruce grunted, only partly in amusement. "That, too."

"Consider me on board." She sipped from an oversized coffee mug as she returned her attention to the myriad screens and pop-up windows. "What do we know so far?"

"The basics," he said. "Percy Wright was considered a Renaissance man in the Gotham of the early 1900s—a renowned artist, scientist, and scion of one of Gotham's most prominent families. He was definitely a member of the upper crust, a man of wealth and privilege, which means he fits the profile for membership of the Court of Owls."

"Then again," Barbara pointed out, "the same could be said of Bruce Wayne... and his ancestors."

"True enough." Bruce appreciated her role as devil's advocate. "In fact, as it happens, Wright was a friend and associate of my great-great-grandfather, Alan Wayne, who commissioned many of the monuments and buildings adorned by Wright's sculptures. Before Alan was assassinated by the Court of Owls, that is."

"Small world."

"Too small," he replied. *As far as Bats and Owls are concerned.*

Barbara scrolled through the data on her screens. "Says here that, aside from his artistic endeavors, Wright dabbled in chemistry, publishing scholarly papers in various scientific journals of the day. A *real* Renaissance man, like you said."

"Chemistry." Instinctively Bruce's voice dropped into the lower register he employed as Batman. "The Owls are fond of their exotic potions and chemicals." He didn't need to elaborate. They both knew about the serums that could revive "dead" Talons from hibernation, and gift them with extreme regenerative abilities. Batman himself had once been drugged with a hallucinogenic compound laced with electrum, causing him to doubt his own senses while trapped in the labyrinth.

Electrum, as had been found in the carbonized remains of Herbert Morse.

"It stands to reason," he said, "that the Court would boast a few cutting-edge chemists in their ranks."

"Like Percy Wright?"

"I wouldn't be surprised."

"But what about now?" Barbara asked. She called up the Wright family tree on the screen, but this was a path he had already explored.

"The Wright family and fortune are currently controlled by Vincent Wright," he said, "whom I know socially, if superficially. The Wrights hadn't come up in our earlier dealings with the Court, but we've only just begun to grasp how deep their claws are sunk into the city. The Wrights are a grand old Gotham family, with a long history of wealth and influence, so if they are involved with the Owls, it shouldn't really come as a surprise."

"But as victims or villains?"

"Too early to say."

Bruce couldn't recall the last time he'd rubbed shoulders with Vincent Wright, most likely at some charity gala or golf tournament.

It's probably time to renew our acquaintance.

"Let me guess," Barbara said. "Vincent Wright just landed on your engagement calendar."

"Being a Wayne does have its advantages." He gazed at the fruits of Barbara's digital sleuthing. "In the meantime, what do we have on that model, Lydia... and her disappearance?"

"Plenty," Barbara said. "Meet Lydia Doyle." She called up a vintage black-and-white photo of an old-fashioned "Gibson Girl," the sort who epitomized femininity back in the early twentieth century. Lydia Doyle was blessed with classically beautiful features, porcelain skin, and dark, entrancing eyes that gazed back at Bruce across the gulf of time. Flaxen ringlets framed her highly photogenic face.

"Another fascinating slice of history," Barbara said. "Although she's largely forgotten today, she was hugely in demand as an artist's model back in the day, so much so that she was once known as 'Miss Gotham' because her likeness could be found all over the city. You could even buy postcards and calendars of her. In a way, she was Gotham's first supermodel and pin-up girl."

"Until she vanished."

"Yep. She went missing in 1918, more than a hundred years ago. The tabloids were all over the story, hyping the mystery for all it was worth. There were scandalous rumors about her relationship with Percy Wright, as well as some suspicion that he was responsible for her disappearance, but nothing ever came of it. At this late date, it's hard to sift through the sensationalism to get to the real story. Eventually the police extracted a confession from"—she squinted at a vintage newspaper clipping—"Billy Draper, a jealous suitor who claimed to have killed Lydia and disposed of her body in a furnace. No evidence of her remains was ever found."

An ancient newspaper photo of Draper depicted a sullen-looking perp with a lantern jaw, bad skin, pomaded hair parted straight down the middle, and wide staring eyes of the sort that Bruce had encountered in far too many psychopaths. He certainly looked the part of a stalker, circa 1918.

"Which begs the question," Bruce said, "of whether or not he was just a patsy set up by the Court to take the fall instead of Wright."

"Or maybe the police just wanted to pin the disappearance on someone to appease the press?" Barbara suggested. "As a cop's daughter, I hate to cast aspersions on law-enforcement, but you and I both know that the GCPD has a dubious history at best. Maybe they just wanted to close the books on the case, regardless of whether Draper was guilty or not."

"That doesn't explain the Court's present interest in Joanna Lee and her research. I can't imagine they'd dispatch a Talon to cover up a long-forgotten tale of an unlucky model murdered by a stalker." He shook his head slowly. "The Owls had to have been involved in Lydia's disappearance… and they need to have a good reason for still wanting to keep the truth under wraps, a full century later."

Barbara contemplated the lurid old headlines, which screamed at them from a century past.

**SAD END TO MISSING
MODEL MYSTERY**

**BEAUTY'S CURSE!
SPURNED SUITOR SLAYS
CELEBRATED SIREN**

**LOVE-CRAZED MADMAN
PLEADS GUILTY TO
MISS GOTHAM'S MURDER**

"You think Wright had her killed?" she asked.

"I don't think anything yet," he replied, "but to all appearances he *was* obsessed with her, even after her disappearance." He recalled what Claire had said. Joanna was convinced Percy Wright's sculptures held secrets of their own. "Let's see her again—both in the flesh and otherwise."

"Easy enough." Her fingers danced across the keyboard. "Hello, Miss Gotham." Multiple images of Lydia Doyle appeared on the screens, smiling for the camera, carved out of stone, cast in bronze, and even embossed on commemorative coins and medallions. Often draped in flowing robes, or wearing nothing at all, she adorned archways, parks, gardens, monuments, and mausoleums. An angel on a stained-glass window bore her features. A decorative frieze depicted her in bas-relief. She reigned as the Queen of Hearts on an old playing card, where her blonde curls and striking blue-gray eyes were shown in full color for once.

Was he just projecting, or was there often a hint of sorrow there? Her smiles seemed like sad ones.

Reflecting her life, Bruce wondered, *or sculpted after her death?* The number and variety of the works—most but not all by Wright—testified to Lydia's popularity, or perhaps to his obsession with her.

One particular image caught his eye. It was a marble fountain featuring a graceful young woman relaxing at its center, her figure reclining on her side at the water's edge. He recognized it immediately.

"That fountain," he said. "It's on the grounds of the Manor." His throat tightened. The fountain, which graced the rose garden outside the west wing of the mansion, had been one of his mother's favorite spots when he was a boy. Memories flooded him as he recalled countless lazy spring and summer hours sharing the garden with his mother, sometimes sailing paper boats in the fountain as she relaxed with a book or magazine.

Other times, in his younger days, she had read to him by the fountain. He had first discovered *The Wind in the Willows* in that garden, and the Oz books and *The Black Stallion*. The girl in the fountain had shared those precious moments with Bruce and his mother. She had been their silent companion, smiling and serene, through many treasured afternoons of peace and togetherness—before Crime Alley changed everything.

"Right," Barbara said. Her eidetic memory was an archive in its own right. "In that pretty little garden outside the screen doors."

The fountain was still there, the garden meticulously maintained, but Bruce couldn't recall the last time he had spent any time there, relaxing or not. His mission didn't allow for such luxuries, while the memories had been best left undisturbed. The girl in the fountain had been neglected, her lonely presence barely registering on him even when he passed by her on his way from one spot to another. He hadn't truly looked at her, *seen* her, since his mother died.

Until today.

"Lydia."

He knew her name now, and something of her history. His expression darkened along with his mood, as he realized that the Owls had intruded upon yet another cherished corner of his past. The fountain had been a place of refuge, a repository of precious memories, and now it served as a reminder of yet another victim of the Court.

His fists clenched at his sides.

"Bruce?" Barbara looked up at him with concern. Like Dick, she knew him better than most. "Are you okay?"

"I'm fine," he lied. "Keep digging."

11

Harbor House, Gotham City, 1918

Percy's face itched beneath the smooth white porcelain mask with a beak and wide, deep-set eyes. He longed to lift it to scratch the itch but, of course, that was quite impossible.

To the world at large, Harbor House was an exclusive social club frequented by Gotham's elite. On nights such as this one, the looming Gothic edifice hosted gatherings of a more clandestine organization, whose interests went far beyond simple socializing. The Court of Owls sat around a long oak table in a windowless room on the uppermost floor of a turret. A candlelit chandelier, along with a row of candelabras lined up on the table, cast an animated light across the gloomy chamber, which housed an intimidating collection of artwork.

Oil portraits of wide-eyed raptors were framed upon the walls. Owls of bronze and jade and gold perched on shelves and the mantle of the fireplace. Examples of the taxidermist's art, which Percy found distasteful, hung suspended above the conference, spreading their wings as though in flight. The lack of subtlety appalled him.

Heaven forbid we should forget our esteemed totem.

Porcelain masks, identical to the one discomforting Percy, hid the faces of the well-dressed men and women convened around the table. Many of the masks, he knew, were family heirlooms passed on from one generation to another. Percy had inherited his own mask from his late father, who had received it from his father before him and so on, all the way back to the colonial era. The Court of Owls was not for the nouveaux riches. Its wealth was old wealth, accumulating over time.

The Grandmaster, an elderly fellow now stooped with age, rose with visible effort to lead the Court in the customary invocation.

"Beware the Court of Owls that watches all the time…" he began, and the others joined in. Percy recited the rhyme along with the rest of the assembly. In truth, however, he found these theatrics faintly ridiculous. Gotham's upper crust was not so large that he couldn't guess whose faces were behind most of the masks, yet the Court was nothing if not devoted to preserving its hallowed traditions—and power.

"Let us get on with the conclave," the Grandmaster said, the ritual complete. He sank with obvious relief back into his seat at the end of the table, wheezing audibly behind his mask. Rumor had it the old man was not long for this world. "We have much to discuss."

"Indeed." Margaret was quick to agree. She sat to Percy's left, her own expression concealed. Her family, the Addisons, was equally well established in the Court. "These troubled times demand vigorous action on our part."

Despite himself, Percy was amused by his wife's eagerness to speak up. That she had ambitions of rising in the Court, and perhaps even taking the aging Grandmaster's place someday, was to be expected. It was not in her nature to settle for less.

"Such as?" the Grandmaster inquired.

"The unfortunate incident at the Pyramid Garment Factory," she answered, referring to a recent tragedy in which more than a dozen seamstresses, many of them immigrants from overseas, had perished during a fire. Their workplace had been ill equipped with fire escapes and exits. Percy had read the newspaper accounts with sorrow, but Margaret had her own concerns regarding the disaster. "Already the usual malcontents are seizing upon this freak accident to stir up discontent among the lower classes, shamelessly taking advantage of the deaths to press for excessive regulation of free enterprise, disruptive labor actions, and unionization of the garment trade."

Her contemptuous tone conveyed disapproval, which was shared by many of her fellow Owls. They muttered and grumbled at such radical notions, which ran contrary to the best interests of the Court and its members. The Bolshevik uprising in Russia, barely a year in the past, had instilled in the Owls a positive loathing for any sort of workers' revolt. They were by no means inclined to share their power with the common herd.

"And how do you propose we counter these alarming initiatives?" the Grandmaster asked, and again Margaret was quick to respond.

"Let us promote the story that the fire was started by foreign anarchists, who callously sacrificed the lives of innocent women in their fanatical crusade against modern industry," she suggested. "Ideally, this will shift the conversation away from empowering the unwashed masses, while providing a timely excuse for the authorities to crack down on those subversive elements intent on sabotaging the proper social order."

"Anarchists?" Percy murmured to his wife. "Is that true?"

She shrugged. "Does it matter?"

"An intriguing proposition," the Grandmaster said. "Certainly worth further consideration."

Percy imagined Margaret beaming behind her mask. A lively discussion followed, then the conclave moved on to other pressing issues. One member of the Court proposed curbing the circulation of tabloid newspapers that were not yet under their editorial control. Another wished to discredit a stubbornly reform-minded political candidate by ensnaring him in an unsavory sex scandal. It was suggested that they acquire, by fair means or foul, several choice pieces of real estate that were bound to appreciate in value once various public and private works were made to happen. Also on the agenda: determining the outcome of the upcoming elections, bribing a Federal judge, and convincing Gotham's latest district attorney that it would be unwise to press charges against the errant son of a prominent family, who had recently run over a young girl while taking a joy ride in his new motorcar.

Percy squirmed restlessly in his seat.

Unlike Margaret, who was in her element, he had little interest in matters of politics and finance. His passions were art and science, which he judged to be of greater lasting value than the ephemera of current affairs. Although they had both been born into the Court, Percy was more than content to let Margaret play politics. As the tedious meeting wore on, he occupied himself with the hypnotic dance of the candle flames, while he pined for his studio and Lydia.

In his mind's eye he began to conceive a new work for which Lydia would be perfect—Cassandra foreseeing the Fall of Troy—and he was eager to commence work on it. Although he was still toying with the precise details, he could almost see the finished piece. No doubt Lydia would improve on whatever he could devise—

"Pay attention!" Margaret hissed *sotto voce*, breaking his reverie. She nudged him below the table. "The Grandmaster is speaking to you."

Dear God, he thought, experiencing a moment of panic. He thanked Providence for the mask that concealed his alarm and confusion as he sought to recover from his inexcusable lapse of attention. "Forgive me, but can you repeat that?"

"I asked," the Grandmaster said huffily, "for the status of the renovations to the Labyrinth."

The Court's underground prison, torture chamber, and on occasion gladiatorial area was showing its age, in particular a large marble figure of the Great Owl. Percy had been drafted to sculpt a replacement on an even grander scale, the better to reflect the Court's growing power and influence in this bold new century. *That* at least was a way in which his talents and the Court's interests coincided.

"It's an ambitious project," he replied, regaining his composure, "which will require a great deal of time and labor. I am confident, however, that the final result shall more than justify the effort. I am already in the process of acquiring a truly monumental block of the finest Italian white marble from which I will personally liberate the Great Owl of hallowed tradition."

The Grandmaster nodded, seemingly satisfied with Percy's report. "I look forward to beholding the culmination of your labors and artistry. Our sacred Labyrinth deserves nothing less than an idol worthy of this Court."

"Quite so," Percy agreed diplomatically. Quietly he breathed a sigh of relief. Then the Grandmaster spoke to him again.

"And what of your scientific pursuits?" he asked. "I hear rumors of a promising new elixir."

Caught flat-footed by the query, Percy glanced in dismay at his wife. As far as he knew, she alone was acquainted with the arcane nature of his experiments. His private laboratory occupied the basement of his house in the city—the same building that held his studio. By confiding in her, he had sought more time alone there. Now he cursed himself for doing so. He should have guessed she would seek to turn his discoveries to her own advantage.

"My... elixir?" He stalled, uncertain how much the Grandmaster already knew. "My experiments appear to date to bear out my theory, but it would be... premature to consider any practical applications at this point. There is still much work to be done to eliminate certain... incendiary... side effects that render the current formulas lethal in the extreme." This was not dissembling. A discouraging heap of charred laboratory mice and rabbits could attest to it.

"Is that so?" the Grandmaster wheezed. "What a pity. From what I hear, this discovery of yours could be of incalculable value to the Court." He peered at Percy through the holes in his mask. "I trust you appreciate that."

His eyes seemed to go cold.

Percy swallowed hard. "Fully, sir."

"Good," the Grandmaster said. "Then you must expend every effort to perfect your elixir, and make it available to the Court as soon as is possible."

"Have no fear, Grandmaster," Margaret said beside him, and he jumped. "*We* understand perfectly, don't we, dear?"

Percy felt like one of his own test animals, trapped in a cage he could not escape.

"Yes, of course."

•

A horse-drawn carriage waited to deliver them to the Plaza Hotel, where they had booked their usual suite in anticipation of the conclave running well into the evening. It was too late to embark on the long trip back to their mansion in the country and, unsurprisingly, Margaret wanted nothing to do with his private lodgings downtown. This was fine with Percy, who was none too eager to share that refuge with her. What sat less well was the growing certainty that he been placed in a highly difficult position. He waited until the carriage was underway before confronting her.

"How the devil does the Grandmaster know about my experiments?"

She did not look at him.

"I may have mentioned something of the sort during a private tea with him and his wife," she said without a trace of remorse. "At one of those dreary social occasions you can seldom be bothered to attend."

"Why in God's name would you do such a thing?" he pressed, leaning in. "Is this some petty act of revenge because of Lydia?" Then she did look at him, and her gaze burned into him, even in the darkness of the coach. He moved back.

"I'll thank you not to speak that trollop's name in my presence," she said. "And don't be absurd. I have far weightier matters on my mind than your trifling infidelities."

"Such as?"

"My... *our* position within the Court. It remains vital that we demonstrate our unquestionable value to the order. More, that we be seen as indispensable to the Court's future." This time she subjected him to an icy glare. "You may be content to coast on your family's long history, treating your membership as an inconvenient obligation, but I intend to make the most of my birthright. What was the point, I ask you, of consolidating our family fortunes if not to assume a leadership position among the Owls?"

"What indeed?" he asked dryly. "But I flatter myself to think that I have served the Court in my own fashion, as an artist and scientist. My studies into the unique chemical properties of electrum alone—"

"Are all very well and good," she conceded, "but again, we cannot rest on our laurels. It is not enough for us to be of use to the Court. At this critical juncture, we must become pivotal to the organization's success. Your astounding elixir could be the key to our ascension."

"But it is nowhere near ready!" he protested. "You know that. It could be years before I find a solution—if there even is one. Yet thanks to you, the Grandmaster now expects results, and quickly."

"How distressing for you," she said without a trace of sympathy. "Perhaps if you were to spend more time in your laboratory and less in your studio..."

Then he saw through her machinations. She had deliberately

manufactured this crisis out of an insidious mixture of jealousy and ambition.

"That is not how it works," he said, his voice a low growl. "Science cannot be rushed, nor can inspiration be simply diverted from one arena to another. My scientific pursuits and my artistic vision feed each other, but they are not interchangeable. Both are necessary to keep my mind and soul in balance," he continued. "You may suppose that you have spurred me to pursue my experiments with greater alacrity—at the expense of my art—but all you have accomplished is to promise the Court a miracle I... *we* may be unable to deliver. Genius is not so easily manipulated as politicians or the press, and you cannot force inspiration upon me."

"As opposed to your precious muse?" she replied. "Understand me, Percy. I tolerate that creature because, as you say, she plays a part in keeping you 'in balance.' Your artistic career and reputation have undeniably benefited since you discovered her, but if she becomes a distraction or, worse, a liability... well, unfortunate things can befall careless young women who outlive their usefulness."

Fear gripped Percy's heart. "No. You wouldn't dare!"

"You know me, Percy. Do you truly believe that?"

12

The rundown fishing cabin was tucked away in the woods overlooking Lake Miagani. An overgrown dirt trail led to the cabin, forcing Batman to park alongside a dimly lit mountain road a short hike away. This was just as well, since he preferred not to alert or alarm any occupants prematurely. It had been a long drive from Gotham City.

With any luck, the trip would be worth it.

The cabin was owned by Dennis Lewton's maternal grandfather, who currently resided in a nursing home in Blüdhaven. The isolated retreat was at least a quarter-mile from any other residences. With the summer over and hunting season not yet begun, most of those were likely to be empty. So if Dennis—and perhaps even Joanna—wanted to hide from the Court of Owls, grandpa's cabin might have seemed like a good option. As long as the Talon didn't follow the same paper trail that had led Batman here.

The moon and stars were in hiding, as well. It was a cold, misty autumn night cloaked in the sort of deep, primeval darkness found far from the lights of the city. A bitter wind rustled the treetops while small animals scurried through the brush. Dampness clung to every surface and softened the ground beneath his feet. An owl hooted, eliciting a scowl from the caped figure.

Night-vision lenses allowed him to study the cabin as easily as if it were daylight. Little more than a one-story wooden shack with peeling paint, asphalt shingles—several of them missing, a sagging front deck, and a brick chimney, the place was off the electrical grid and didn't even seem to have a phone line. Not far away a dilapidated outhouse implied the absence of indoor plumbing. Cardboard had been used to patch broken windows. No light escaped the premises and no smoke rose from the chimney.

At first glance, it appeared as if the cabin had been deserted for some time. Closer inspection suggested otherwise. Modern blinds were drawn over the few intact windows. A waterproof polyethylene tarp protected a fresh supply of firewood. A motorcycle was hidden in the bushes behind the cabin, safely out of view from the approach. The license plate confirmed that the bike was Lewton's.

Bingo.

The sagging deck creaked beneath Batman's weight as he approached the front door, which he found riddled with bullet holes. Somebody had fired from inside the cabin—perhaps in self-defense?

The perforated door swung freely open, admitting him to the cabin's sparsely furnished, one-room interior. Signs of a struggle were everywhere. Chairs, cots, and a table were overturned. A fallen shotgun had been smashed to pieces. Twelve-gauge shell casings littered the floor, along with a pair of crumpled sleeping bags and various articles of clothing. A hint of gunpowder lingered in the air, and he grimaced beneath the mask.

He didn't like guns.

A cast-iron wood stove was cold, implying that some time had passed since the altercation, as did the dried blood splattered on the interior side of the door. No bodies were to be seen, charred or otherwise, which offered both a puzzle and a modicum of hope. Mere bullets weren't enough to put a Talon down, at least not for long, but what had happened to Dennis and Joanna? The twin sleeping bags suggested that they had been hiding here together.

Had they been abducted? It was a grim prospect, yet certainly better than the alternative.

He stepped back out of the cabin to survey its surroundings. A moss-covered picnic table recalled happier days. A winding trail led down to the shore of the lake where a wooden dock, extending out onto the water, could be glimpsed through the trees. No boat was visible, but someone still could have come or gone by water.

Leaving the cabin behind, he headed down to the shore, where a grisly sight awaited him. A charred body lay by the shore. Water lapped against the blackened corpse which was half-in, half-out of the shallows, lying facing down on the damp, rocky ground. A rapid inspection revealed that the victim was male.

Dennis Lewton, Batman assumed, although the corpse's face had been burnt beyond recognition. He allowed himself a selfish moment of relief that it wasn't Joanna, even as he regretted arriving too late to save her boyfriend. One more life lost to the Court of Owls and their latest Talon, whose incendiary methods still posed a mystery.

He's not going to get away with this, Batman vowed silently. *There's a cell in Blackgate waiting for him.*

Scanning the surroundings, he attempted to reconstruct the events that had led to the murder. There were overt signs of a struggle, and several more shell casings. His best guess was that Dennis had attempted to defend himself with the shotgun, but that hadn't been enough to stop the indestructible Talon. Fleeing the cabin, Dennis had been herded toward the lake, where he would have had nowhere to run before the Talon caught up with him. A struggle had ensued, kicking up a great deal of gravel, much of it now charred.

The question that remained, however, was whether or not Dennis had delayed the Talon long enough for Joanna to escape. There was no sign of her.

Please let her be safe. Batman knew firsthand what it was like to endure the sadistic hospitality of the Court of Owls. The thought that Joanna might have fallen into their hands sickened him.

Kneeling next to the body, he examined it closely. Sure enough, stab wounds suggested that, like Professor Morse, Dennis had been brutally interrogated before immolation occurred. As ugly a picture as that painted, it also suggested what might have happened to Joanna. Why would the Talon have questioned Dennis if he already had Joanna in his grasp? Perhaps Dennis hadn't died in vain—it might be that his doomed battle with the Talon had at least bought her time to escape, possibly by boat.

A vivid image played in his mind's eye—of a screaming Dennis plunging into the water even as he burned up from the inside. He had never met the young man, but hoped the frigid lake had provided him some small measure of relief before he died.

It was cold comfort, however.

After inspecting and digitally recording the crime scene, Batman dragged the body further up onto the shore. He would need to alert the local police to the body's location, but first he wanted to take another look at the cabin. Returning to the violated structure, he conducted a swift but efficient search—this time with a powerful flashlight. A small stockpile of woman's clothing supported the idea that Dennis had not been alone.

Only the Talon's blood had been spilled inside the cabin, implying that Dennis had been tortured outdoors. The assassin had removed any records of Joanna's thesis from Morse's office, so Batman assumed he'd searched the cabin as well.

Was there a chance he had missed something?

There was a conspicuous absence of any electronics—laptops, phones, or tablets. Not even a smart watch. Granted, the remote cabin was off the grid, but Batman doubted either Dennis or Joanna would have abandoned their devices entirely when they retreated into the wilderness. Joanna in particular would have hung onto copies of her work, if at all possible. While it was likely that the

Talon had already made off with any devices he had found, he was an assassin—not a detective.

It's worth another look, Batman thought. *Any chance to learn more about what she was working on.*

Pulling an advanced sonic scanner from his utility belt, he used it to inspect the cabin's interior from one end to another, but found nothing hidden in the floor, ceiling, or even the linings of the sleeping bags. The wood stove held nothing but ash.

The outhouse? He rejected the notion quickly. Joanna surely had more respect for her labors than that. In addition, the decrepit structure was hardly secure from the elements, let alone waterproof.

Waterproof...

A possibility struck him. Rushing out of the cabin, he yanked the waterproof tarp off the woodpile and began rooting methodically through neatly stacked firewood. Within moments his efforts were rewarded by a plastic case sealed inside a Ziploc plastic back for extra protection. Opening the bag and cracking open the case, he found a single thumb drive tucked away for safekeeping. A rare smile lifted his lips.

Good girl, Joanna.

Batman hoped the drive held at least some of the answers he needed.

For Gotham's sake.

13

Wheeler-Nicholson Exposition Grounds, Gotham City, 1918

The grand Gotham City International Exposition was in full swing. For weeks it had drawn throngs to the colossal fairgrounds, which had been created on the grounds of a sprawling estate just for this monumental event. Although Metropolis, Star City, and St. Roch had all bid to host the 1918 World's Fair, Gotham had triumphed over the competition and had spared no expense in mounting the Exposition, the better to show off their rising preeminence as one of the nation's great cities.

Spacious boulevards wide enough to accommodate legions of visitors connected hundreds of acres of ornate courts and pavilions boasting exhibitions from all across the globe. Sparkling white towers studded with cut-glass "jewels" of myriad hues rose to the heavens. Temples of science and industry displayed the wonders of the modern age, from a transcontinental telephone connecting Gotham with far-off San Francisco to assembly lines and baby incubators and even a working model of the world's first radio-controlled airplane.

Clanging trolleys carried wide-eyed fairgoers from one end of the Exposition to another, while a veritable galaxy of bright electric lights set the warm summer night aglow. Colored spotlights reflected off the jeweled towers. Lydia had read that more than twenty million people, including sightseers from all over, were expected to pass through the imposing arched gates. Looking about, it seemed to her that all of them had chosen to visit the fair the very same night as she.

"It's astonishing," she marveled aloud. "Like a city of stars."

Arm in arm with Percy, she strolled down a boulevard, trusting in the anonymity of the crowd to protect them from undue scrutiny. There was almost too much to see. She didn't know where to look first.

"Just wait," he said. "I have a surprise for you."

A silk top hat perched rakishly atop his head gave him a jaunty air. Beneath the electric glow of the lights, she admired his lean, distinguished features. His noble brow and high cheekbones conveyed remarkable intellect and breeding, while his angular features were softened by a magnificently fulsome mustache. Her own hair was done up in the bouffant style of a Gibson Girl, beneath a wide feathered hat. She flattered herself that they made a handsome couple, which caused her to worry just how inconspicuous they truly were, even in the midst of thousands of other fairgoers.

"Percy, this is heavenly," she said, keeping her voice low, "but is it truly safe for us to be seen together? Your wife—"

"Is not here," he replied firmly. "We are but one of many couples taking in the Exposition. Its sheer spectacle all but guarantees that no one is looking at us when there are so many other attractions on which the eye may feast." He smiled to reassure her. "In the unlikely event that anyone should ask, you are merely my niece from Chicago, come to experience the Fair like countless other out-of-towners."

He made a good point, she conceded. Every day, trains and steamboats and coaches unloaded yet more visitors to Gotham. Hotels and inns were booked for months with nary a room to be had for love or money. Some enterprising citizens had even taken temporary lodgers into their homes and apartments, causing ad hoc boarding housings to spring up all across the city. Yet even allowing for such a flood of new arrivals, she could not help feeling as though she and Percy might be pressing their luck by parading out in the open together.

"It is still a risk," she insisted. "You didn't have to do this for me."

"I beg to differ," he said warmly. "You deserve it, after being cooped up in my studio for hour on hour, day after day. *We* deserve this." He looked at her longingly. "Alas, my scientific efforts are likely to consume much of my time and concentration in the coming weeks and months, which means, sadly, that we shall not be able to see each other as much as we might prefer. This being the case, I believe that we are damn well entitled to a night out, before my experiments tear me away from you."

"Your experiments?"

"Have reached a critical juncture, I'm afraid. I believe I am on the verge of an important breakthrough, but I cannot say for certain how much time may be required."

"I have faith in your genius, darling," she said, a hint of sadness in her voice. "You are bound to succeed brilliantly, and in no time."

"Thank you, dearest. Your confidence in me bolsters my spirits."

"You have it always," she said. "Never doubt that."

Despite her disappointment at his upcoming absence, she could hardly object to the experiments that impinged on their romance, since his remarkable mind was one of the attributes she most admired in him. That he was both an artist *and* a scientist— altogether cultured and worldly—had attracted her from the start.

There was so much more to Percy than the callow Stagedoor Johnnies who had attempted to woo her during her short-lived career as a chorus girl, before she discovered that she was better suited to posing as a model than prancing about on stage. She had never intended to become intimately involved with one of her employers, let alone with a married man, but the magnetic pull between them had been impossible to deny. It was worth whatever challenges and inconveniences their unlikely relationship entailed.

"I'll do no more fretting," she promised. "Let us put the future aside for the moment, and make the most of tonight while we can."

He gently squeezed her arm. "I couldn't agree more."

They strolled past the Temples of Agriculture and Invention as ragtime music played from a bandstand. Fireworks erupted in the sky, eliciting appreciative gasps and applause from all around. Immense bursts of brightly colored sparks expanded outward to fill the firmament, accompanied by the bangs and pops of the exploding gunpowder. Lydia squealed in excitement. She had always loved fireworks.

"A teddy for the lady?" a raspy voice called out. "Get yerself a cuddly teddy bear here."

A peddler was hawking his wares near the illuminated entrance to the Amusement Zone, where the sideshow attractions, concessions stands, souvenir shops, and mechanical thrill rides were cloistered. Stuffed bears upholstered in tawny mohair sat atop wooden crates, waiting to be adopted. Truth be told, Lydia had never quite seen a resemblance between the popular toys and the rambunctious former president, but the furry animals were quite appealing in their own right.

"Oh my," she exclaimed. "Aren't they adorable?"

"That they are, miss!" the peddler agreed enthusiastically. "Go ahead, gent. Treat the pretty lady to a teddy. You won't be sorry."

"Why not?" Percy traded a silver dollar for a bear and handed it to her. "To keep you company while I'm slaving away over my test tubes and retorts."

"I'll cherish him forever!" She hugged it to her bosom, then kissed it playfully on the snout. "Perhaps I'll name him Percy, so that he will always remind me of this magical evening."

"The best is yet to come," he responded. "Follow me."

Leading her through the crowd, he steered them toward one of the Fair's most elegant structures. The Temple of Fine Arts was comprised of a wide, semi-circular art gallery built around a huge domed rotunda on the shore of a shimmering artificial lagoon. They made their way through one of the rotunda's tall archways to the interior of the building, which was packed with sightseers gawking at its classical splendor. To Lydia's eye, it seemed as glorious as any monument that might be found in Greece or Rome.

Not that she had ever personally ventured overseas.

"It's very impressive," she told Percy. "And right here in Gotham City."

"Look up," he said.

Lifting her gaze to the domed ceiling, she saw three female figures painted on a mural high above her head. She had learned enough about art over the last year or so to recognize them as the Three Graces of pagan mythology, clad only in diaphanous wisps of cloth. Then she let out a gasp.

"It's me," she whispered.

"In triplicate," he said. "Each as lovely as her sisters."

"But when?" Looking more closely, she recognized each of the three poses from past sessions in Percy's studio, studies for coming sculptures. "How?"

"Have you forgotten that I have a talent for painting, as well?" he said. "It took very little effort to persuade the organizers of the Exposition that I had 'located' the perfect model to represent the Graces and all they embody, then to allow me to execute the mural."

"It's beautiful," she said, then she covered her mouth. "If that's not too vain to remark."

"You are the fairest beauty to ever grace Gotham," he said, and with a wave of his hand he indicated the crowds that surrounded them. "The whole world is flocking to admire you."

Staring at the mural, she was filled with pride. She had seen her face and figure reproduced before, of course, on everything from postcards to building façades, but it still took her breath away to discover that she was part of the great Exposition, being viewed by hundreds of thousands of strangers every day. If only her family could see her now, she thought. They had not approved of her running off to the big city to seek her fortune, nor had they approved of the vocations that had been available to her. Yet here she was, part of the Temple of Fine Arts, no less.

Not too shabby for a former chorus girl.

Suddenly self-conscious, she peeked at the fairgoers who surrounded them. None appeared to note her resemblance to the goddesses on the ceiling. Indeed, she felt like a princess in disguise, wandering incognito through her fairy-tale kingdom, unrecognized and unseen. Percy was right. Lost in the crowd, they were all but invisible.

"Why, Miss Doyle. Fancy meeting you here."

Her heart sank as she saw a man elbowing his way toward them. As usual, his smile was a little too broad, the gleam in his eyes rather too bright. A straw boater capped his head.

Billy Draper was a young man about town, a dilettante playboy whose primary vocation was squandering his sizable allowance on music halls and showgirls. He had been pursuing her for some time, despite her polite attempts to dissuade him. Indeed she wondered about this chance meeting. It was hardly the first time that they had "accidentally" crossed paths.

"Hello, Billy," she said courteously. "Are you enjoying the Fair?"

"Very much so," he said brightly. "And all the more so now that I've come upon your delightful presence." He attempted to kiss her hand, but the teddy bear conveniently obstructed his efforts.

Good teddy, she thought.

"I don't believe we've been introduced," Percy said stiffly.

"Billy Draper, of the Blüdhaven Drapers." He extended his hand to Percy, who grudgingly accepted it. Billy beamed at Lydia. "I'm Miss Doyle's greatest admirer."

"Is that so?" Percy said. He was clearly displeased by the younger man's intrusion, but was hardly in a position to protest.

"Billy, this is…" Lydia hesitated, uncertain how to proceed.

"There's no need to introduce your esteemed companion," Billy said. "All of Gotham knows the illustrious artist Percy Wright." There was a sarcastic edge to his voice. "And of course, your good wife, who is justly celebrated for her social and philanthropic pursuits. I trust she is well?"

"Quite," Percy said tersely.

Lydia searched for some way to defuse the awkward situation, since she could hardly pose as a visiting niece.

"Have you noticed the mural on the ceiling? Percy was kind enough to escort me to the Fair tonight, so that I might have the opportunity to behold my triplets."

Following her gesture, Billy looked up, and his eyes went wide. For a moment, he seemed lost in rapt admiration, to a degree that Lydia found somewhat discomfiting.

"Billy?"

He snapped out of his trance. His eyes narrowed suspiciously as he turned toward Percy.

"Your work, sir?"

"Precisely," Percy replied, taking his cue from her. "It seemed only fitting to accompany Miss Doyle to her first viewing of it."

"That was most chivalrous of you, sir." Billy said sourly. Lydia feared he was vexed at the thought of her posing thus for Percy.

"It was the least I could do," Percy replied. "I could hardly allow the young lady to brave this teeming sea of humanity without an escort. Heaven knows what sort of ill-intentioned jackanapes she might encounter."

Billy scowled. "Or lascivious old men, for that matter."

Oh dear, Lydia thought, alarmed at the direction the encounter was taking. Another woman might savor the spectacle of rival suitors vying for her favors, but she felt otherwise. This could not possibly end well for any of them.

"Excuse me, Percy, but I believe we are expected elsewhere." Grasping his arm, she turned him toward the nearest exit. He did not resist. "It was lovely running into you, Billy, but I'm afraid we must be going. Do enjoy the rest of the Fair." She hurried Percy away before Billy could invite himself to join them. To her relief, he was not *that* forward. They left him standing in the rotunda with a stricken expression on his face, and Lydia felt a twinge of pity for him.

She disliked injuring anyone's heart.

Percy was less forgiving. "That impertinent pup. The nerve of the man."

"It's a shame we ran into him," she agreed, "but I suppose this proves what they say, that all the world is attending the Exposition."

For fear of upsetting him further, she chose not to mention her suspicions that Billy might have followed her to the Fair. Percy fumed nonetheless.

"How is it you know that cad?"

"Just a sadly persistent admirer, no more."

"Should I be jealous?"

"Not in the slightest," she assured him. "Alas, matters being what they are, I can hardly inform anyone that I am already spoken for." She smiled wryly. "An unfortunate drawback to being the other woman."

"I suppose," Percy said, acknowledging the delicacy of her position. "Would you like me to do something about him? For better or for worse, I have some acquaintances who might be prevailed upon to… discourage… him from pestering you any further."

Lydia assumed he was referring to hired bodyguards or detectives. A man in Percy's position would sometimes be forced to deal with such men, but she was appalled at the notion of sending a Pinkerton around to physically intimidate Billy—or worse.

"Oh, no, you mustn't think of that," she said quickly. "Billy is harmless. In time, he will surely transfer his affections to some other poor showgirl or model."

"Are you quite certain of that?"

"Absolutely." She squeezed his arm affectionately and attempted to make light of the topic. "In any event, this is all your fault after all."

"How so?"

"Why, by displaying my charms all over Gotham, of course," she replied. "How could any man be expected to resist?"

14

"'My muse is a muse of fire,'" Barbara read aloud, "'a deathless inferno that consumes my soul, as it will someday consume all of Gotham.' Percy Wright, 1925."

Her face appeared on the Batcave's main monitor while various text files, photos, and scans from the flash drive occupied peripheral screens and windows. Joanna had encrypted her files, but this had posed little challenge to Oracle. The data security measures available to an ordinary grad student were child's play compared to some of the codes they'd each cracked in the past. The Riddler would have laughed at the encryption—if he wasn't currently locked away in Arkham Asylum.

"Joanna was—*is* quite the researcher," Barbara said appreciatively. "She's pulled together an impressive amount of material from a wide variety of primary sources, many of them obscure. She's skilled at locating stuff that fell between the cracks."

"Too much so, perhaps," Bruce replied, "as far as the Owls are concerned." For all he knew, the Talon had already captured her for the Court. Not for the first time, he wondered what had sent Joanna into hiding in the first place. If Joanna had disappeared before Professor Morse's death, how had she discovered that the Owls were targeting her?

"You'd like her," Bruce told Barbara.

"Can wait to meet her," Barbara said, "if—"

"When," Bruce insisted.

"Yes, of course. I didn't mean—"

"You were saying something about material that fell between the cracks?" The files on the drive had been fragmentary. Dozens of notes and drafts and documents ranging from antique newspaper clippings to architectural drawings and blueprints. Joanna must have been constructing her thesis when danger emerged from the shadows, so her work consisted of bits and pieces that would require considerable effort to collate and review. A jigsaw puzzle in its own right.

"Take that quote I just read you," Barbara replied, "about 'a muse of fire.' Joanna found that buried in the self-published memoir of one Basil Irvine, a now-forgotten patron of the arts and, apparently, an inveterate name-dropper. In his book—which was little read then and even less so now—he recounted a reception thrown for Percy Wright several years after Lydia's disappearance, at which the guest of honor had too much to drink. According to Irvine, the great man started rambling and was swiftly hustled away by his friends and family, 'lest he embarrass himself further.' This anecdote never made it into the press of the time, or even Wright's official biography. It only survives on a single page of Irvine's obscure little tome. God knows how Joanna unearthed it."

Bruce was impressed. Searching the files, he quickly located the excerpt in question, along with some of Joanna's notes and annotations on the incident. Scattered pieces of data came together as he realized that this forgotten snippet of gossip formed one of the foundations of her thesis. What he read disturbed him.

"Not just a message," he muttered under his breath.

Barbara peered at him over the top of her glasses. "What is it, then?"

"According to Claire Nesko, Joanna's theory was that there was a message hidden in the figures of Lydia that Percy sculpted after her disappearance. From what I'm seeing here, however, Joanna believed it was more than a message. It was a prophecy, warning of an 'inferno' that would occur in Gotham's future."

"That seems like a leap," Barbara said skeptically. "Sure, Wright was obsessed with her. Maybe a guilty conscience drove him to leave some sort of confession behind, but a prophecy of doom, hidden in some old statues? Sounds like a fable, not reality."

"That's what I thought about the Court of Owls," Bruce reminded her. "Once upon a time."

"Point taken."

"Perhaps Percy knew something we don't," Batman said, following the thread. "Something from the past, that would bring about a disaster in the future."

Barbara shrugged. "Or maybe he was just crazy."

"That still doesn't explain the Court's involvement," he said. "I doubt they would be this concerned about the feverish delusions of a long-dead artist. There has to be something more..." He stroked his chin, which needed a shave. "The Owls are always playing a long game, scheming through history. We can't rule out the possibility that Percy was hinting at something ominous planted in Gotham's past. Something in which he may have had a hand."

"Now *there's* a reassuring notion," Barbara said wryly. "But speaking of 'feverish,' I've been digging through some info from early-twentieth-century Gotham, as you requested. A curious 'coincidence' turned up."

"I don't believe in coincidence," he said.

"Then you'll love this," she continued. "It seems that not long after Lydia disappeared, a mysterious 'fever' broke out in the poorer parts of the city. According to the tabloids and yellow journalists, the victims of this plague literally burst into flames, although the authorities of the time dismissed the reports as 'exaggerated.' The 'Burning Sickness' actually drove the Lydia Doyle mystery off the front pages for a while, with the fever being blamed on everything from the 'wrath of God' to a secret plot by the Bolsheviks."

"I've met the Wrath of God," Bruce mused. "Killing innocents isn't Corrigan's style." He studied the computer monitors as Barbara called up various tabloid articles for his inspection. As she'd said, the dates placed the outbreak in the weeks and months following Lydia Doyle's disappearance. He recalled the coroner's report that compared Morse's spontaneous combustion to a fever originating in his overheated brain. "So what happened with this fever, back in Percy's time?"

"From what I can tell," Barbara said, "the authorities never determined the source of the outbreak, but it eventually burned out on its own, so to speak. That's not the end of the story, though. Intrigued, I ran a search for other alleged instances of spontaneous combustion, and discovered that there have been intermittent episodes recorded throughout Gotham over the last century, ever since that first outbreak in 1918. None of the subsequent incidents claimed as many victims as the initial scare, but it appears as though the 'Burning Sickness' has been visiting Gotham on and off for the last hundred years."

"Ever since Lydia vanished," Bruce said grimly. A thread was forming here—or perhaps a smoking fuse. "Billy Draper claimed he burnt Lydia's body after he killed her. Percy Wright allegedly planted clues warning of an 'inferno' awaiting Gotham. People are spontaneously combusting again, just as before, and, somehow, the Court of Owls is in the thick of it." He tried to make sense of a pattern that was only just beginning to emerge.

They still hadn't proved conclusively that the Owls were involved with Lydia's disappearance back in 1918, but Bruce would have been willing to bet a good deal of his annual earnings on it. His gut told him they were on the right track.

"All those people burning alive, over all these years." Barbara's voice grew hushed as the implications of what they were learning sank in. "My God, Bruce, how big is this thing?"

"I don't know... yet," he said. "Bigger than I prefer to think about." Like her, he was appalled to contemplate how many agonizing deaths, stretching across generations, might be laid at the feet of the Court—but that wasn't the worst of it. What worried him now was how many *more* lives might go up in flames. Percy's cryptic prophecy haunted him.

"A deathless inferno that consumes my soul, as it may someday consume all of Gotham."

15

"Care for more champagne, Mister Wayne?"

"No, thank you. I'm good."

A charity gala was underway at the historic Tilden Theater in uptown Gotham City, to raise money to preserve and restore the venerable old edifice, which was one of the oldest working stages in the city. Well-heeled men and women, dressed to impress, mingled in the theater's elegant art deco lobby, where an open bar and tables of gourmet refreshments catered to the city's elite. All had shelled out considerable sums for the privilege of attending the event.

Additional guests crowded the mezzanine as well as the sweeping staircase that led up to it, in anticipation of a special performance of *Pygmalion* that was scheduled to begin shortly. Everybody who was anybody in Gotham was present, which was just what Bruce was counting on.

Looks like I've come to the right place. Decked out in a tailored Italian suit, he took in the scene. His crystal champagne flute actually held ginger ale. Despite appearances, he was on the job and needed to keep his wits sharp.

Batman peered through Bruce's eyes, intent on his mission.

A large ice sculpture dominated the refreshments table. It was modeled after the plaster bas-relief that adorned the ornate pediment about the theater's front entrance, depicting the twin muses of Comedy and Tragedy. Melpomene, holding her frowning mask to her breast, posed beside her more light-hearted sister, Thalia, whose classically beautiful features were only partially hidden by her own grinning disguise.

The muses shared the face and form of Lydia Doyle.

A timely coincidence? he wondered, contemplating the frozen muses. Or simply more evidence of just how ubiquitous "Miss Gotham" had been in her heyday? Lydia was everywhere once you started looking for her. Was that what the Talon had meant when he'd alluded to a secret that had been hiding right in front of Batman all this time?

Small talk, punctuated by occasional laughter, filled the lobby, competing with a string quartet performing in the southwest corner of the chamber. The nouveaux riches mixed with old money, sizing each other up.

Turning away from the ice sculpture, Bruce made his way through the milling throng, skillfully deflecting greetings and invitations from the mayor, at least two members of the city council, several business contacts and would-be business contacts, a rising tech millionaire, an award-winning playwright, a theater critic, gossip columnists, and one bona fide movie sex symbol. He did so as deftly as Batman might evade a barrage of gunfire, politely brushing aside the overtures with practiced ease, while scanning the crowd for one particular face.

"Bruce! Bruce Wayne!"

Vincent Wright held court on the mezzanine, flanked by a pair of attractive young women, one blonde, the other brunette. The dapper heir to the Wright family fortune was roughly the same age as Bruce and swam in the same circles. A shaved skull served as a fashion statement, along with a neatly trimmed blond goatee. Shrewd blue eyes indicated that a life of privilege had not dulled his wits. His attire and grooming were impeccable.

"Hello, Vincent."

The crowd parted to let Bruce join the group. Vincent came forward to greet him, flashing the whitest smile money could buy. Bruce wondered if he was aware that the ice sculpture below was inspired by his great-grandfather's work.

If he was connected to the Court, probably.

"Great to see you, old man. How long has it been?" Vincent held out his hand. Bruce gripped it with something less than his full strength before letting go.

"Too long, I'm sure."

"Without a doubt." Wright placed an arm around each of his comely companions. "Have you met Judith?" he asked, indicating the blonde on his right. "And..."

His memory seemed to falter.

"Lisa," the brunette supplied, an edge to her voice.

"Of course," Vincent said, unabashed. "Glad you could make it, Bruce."

"I almost skipped it," he confessed. "What with this worrisome fever going around."

"Fever?" If Vincent caught the reference, he gave no sign of it. His expression remained blandly affable.

"Didn't you hear?" Bruce said. "A homeless fellow burst into flames down by the market the other day." He made a point of applying hand sanitizer to his palms. "They say he literally burned up from the inside-out, because of some kind of ghastly new fever."

"Oh, right!" Judith chimed in. "That was on the news." She shuddered at the thought. "As if this city wasn't scary enough!"

"Tell me about it," Lisa agreed, not to be left out. "I swear, it's enough to give you nightmares."

"Oh, please." Vincent rolled his eyes. "Really, Bruce, I'm surprised at you falling for such alarmist nonsense. It's surely just clickbait and ratings fodder. Chances are, the man was just a wino who accidentally set his booze-soaked rags on fire while trying to drink and smoke at the same time. Unfortunate, for sure, but hardly cause for a quarantine."

His explanation elicited nervous laughter from the two women.

"I don't know." Bruce glanced around before lowering his voice conspiratorially. "My contacts at City Hall tell me this isn't the only such incident that's happened recently." He tugged nervously at his collar. "What if we're looking at an epidemic?" He had no intention of starting a panic so he leaned into his dilettante playboy persona. Painting Bruce Wayne as a hypochondriac was a small price to pay for trying to provoke a reaction from Wright.

"Are you serious?" Vincent scoffed. "This is Gotham. People come to bizarre ends all the time. At worst, this is merely the work of yet another flamboyant maniac like Mister Freeze or the Scarecrow. For better or for worse, a few colorful murders every now and then are the price we pay for living in one of the greatest cities in the world."

"I wish I could believe that," Bruce said, quite sincerely. "But an expert of my acquaintance informs me that outbreaks of spontaneous human combustion have occurred throughout Gotham's history, for at least a century or so. They used to call it the 'Burning Sickness,' or so I'm told."

"Really?" Lisa fished a small bottle of hand sanitizer from her purse. "Holy crap."

"Here, let me have some of that." Judith reached anxiously for the bottle.

"In a minute." Lisa applied the gel to her palms. "Better safe than sorry."

Vincent clucked at them. "You're all taking this way too seriously. Gotham is awash in spooky legends and folklore. Hell, you can take a ghost tour of the city most any night of the week. This 'Burning Sickness' is just another historical horror story, blown all out of proportion."

"Like the Court of Owls?" Bruce asked.

It wasn't subtle, but sometimes brute force got the job done more effectively than any intricate strategy. The Owls already knew that Bruce Wayne and Batman were one and the same, so there was little danger of exposing his true identity. He watched intently for any telltale reaction on Vincent's part.

There!

Was it his imagination or did the provocation hit a nerve? Just for a moment, Vincent stiffened and his eyes widened, then narrowed in suspicion. His charming smile never slipped, but it suddenly looked a bit more forced, if only for a heartbeat. A certain wariness entered his body language, as well. His cultivated poise seemed more... artificial than before.

"Yes, precisely," he said, recovering smoothly. "Exactly like the so-called 'Court of Owls.' Unsubstantiated rumors and legends."

He was a cool customer. Most people wouldn't have noticed his micro-tells. Bruce, however, wasn't "most people."

"But, Vinnie," Lisa protested, "I heard the Owls were real. Remember when all those politicians got assassinated a while ago? People said it was the Talons, like out of the stories. That wasn't just talk. That was on the news."

She wasn't wrong. Not too long ago, during the so-called "Night of Owls," the Court had briefly thrown their traditional secrecy to the winds and dispatched a squadron of reanimated Talons in an all-out assault on Gotham's movers and shakers, with an eye to asserting their dominion over the city once and for all. Several prominent citizens had been assassinated before Batman and his allies had succeeded in neutralizing the threat. It was a drastic overreach that had cost the Court dearly.

They had been more circumspect since.

"Yet more clickbait," Vincent said dismissively. "Yes, of course, we all remember when some masked terrorists or gang members went on a horrific killing spree. Gotham lost many fine public servants that terrible night. And, yes, from what I understand, the killers dressed up as the 'Talons' from the old nursery rhyme, probably just to scare people. Gotham criminals love their theatrics after all, not unlike a certain Dark Knight I could name."

He glanced pointedly at Bruce.

"So you don't believe in the Court of Owls?" Bruce pressed.

"No more than I believe in the tooth fairy or the boogeyman." Vincent yawned, as though growing bored with the topic. "Seriously, my family has been rooted in Gotham almost since its founding. If the Court of Owls were really nesting in the city's nooks and crannies, I like to think my distinguished ancestors would have run across them at some point."

"Well, my family *has* been in Gotham since its very beginnings," Bruce reminded him. "And I've learned never to underestimate what might be hiding in its shadows."

A tense pause ensued before a contrite look came over Vincent's face. He smacked his forehead.

"As in Crime Alley, of course," he said. "I'm so sorry, old man. Given your personal history, I can understand why you—of all people—should be wary of Gotham's darker corners. I should have taken that into account before pooh-poohing your concerns so insensitively." He feigned sympathy convincingly enough. "But trust me when I tell you that, as far as I know, the Court of Owls is just a bedtime story."

"And the Burning Sickness?"

"Hype and hysteria, I'm sure."

"If you say so." Bruce decided to bring the skirmish to a close. He'd seen what he was looking for, or thought he had. Vincent was on guard now. It was unlikely he was going to let anything else slip.

The lights flickered overhead, signaling that the curtain would be rising soon. The crowd began filing into the auditorium to claim their seats, grabbing perhaps one last drink or canapé before the play began. The musicians put down their instruments.

"Ah, show time!" Vincent announced to his companions. "We should seek out our private box. You're welcome to join us, Bruce, unless you've made other arrangements."

"I'm going to pass on the play," he replied. "With due respect to George Bernard Shaw, I don't need to see *Pygmalion* again."

"Can't blame you there," Vincent quipped, all chummy cordiality again. "Just so you know, though, I'm throwing an after-party at the Plaza later on, exclusively for a few very special friends and associates. You should definitely drop by, and please feel free to bring a guest if you like or, if you're truly going stag this evening, I'm certain we can find suitable company for Gotham's most eligible bachelor."

"Oh, yeah," Judith said invitingly. "I don't think that would be a problem."

"No problem at all," Lisa confirmed.

"Thanks for the invitation," Bruce replied, noting the women's obvious disappointment, "but I'm afraid I have other plans for the evening."

•

Batman glided over the streets. His scalloped black cape fanned out behind him as it caught the air currents that held him aloft. Despite the hour, the lights of the city glittered beneath him, combating the darkness. Aging chimneys and water towers shared rooftops with modern solar panels and satellite disks. The pedestrians enjoying Gotham's nightlife remained unaware of the stealthy figure soaring high above the streetlamps.

Expertly guiding his descent, he touched down on the rooftop of a pricy penthouse atop a gleaming new high-rise condominium. His boots made no sound as he landed, even though, in theory, there was no one to hear him in the apartment below.

Vincent Wright's party at the Plaza Hotel would be well

underway by now. The discovery that Vincent would be away for the evening had been a welcome fringe benefit of their encounter at the theater, and it presented an ideal opportunity to search his residence. Batman hoped to confirm his suspicions, and perhaps even discover some reference to the current killings.

How exactly is your family mixed up in this, Vincent?

A very expensive, very sophisticated security system barely slowed him down as he entered the penthouse via a skylight. Infrared sensors in his cowl failed to detect any unexpected heat signatures, confirming that no one was at home. A brisk sweep of the suite revealed nothing incriminating, which came as little surprise. Batman had hardly expected Vincent to leave anything of value out in the open. The Owls guarded their secrets well.

From a shadowed perch, behind granite and lime...

Digging deeper, Batman searched the apartment as swiftly and efficiently as possible. Even though he had every reason to assume that Vincent would be out late, he wasn't inclined to push his luck by lingering any longer than was necessary. Wright's well-equipped home office was the logical place to focus the search, so he began by firing up Vincent's home computer and starting the process of downloading its contents, encrypted or otherwise, onto a flash drive programmed to bypass all but military-strength security measures.

The download required several minutes to complete, and he used those minutes to take a closer look at Vincent's personal library, which included a few of the standard books on Percy Wright and his art, as well as a sizable number of advanced scientific texts on biochemistry. Vincent, it appeared, took after his illustrious ancestor when it came to scientific curiosity. Much of the Wright fortune was invested in pharmaceuticals and biotech, and Percy Wright had been a chemist, as well.

A family tradition, perhaps?

Vincent also seemed to share his ancestor's interest in art.

Framed on the wall of the office was what appeared to be a rough pencil sketch of a nude model striking a dramatic pose. The woman's face was turned away from the artist, but by now Batman recognized the familiar contours of Lydia Doyle. Percy Wright's signature was scribbled in the lower right-hand corner of the sketch, which might have been a preliminary study for some sculpture. Batman made a mental note to compare the sketch to Wright's known oeuvre.

Perhaps Vincent shares Joanna's fascination with Lydia.

He reminded himself that the portrait wasn't necessarily a smoking gun. There were perfectly innocent reasons why Vincent might want to proudly display his ancestor's work, just as it was hardly a crime to take an interest in chemistry. But coupled with the Court's scorched-earth response to Joanna Lee's research, the portrait's presence was provocative, to say the least. Where there was smoke, there was often fire—perhaps even spontaneous combustion.

What other secrets might "Lydia" be hiding?

Carefully removing the framed portrait from the wall, he uncovered the built-in safe hiding behind it. Unlike the drawing, it was far from vintage, being a top-of-the-line steel-and-cement composite with a digital keypad. It was a serious container meant to protect serious valuables. Or secrets.

Selina would find this irresistible. Batman knew the feeling, at least in this particular instance. He wasn't leaving without finding out what Vincent was hiding, although he considered his options as he retrieved the spy-drive from Vincent's computer. Having studied under the finest safecrackers on six continents, and taken pains to keep abreast of the latest innovations in the field, he was confident that he could break into the safe in due time. But time was indeed an issue.

There was no way of knowing for certain when Vincent might come wandering home, alone or with company, and Batman was in no hurry to get caught breaking and entering. There was also the danger that in breaching the safe's defenses, he might leave behind evidence that it had been tampered with, thus tipping his hand. Perhaps it was worth trying a less invasive approach?

Batman considered the keypad. His gaze darted over to the portrait, which he had placed atop Vincent's desk.

"Hmm," he grunted. Playing a hunch, he took a stab at the password.

LYDIA.

A digital display replied.

PASSWORD INCORRECT

Batman tried again.

PERCY.

PASSWORD INCORRECT

He paused. Safes of this make and model often only allowed a limited number of false guesses before denying access and likely triggering an alarm. He could only risk one more guess. Searching his mind, he recalled what he knew of Percy and Lydia. The ice sculpture back at the theater glistened in his memory as another possibility came to mind. He recalled that old quote from Percy that Joanna had turned up, his rambling remarks at that long-ago reception in his honor.

Batman keyed in another password, oddly confident of the results.

MUSE.

PASSWORD ACCEPTED
ACCESS GRANTED

A metallic click indicated that the safe was unlocked. Batman found the recessed grip and pulled the door open, exposing the contents. A sharp intake of breath betrayed his reaction to what he found.

A white porcelain Owl mask was propped up on a stand. Unlike the black leather hood and metal goggles worn by the Talons, a mask of this sort was worn only by a high-ranking member of the Court, and typically only at one of the Court's clandestine meetings. The stylized mask was both elegant and eerie in its simplicity. Oblong eyes and a hint of a jagged beak sufficed to give the impression of a distinctly owlish mien. Batman recognized the mask at once.

He could never forget it.

Once again, his mind threw him back to the Labyrinth. He was trapped in a gladiatorial pit at the heart of the maze, penned in by towering marble walls, as the Court of Owls peered down on him from their lofty galleries high above his head. Their faces were concealed by masks like this one.

Starved, drugged, and battered, Batman hadn't even been able to trust his own senses, so that the masks had seemed to come alive, transforming the Owls into nightmarish, half-human, half-avian monstrosities, hooting shrilly as they prepared to feast upon his flesh and bones. A colossal white marble statue of an owl loomed majestically over the scene, tainted water spilling from its beak into an elegant fountain. Blinding lights had exposed Batman to the Court's relentless scrutiny as they'd voyeuristically delighted in his suffering. Masked men, women, and even children had shed their humanity, along with any trace of mercy or compassion…

Batman repressed a shudder as he forced the hellish memory back into the past where it belonged. He'd escaped from the Labyrinth, that was what mattered.

He reached for the mask, then reconsidered. There was no

law against possessing an Owl mask, and taking the object would merely alert Vincent to the incursion and put him further on guard. Batman had found the confirmation he sought. Better now to slip back into the night with the captured data from the computer, leaving Vincent none the wiser.

"Hoo goes there," a voice said behind him. "Hoo, hoo."

Batman spun around to find the Talon standing in the doorway, knives drawn. Batman was impressed. It took skill to sneak up on him.

Maybe if I hadn't let memories distract me...

But he could castigate himself later. Snatching the Owl mask, he flung it at the assassin who, predictably, dropped one of his knives to rescue it, snatching it out of the air before it could shatter against a wall. At the same time the Talon hurled his remaining knife at his opponent's face.

Batman turned his head just in time to avoid the missile, which smacked into the wall behind him, missing him by inches. He snatched the flash drive from the computer and overturned Vincent's desk, spilling the computer and other desktop items toward the Talon, forcing him backward into the spacious living room that lay beyond.

Springing over the desk, he took the fight to the Talon, who flung the captured mask onto a plush sofa to get it out of harm's way. Batman threw a hard punch at the Talon's jaw, putting his weight into it. The blow knocked the Talon's head to one side, and Batman followed it up with a right, a left, and an elbow to the face. The last strike cracked one of the yellow goggles that hid the Talon's eyes.

The Talon retaliated by slashing out with his eponymous claws, which raked across the embossed Bat-emblem on the hero's chest. A hideous scraping noise assailed Batman's ears, making him grateful for the extra layer of Kevlar that lay beneath the symbol. The men grappled furiously until the Talon managed to shove Batman backward over a glass coffee table, which shattered beneath his weight. Batman landed hard, the debris digging into his back.

"Mister Wright said you might come snooping around." The Talon drew a sword from the scabbard on his back. "I still owe you for that zap back by Claire Nesko's place."

"Consider it on me," Batman said.

"Oh, I always pay my debts," the Talon replied, "but I wouldn't advise trying that taser-toy again. I'm ready for it now."

Good to know.

Raising the sword above his head, the Talon swung it down at Batman, who rolled out of the way to avoid being bisected, even as he hurled a Batarang at his foe with all his strength. The Talon's reflexes were too fast, however, and he caught it in mid-air, despite the razor-sharp edges which cut through his leather glove and into his palm. Blood streamed from his hand, but the stream rapidly slowed to a trickle, then a halt, as the killer's sliced flesh healed with terrifying speed. He snarled as he tossed the bloody Batarang aside.

Adrenaline accelerated a Talon's regenerative abilities.

"How is Claire doing these days?" the assassin asked. "Don't suppose you want to tell me where I can find her… or Joanna."

Bingo!

"Not particularly." Batman sprang to his feet, fists clenched and ready. "I've seen what you did to Dennis Lewton and Professor Morse. What's with the spontaneous combustion gimmick? That's not from your team's usual playbook."

"What can I say?" the Talon responded with a shrug. "Everything old is new again." He came at Batman again, swinging his sword horizontally this time, aiming for his midriff. Batman leapt above the assault, pulling his legs up so that the blade sliced through the empty air beneath him. Turning his defense into an attack, he delivered a snap-kick to the Talon's chin that caused the hooded assassin to lose his grip on his sword, which went flying across the room.

Batman dropped back onto his feet, wanting to keep the Talon off-balance. He came in close to deliver a rapid-fire series of blows he hoped would stun the Talon long enough to immobilize him. A kidney punch, followed by an open-handed chop to the man's throat, elicited a grunt of pain from the assassin. A solid left hook to his jaw whipped his head to the side—but still didn't put the Talon down for the count.

"My turn," he growled.

Grabbing his foe by the shoulders, he hurled Batman across the room. He crashed into a glass display case holding various expensive artifacts. The impact jarred Batman even through his protective suit. Bruised ribs ached in protest. His mouth tasted of blood.

"You getting it now, Bat?" the Talon crowed. He threw out his chest as he postured before a large plate-glass window that overlooked the city. "You may have beaten some of those old Talons before—barely—but you don't stand a chance against me. There's a reason the Court took me in, and trained me to within an inch of my life. I'm a legend in the making."

"That's what they all say," Batman replied. "And you know what? I'm getting damn sick of legends."

The bright side to the Talon's indestructibility was that Batman didn't have to hold back. Springing into the air, he grabbed onto a hanging ceiling lamp and swung feet-first at his opponent, letting go of the lamp in order to clear the distance between them. The soles of his boots slammed into the Talon's chest, knocking the killer right through the plate-glass window—and sending both men flying out into the sky high above Gotham.

Burglar alarms shrieked over the sound of broken glass as gravity seized the two. The Talon grabbed onto Batman's right leg as they plunged toward the street, forcing the hero to drive his left heel into the killer's hooded face. He kicked repeatedly even as he fired his grapnel gun at a balcony on the skyscraper across the street. Ordinarily, he would want to save his foe from falling, but this was a Talon. Batman knew from experience that even a multi-story fall would only slow him down.

"Let go of me, you maniac!"

The micro-diamond drill head at the business end of the Batrope dug into the underside of the balcony, taking hold in the concrete. The line went taut as the de-cel jumpline arrested Batman's descent, sending him swinging above the street, but the Talon held on just as tightly, despite the hard rubber heel slamming into his face.

Showing no mercy, Batman plucked a miniature flash-bang grenade from his belt and threw it straight at the assassin's face. He averted his own eyes as the grenade went off, but the sudden blast of glare and noise jolted him even through his protective cowl. The flash-bang did the trick, however, dislodging the Talon, who tumbled helplessly toward the ground where a construction tarp and wooden scaffolding had been erected over some sidewalk repairs. The plummeting figure crashed through the tarp, vanishing from sight.

Damn it, Batman thought. *I need to keep eyes on him.*

The swinging rope carried him toward the face of the other skyscraper. He used his heels to keep from slamming into the building, then extended the cable to descend rapidly to the sidewalk, where startled night owls of a more innocent variety gaped at him. Brakes squealed as cabs and limos halted to catch a glimpse of Gotham's near-mythical defender. People reached for their phones to snap a picture. Ignoring the bystanders, he rushed to the construction site, hoping that the fall had injured the Talon long enough for him to be apprehended.

Escaping from the Talon wasn't enough—the assassin still needed to face justice for the deaths of at least two people. Nor would his other targets be safe until the Talon was under wraps and the Court's secret agenda was exposed to the light of day. In the past, Batman recalled, extreme cold had been effective in keeping Talons in a state of suspended animation so that they no longer posed a threat. He wanted to put this Talon on ice as well.

Trading the grapnel gun for a fresh Batarang, he cautiously entered the site. Posters advertising local bands and nightclubs were plastered over the scaffolding. A ragged hole in the tarp flapped around the edges. A depression in the gravel indicated exactly where the falling Talon had landed. Blood splattered the debris.

The Talon was gone.

Batman silently cursed the assassin's preternatural ability to heal. Crimson streaks and droplets suggested that the Talon has indeed managed to drag himself away in the time it had taken Batman to descend—rather less spectacularly—to street level. The bloody trail, which diminished noticeably as Batman followed it, led to an open manhole just beyond the demolished sidewalk. He stared down into the sewers, which offered a variety of subterranean escape routes.

He fought the temptation to chase after his prey. As much as he wanted to end this tonight, he knew that realistically there was little chance of finding the killer now that he had vanished into the byzantine depths of Gotham's substructure. Nor was Batman eager to rush into an ambush without any real plan on how to subdue his foe. Frustrated, he turned away from the beckoning manhole.

Police sirens closed on the vicinity, no doubt responding to the burglar alarms triggered by Batman's shattering exit from the penthouse. He wouldn't be surprised if Vincent had his own private security team, as well. Disappearing into an unlit alley, he verified that the flash drive storing Vincent's stolen data was still secure within a compartment on his Utility Belt.

Throbbing ribs demanded Alfred's services as a medic. Batman consoled himself that tonight's expedition hadn't been a total waste. He now knew for certain that Vincent Wright, great-grandson of Percy Wright, belonged to the Court of Owls.

That would have to be enough for the present.

Next time, he promised the assassin.

16

It was late, and the Gotham Museum of Natural History had been closed for hours. The regular cleaning and security staff had all been sent home, the better to accommodate a very private gathering in the museum's avian wing.

The Court of Owls convened around a long rectangular conference table beneath a large stuffed condor that hung suspended from the ceiling. The lighting was dim, rendered warm by the dark wood of the decades-old chamber. The murmurs of conversation mingled to create ambient noise. Drawn drapes concealed the conclave from the outside world, but not from Batman, who crouched atop the condor.

Masks, identical to the one he had found hidden in Vincent's office, hid the identities of more than a dozen or so men and women seated at the table, but their fine attire attested to their wealth and privilege. Stone-faced bodyguards, no doubt armed to the teeth, were stationed around the perimeter of the chamber, yet the Talon was nowhere to be seen.

This worried Batman.

The data captured from Vincent's home computer, once decrypted, had contained little evidence of his involvement with the Court—apparently he kept his owlish endeavors carefully segregated from his less clandestine pursuits. A close examination of his calendar, however, had turned up one seemingly innocuous engagement—a late-night appointment labeled simply "PARL."

Batman had learned more about owls than he would have preferred. He knew that a group of owls was properly known as a "parliament." It was why he'd tailed Vincent to this meeting, keeping a wary eye out for the Talon the entire time.

The condor's impressive wingspan hid his presence from the Court. Nevertheless seeing so many Owls gathered in one place, for the first time since he'd escaped the Labyrinth, troubled him more than he'd anticipated. Despite his past victories, the Court endured, just as it had down through the generations. Was he fooling himself to think that he could ever bring the organization down permanently? Or would it outlive him, after all?

"Let us get down to business."

A female Owl stood at the head of the table, raising her voice to be heard above the various murmured conversations. Delicate gold filigree around the edges and eyeholes of her mask indicated that she was the current Grandmaster of the Court, as did her imperious tone and bearing. A mink stole warmed her shoulders above an elegant black evening gown suitable for a red-carpet entrance. Tasteful silver jewelry gleamed on her fingers and around her neck. Lustrous black hair, done up in a chignon, could be glimpsed at the back of her head.

"Times being what they are," she added, "we should avoid congregating in one spot for any longer than is absolutely necessary, so it behooves us to conduct this conclave in a brisk and efficient manner. We do not have the luxury of engaging in idle chatter."

The woman's voice wasn't familiar, either from the Gotham social scene or from his past dealings with the Court. She would have been newly installed as the Grandmaster after the Court's recent reverses, which had included some bloody internal power struggles. More than a few of the Court's previous leaders were behind bars, in exile, or six feet under. Batman wondered how exactly this new Grandmaster had snagged the top spot, and just how secure her position might be. Internecine conflicts could sometimes spill over into the city itself, endangering the innocent as well as the guilty.

The hubbub died down as the Grandmaster continued to address the Court.

"Thank you all for taking time out of your busy schedules to attend this conclave," she said, "and my gratitude to those members of the Court who quietly arranged to make this apt location available for the night." An older Owl harrumphed at his seat. His stooped back, as well as the cane leaning against his chair, implied both age and infirmity.

"Still doesn't feel right holding these meetings all over town, instead of at the Harbor House," he growled. "It lacks tradition… *history.*"

In addition to their underground sanctuary, the Owls had once held Court at a venerable old edifice on the city's South Side. It had appeared to be an elite social club catering to Gotham's upper crust, but Batman had seen past that façade, forcing the Owls to abandon their long-time lair. Harbor House had remained empty ever since. Whispered rumors about its dark history had discouraged even the most avaricious would-be developers.

"I understand how you feel," the Grandmaster replied to the querulous old man, "but we both know that it is no longer safe to frequent certain old haunts. Ever since the Batman turned his eye toward us in earnest, the Court has opted never to meet twice in the same place. Nor do we need to, given our ready access to any number of suitable locales."

No wonder I haven't tracked down their new meeting-place, Batman mused. *It's become a moving target.*

He was tempted by the opportunity to apprehend the gathered Owls in one swoop. The bodyguards posed a challenge, but he had faced stiffer odds before, and was confident that he could take them down, if necessary. But the altercation might allow the Owls to escape, rendering the effort futile. And there was still no sign of the Talon. It concerned Batman that the Court's most formidable defender remained unaccounted for.

Weighing his options, he waited to hear what the Owls had to say before deciding on a course of action.

"It is a wise and prudent policy, Madame Grandmaster," a dapper Owl stated at the opposite end of the table. Batman instantly recognized Vincent Wright's voice and mannerisms. "I commend your caution… as long as we don't become too scared of our own shadows. Or the shadow of a certain bat." That started a new round of murmuring, which their leader cut off with the raising of a single hand.

"'Grandmaster' will suffice," she said archly, "and while we appreciate your approval of this Court's decision, we hardly deem it necessary."

"My apologies… Grandmaster," Vincent replied. "I meant no disrespect."

"See that you don't." Her beady black eyes fixed on him. "Particularly since I, and various other members of the Court, grow increasingly concerned about recent efforts you have undertaken in the Court's name, namely deploying our Talon to re-bury a forgotten scandal concerning your family."

There it is, Batman thought. Masks or no masks, the Grandmaster wasn't even pretending to shield Vincent Wright's anonymity. Was it a careless breach of protocol, or a deliberate attempt to put Vincent in his place?

"Everything I've done was in the best interests of the Court," Vincent insisted, "and as you know, it was done with your authorization. I would never think to go behind the Court's back."

She nodded. "We agreed that the Lee girl's investigations warranted action, yes, but your aggressive approach to the matter has caused it to escalate at an alarming rate, attracting the attention of our greatest enemy," the Grandmaster said. "In hindsight, perhaps we should have let sleeping dogs lie. Why go to such lengths over a dusty bit of history from a century ago?"

Masked heads nodded near her end of the table. Perhaps half of those assembled appeared to share the Grandmaster's concerns. The other half, seated at Vincent's end, refrained from nodding. Muttered voices conveyed unrest among the Owls.

"Surely the secrets of the Court must be protected from scrutiny?" Vincent said calmly. "Hasn't that always been our way? 'Speak not a whispered word of them,' and all that?" Now the Owls seated near him nodded in agreement. It appeared there was indeed a degree of dissension within the Court. A rival faction, perhaps, jockeying for power in the wake of recent setbacks? Or simply disagreement on this one point?

How ambitious are you, Vincent?

"Guarding our past cannot endanger our present," the Grandmaster said. "Particularly when it brings the Batman to your very door." She clucked in disapproval. "Did you expect that his nocturnal visit to your penthouse would escape our notice, or that this would not concern us?"

"Not in the least," Vincent replied, "but I wouldn't make too much of the incident. The Talon repelled the incursion and now... what? The Dark Knight is working against us? What else is new?" He scoffed. "A reasonable degree of caution is one thing, but we can hardly curtail our operations at the first sign of trouble. If that's our policy, we might as well withdraw from Gotham altogether, which I doubt anyone here favors." He gave a dramatic flourish of his hand.

"Hear, hear!" another Owl agreed, thumping the tabletop for emphasis. "This is our city, not that damn vigilante's. He's the one who should be running scared."

The Grandmaster glared at the speaker, silencing him with a pointed look, then turned her gilded mask back toward Vincent.

"Are you accusing this Court of cowardice?"

"Certainly not," he answered. "I'm simply recommending that we not let Batman intimidate us. With all due respect, an excess of caution could prove as much a mistake as underestimating him."

"Perhaps," the Grandmaster said skeptically, "but a wise owl chooses its battles. I remain unconvinced that this old business of yours merits further exposure, let alone going to war."

"The Court is already at war, and has been for some time," Vincent argued. "That's not going to change, regardless of what we decide tonight. And there's far more to this current affair than merely some 'dusty' old history, as you put it. There's an opportunity to be grasped, a chance to locate a priceless asset that has eluded us for a century!"

That got Batman's attention.

I knew there was more to this case than a scandal...

"Percy Wright's fabled elixir," the Grandmaster said mockingly. "It's nothing but a pipe dream."

"Far from it," Vincent insisted, leaning forward. "We know from our own secret histories that the elixir existed, which is why my family has been diligently trying to recreate it for generations— minus its... incendiary side effects."

"Yet you have nothing to show for it," the Grandmaster observed, "other than the occasional charred cadaver or two, or three, or four..."

The Burning Sickness, Batman realized. *It's not a fever then, but a failed experiment.* From the sound of it, Wright and his ancestors had been testing this mysterious "elixir" on human guinea pigs ever since Percy's time. But what kind of chemical were they talking about? What made it so valuable?

"Casualties among the lower classes," Vincent replied, "and only when a promising new approach presented itself." He sat back again. "Still, I confess that the project has encountered a frustrating number of false leads over the decades. Eliminating the lethal aspect has proven more challenging than one might expect."

Batman felt his frustration growing. So many hints, yet nothing concrete.

Why human subjects? he wondered. *Why not test on animals?*

"We've heard all this before," the old Owl with the cane said. "From you, and your father before you. What has changed?"

"Joanna Lee," Vincent said. "We've long known that Percy, for his own reasons, withheld data from the Court. This he confessed in a letter that was delivered after his death. In that message he claimed to have developed a version of the elixir that did not induce spontaneous combustion in its subjects. Despite that fact, he swore that the formula would be lost to history, 'for the sake of the future.'" The tone of Vincent's voice revealed how little he thought of his ancestor's scruples.

"Needless to say," he continued, "my family has sought Percy's secret formula ever since, but until recently I thought had exhausted all avenues of investigation. Fortunately, as you know, the Court has mechanisms in place to alert us if anyone digs too deeply into our affairs, past *or* present. When Joanna Lee began consulting certain records, conducting specific searches, and posting her notes to the university's cloud-based backup system, I became aware of her investigation into my ancestor's colorful history… and of her provocative new theory that Percy had, in fact, hidden a secret message in his work.

"Needless to say, I was intrigued."

So Vincent, at least, was taking Joanna's theory seriously. Now if only he would explain the nature of Percy's work…

"At which point, naturally, our agenda has become two-fold," Vincent said. "First, to obtain Ms. Lee and obtain whatever fresh insights and information we can extract from her, while simultaneously containing the situation by eliminating anyone who might be familiar with her studies."

"And what, may I ask, is the current status of the operation?" the Grandmaster said acidly.

"Joanna is in hiding, but cannot long elude us. Our eyes and ears are everywhere, after all."

"What of the roommate?" the Grandmaster asked. "The one Batman rescued from the Talon? You had hoped to use her as leverage to ensure Joanna Lee's cooperation if and when you secured her."

"Claire Nesko?" Vincent said with a chuckle. Batman could practically hear him smirking behind his mask. "There we have had greater success. Despite Batman's best efforts to hide her, the Talon is on his way to retrieve her even as we speak."

Batman stiffened, and it was all he could do not to react—not even a sharp intake of breath. Suddenly he was faced with a harsh dilemma. He knew now where the Talon was. Should he take on the Court—bodyguards or no bodyguards—while they were gathered in one place, or rush to Claire's rescue?

The Court of Owls posed a threat to all of Gotham. Many more lives than Claire's could be in play here, especially if the Court got their hands on this elusive elixir. Or if they continued to experiment on helpless citizens, resulting in another "outbreak" of the Burning Sickness.

Yet an innocent was in danger. An innocent he had promised to keep safe.

There was no choice, really. He couldn't let Claire become the Talon's next victim. Moving with intense focus, he pulled a secure phone from his belt and texted a priority alert to Nightwing.

> Talon coming for Claire.
> On my way.

The conclave wasn't over yet, but it was time to go. Eschewing stealth for speed, he plucked a handful of miniature smoke-bombs from his belt and hurled them at the assembly below. Billowing black fumes engulfed the Owls and their guards, shielding Batman from view. An acrid odor polluted the air, further distracting his foes. Agitated shouts and coughing could be heard through the swirling smoke-screen.

"The Batman! He's here!"

"Kill him!"

Gunfire peppered the dead condor. The cables were shot apart, causing the stuffed bird to swing alarmingly, but he had already abandoned his perch there. Embedding a grapnel in the ceiling, he swung above the fogbound Owls toward the nearest draped window, tossing an explosive charge ahead of him. It blew out both the curtains and the window to speed his retreat. Broken glass rained down on the guards below.

Bullets chased him, chipping away at the walls and exhibits, but by the time the gunfire swung toward the breach, Batman was clear of the building and dashing toward the Batmobile, hidden not far away. It would take him several minutes to reach the safe house where he'd stowed Claire, which might not be fast enough if the Talon was already closing in.

Every moment counted.

Keep her safe, Dick.

And watch yourself, as well.

17

The mugger barely qualified as a workout. Nightwing stood over the fallen figure, who was sprawled unconscious on the floor of an alley not far from the safe house. A switchblade gleamed on the pavement just beyond the crook's limp fingers. He kicked it out of the way, just in case the would-be thief was playing possum, then bound the man's hands behind his back with zip-ties.

An elderly couple, who had been making a midnight run to the local all-night deli, looked on anxiously. A black eye and busted lip were all the mugger had to show for his efforts. He moaned weakly.

"You okay?" Nightwing asked the couple.

They nodded, clutching each other.

"You'll be fine now," he assured them. "I've paged the police, who should be here shortly. Just tell them what happened." He figured their testimony would be enough to put the mugger away for a while. Chances were, the crook already had an extensive rap sheet. Nightwing hoped they threw the book at him. Preying on senior citizens was about as low as it got.

"Thank you," the old woman managed, clearly shaken by her close brush with becoming a crime statistic. "If you hadn't showed up when you did…"

"No problem." Nightwing re-bagged the seniors' groceries, which had spilled onto the pavement, and handed the brown paper sack back to them. "I just happened to be in the neighborhood."

It was true.

As Batman had requested, Nightwing had been keeping an eye on the safe house where Claire Nesko was being held. While not staking out the building all night every night, he had stuck close to the location, particularly after sundown, regularly and discreetly checking on it to make certain nothing was amiss.

Last time he'd swung by, less than thirty minutes ago, a pair of plainclothes police officers were still stationed outside the building, looking bored. The electronics surveillance devices he and Batman had covertly planted inside the safe house had picked up nothing alarming, nor had the regular GCPD feeds. Nightwing had been almost grateful to stumble across the attempted mugging while patrolling the neighborhood. It was the most excitement he'd had in days, even if the low-level hoodlum wasn't exactly the KGBeast.

Beggars can't be choosers.

A siren indicated an approaching police car, which meant it was time to get a move on. He hoped the couple he'd rescued would stick around long enough to press charges, but as a vigilante he could hardly accompany them down to the station to make an official statement. The trussed-up mugger and the telltale switchblade were the only evidence he could personally provide. With an acrobatic leap, he propelled himself onto the lower rung of a nearby fire escape, and swiftly scaled the side of the building to reach the rooftop.

The exercise invigorated him. Sitting still had never been his style, not even in his Boy Wonder days. He liked to think that he had inherited that restlessness from his daredevil parents, circus performers from a long tradition.

A vibration in his facemask alerted him to an incoming transmission from Batman. The HMD tech in his lenses flashed an urgent message before his eyes.

Talon coming for Claire.

On my way.

Nightwing swore under his breath. Now he was regretting the detour. If something had happened to Claire Nesko while he'd been out taking the air, he knew he'd never forgive himself.

By now he knew the neighborhood like the back of his hand. The safe house was only a few blocks away, and he leapt from the roof onto a convenient power line, which he ran along as fearlessly as a tightrope walker performing without a net. The insulated soles of his boots protected him from any high-voltage shocks while providing excellent traction on the taut cables. Cars and buses passed underneath as he took the high road over the public streets and sidewalks. An express train rumbled along the nearby tracks.

Tuning out the sounds of the city, he activated the bugs they had placed throughout the safe house. For privacy's sake the concealed listening devices were only located in the house's common areas, but would be effective in letting him know if there was any commotion on the premises. Listening in, he was relieved to hear nothing out of the ordinary. If anything, the audio was reassuring in its mundanity.

"It's getting late, miss," a cop said, yawning. "Sure you don't want to turn in for the night?"

"Like I could sleep anyway," Nesko replied, "with an owl-faced assassin after me. Sorry to keep you boys up." She sounded out of breath, and he could hear the steady hum and *thump thump thump* of a treadmill. They had to be in the gym on the top floor of the one-time boarding house.

"Just doing our duty, that's all," another voice assured her. "And we're not getting paid to sleep on the job. Which reminds me, Jerry, there any coffee left in the kitchen?"

Flicking through a sequence of audio channels, he eavesdropped on other parts of the safe house—the living room, the basement, the garage, the main stairs, and so on—but heard nothing out of the ordinary. A TV set on low, a hissing radiator, a grumpy cop bitching about an extra shift, and, yes, a pot of coffee brewing in the kitchen. All seemed well—for the moment.

Perhaps he wasn't too late to protect Claire from the Talon. Nevertheless, Nightwing didn't slow down as he neared the building. Shuttered windows hid the top floor from view, but some light still seeped through the blinds. He switched back to the bug in the gym.

"Just give me a few more minutes to burn off some energy," Claire said, huffing a bit. "I'm going stir-crazy cooped up in this place, no offense. Any idea when it will be safe for me to go back to my life?"

"'Fraid not, miss. That's up to the Commis—"

A whooshing sound cut off his answer. Something landed heavily—and wetly—on the floor.

"What the hell? Where did you—"

Another body thumped loudly and Nightwing heard Claire gasp out loud. A new voice came through Nightwing's earpiece.

"Hoot, hoot."

His heart sank as he kicked himself for not being faster. Leaping from a power line onto the window sill outside the gym, he fought the urge to charge to the rescue without first assessing the situation, the way Robin might have back in the day, before Batman had taught him better than that. Switching to infrared, he scanned the gym and detected four heat signatures on the other side of the window.

Two were cooling fast.

Damn it.

"Hello again, Claire," the Talon said. "Think twice about screaming or shouting, unless you want to get more cops killed."

His movements were too stealthy to hear over the hidden mikes, frustrating Nightwing. "Now then, refresh my memory—where did we leave off again?"

"No, please," Claire said softly. "Why can't you just leave me alone?"

"Blame your runaway roommate," the Talon taunted her. "She's the one who opened this can of worms, unluckily for you." His heat signature advanced on hers. "Claire Nesko, the Court of Owls has—"

Nightwing had heard enough. Retracting the infrared lenses, he grabbed the eaves above him with both hands, then swung feet first through the window, crashing through the glass and blinds as he launched himself into the gym with a spectacular lack of subtlety. He took in the scene in an instant: the converted attic filled with exercise equipment; Claire retreating behind the treadmill. She clutched a ten-pound dumbbell for protection, as the Talon stalked toward her, unconcerned, sword in hand. Two decapitated cops sprawled on the floor, taken unawares by the Talon before they could even draw their weapons.

The poor guys hadn't stood a chance.

Two more deaths crying out for justice.

The momentum of Nightwing's entrance carried him into the Talon, knocking him away from Claire. Recovering instantly from the attack, the Talon lunged at him, and Nightwing ducked beneath the killer's swinging blade to deliver a brutal snap-kick to the assassin's kneecap. The Talon collapsed to the ground, clutching the dislocated joint, but Nightwing knew from experience that the crippling injury would heal within minutes. This fight was far from over.

"Run!" he shouted to Claire. "I'll hold him back as long as I can!"

Nodding rapidly, she dropped the weight and sprinted out through the exit. As her steps pounded on the stairs, Nightwing drew his Escrima sticks from their holders on his back. The unbreakable polymer batons were his primary weapon of choice. Effective, but non-lethal, at least when used by somebody who knew what they were doing.

"Easier said than done." The Talon snapped his knee back into place with an audible *crack*. He sprang to his feet as though he hadn't been injured at all. "Well, well, if it isn't the poor man's Batman. As I understand it, you were meant to wear our livery, instead."

Nightwing didn't appreciate the reminder. "What can I say? I dodged that bullet."

"Dodge this," the Talon snarled. He came at his opponent, swinging the bloody sword. Nightwing flipped backward to avoid being sliced. His suit provided a degree of protection in a fight, but he wasn't inclined to test it against the Talon's razor-sharp blade.

A flying kick to the chin staggered the Talon, buying more time for Claire to escape, but only for a moment. Raising his sword high, the Talon brought it down toward Nightwing's scalp, which was protected only by the young hero's tousled black hair. For a split-second, he envied Batman's armored cowl...

Vanity is going to be the death of me.

Parrying the overhead strike with one baton, he jabbed the blunted end of his other stick into the Talon's ribs. His opponent grunted but, with a deft move, landed a blow to Nightwing's shoulder, and his sword bit in, drawing blood. A high kick to the Talon's chin briefly repelled the attack, even as Nightwing grimaced in pain. The wound stung like the devil. Clenching his teeth, he moved a second too slowly and the Talon's sword darted in to gash his cheek, as well.

The strike drew a hiss from between Nightwing's lips.

"Having second thoughts about throwing in with the Bat?" the Talon mocked. "You chose the wrong side in this war."

"War's not over, bro."

Blood streamed from Nightwing's face and shoulder, but he didn't let pain or panic throw him off his game. This wasn't his first rodeo; he'd taken his fair share of licks over the years and still come out on top in the end. Yet his opponent healed so much faster than he did. Without the ability to deliver a finishing blow, he was fighting a losing battle against the unstoppable assassin.

"If the Court could see you now," the Talon said, and he didn't sound even remotely winded. "Starting to wonder what they ever saw in you and your kin."

"Says the brainwashed lackey who performs on command." Nightwing tried to ignore the blood streaming from his cut cheek. Slapping an adhesive bandage over the wound wasn't an option at the moment. "You're just an attack dog let off its leash once in a while."

"I serve the true rulers of Gotham!" the assassin replied. "You're just an apprentice to an imposter."

Then he lunged, thrusting and slashing as the two men dueled. Nightwing blocked the attacks with his batons, but found himself increasingly on the defensive. A jab to the solar plexus barely slowed the Talon down, providing Nightwing with only a moment of respite. The crimson puddles spreading from the bodies of the murdered police officers posed an additional hazard—he had to watch his step to avoid slipping on the pooling gore. The severed heads reminded him of just what the Talon was capable of doing.

Got to keep a cool head if I don't want to lose mine.

Exercise equipment cluttered the ad hoc arena. Ducking behind a hanging punching bag, Nightwing put his whole body into swinging the seventy-pound bag into the Talon, knocking him flat on his back. The hero seized the moment to snatch up Claire's discarded dumbbell and hurl it at the downed man before he could get back on his feet. The killer threw up his sword arm to protect his face and the dumbbell smacked into his wrist. Bone cracked loudly, but he somehow held onto his weapon. He roared with anger.

"You upstart mongrel! You think your cheap tricks can stop me?"

Angrily he threw his sword at Nightwing, who flung himself into the air to avoid being speared. The sword passed harmlessly beneath him and he raised his batons, ready to stay on offensive—

—only to feel two sharp pains penetrate his chest, one immediately after the other. Glancing down, he saw a pair of gleaming throwing knives embedded there, and realized the Talon had tagged him in mid-air. The knives were professional grade and sharp as a Batarang's points.

Nightwing cried out loud as he twisted in the air to avoid landing face down and driving the knives further into his body. His back slammed into the floor, knocking the breath out of him. The jarring impact dialed the pain up another notch... and then some. Worse yet, he lost a baton in the crash.

"Thanks for the target practice, bird-boy."

Two sheathes on the Talon's bandolier were conspicuously empty. Favoring his fractured arm, the assassin climbed to his feet and drew a third knife. A stationary bike blocked his path and he impatiently shoved it aside to come at Nightwing, giving the wounded hero little time to assess his injuries. It didn't seem as if either of the knives had pierced a vital organ or artery, but it wasn't as though he'd been checked out by a medic.

Clambering to his feet, he extracted one of the knives from his chest. It hurt just as much coming out as it had going in. Nightwing gripped the hilt of the bloody knife. Hoping to cripple or maim the Talon long enough to survive a few more minutes, he sprang at the assassin and thrust forward with the blade.

He aimed the knife at the other man's skull, but the Talon, showing no sign of fatigue, easily intercepted the strike. He drove his own knife through Nightwing's outstretched forearm, skewering it. Severed tendons caused Nightwing to lose his grip on the weapon as he yanked his wounded arm back, taking the knife with it. This wound, he knew too well, wasn't going to heal quickly.

"What's the matter?" the Talon gloated. "Having trouble holding on?"

Something like that, Nightwing thought.

Clutching his arm to his chest, with the knife tip pointed away from his body, Nightwing dropped to the floor and rolled beneath a gymnastics pommel horse to put some distance between himself and his foe. The move aggravated his injuries, hurting like hell. Running on adrenaline alone, he jumped to his feet on the opposite side of the horse. The blood loss was getting to him; he teetered unsteadily upon rubbery legs. His head was spinning. A cold sweat glued his suit to his skin. His pulse raced as he felt himself going into shock…

Don't let it show, he thought. *Stay strong.*

"Getting tired?" The Talon moved at a more leisurely pace now, hood and goggles masking his expression, but when he spoke, the smugness in his voice was unmistakable. He flexed the arm that had snapped only moments ago. "This has been fun, but I guess it's time to put you out of your misery, and send Batman a message about who really rules in Gotham…"

"You can try."

Dead on his feet, Nightwing had nothing left but bravado, but he'd be damned if he let this faceless murderer get the last word. If this was his final bow, Nightwing was going to exit the stage with style.

Sorry, Bruce. I did my best…

"Help me, somebody! For God's sake, please help me!"

Filled with fear, Claire's voice rose up from the street outside, entering the loft through the broken window. Grimly Nightwing realized that meant the other cops had to be dead, their communications disabled. He and the young woman were on their own.

143

The Talon spun toward the sound, as if suddenly remembering that his actual quarry was getting away. A frustrated snarl escaped his hood as he turned his back on Nightwing, who no longer posed any serious threat to his mission.

"You lucked out, bird-boy. Duty calls..."

Leaving Nightwing behind, he dashed out of the attic after Claire. Nightwing tried to chase after him, but collapsed against the gymnastics horse before sliding down onto the floor. His own blood mingled with that of the Talon's other victims. His vision blurred. Darkness encroached on his consciousness.

"Run," he whispered faintly. "As fast as you can."

•

Claire fled from the safe house, which was obviously anything but. She hated leaving Nightwing to fight the Talon alone, but what else was she supposed to do? She was no superhero or street fighter— she was just a slightly nerdy anthropology student. All she could do was try to stay alive. Her sweaty exercise togs hardly suited the season, but the autumn chill barely registered as she dashed outdoors. Her heart pounded frantically.

"Help me, somebody! For God's sake, please help me!"

She had found another of the cops in the front room, still sitting in the easy chair. His head was on the floor in a pool of blood. There was no sign of any others, but they hadn't come running once Nightwing smashed through the upstairs window. That suggested the worst.

Standing in the darkened street, she looked around desperately, unsure where to turn. Most of the local shops and business had closed hours ago. The late-night traffic was sparse. A few cars sped past, not wanting to stop for a crazy, disheveled woman shrieking in the street. This being Gotham, she could hardly blame them.

"Miss Nesko?" a man emerged from the back of a nondescript utility truck parked at the corner, and instinctively she shrunk back. He held up a badge. "Officer Mason. What's happening?"

A woman followed him out of the van. Claire realized that the GCPD must have posted the officers to keep watch from the outside. Not that it had done any good.

"The Talon!" She ran toward them. "He's in the house! He killed the other police officers. Nightwing is fighting him!"

"Crap!" Mason shot an urgent glance at his partner as he drew his sidearm from a holster beneath his jacket. "Get her into the van, pronto! And call for reinfor—"

A knife came out of nowhere, spearing his eye. He crumpled to the pavement, already dead.

"Dan!" His unnamed partner gaped in horror, right before another blade struck her in the throat. She dropped to the ground, choking on her own blood. Unlike Mason, she did not die instantly.

"No, no, no…" Claire backed away from her dead and dying rescuers. Trembling, she looked back over her shoulder in time to see the Talon jogging toward her.

"Alone at last," he said. "No more playing hard to get. How about we go someplace where we can have a private conversation, without all these third wheels cramping my style?" He crossed the street toward her. "I'm thinking maybe a fireplace chat… with you as the fire."

Her gaze darted toward Mason's gun, which was lying on the pavement only a few yards away. Could she possibly snatch it up in time to defend herself? She had never actually fired a gun before, but maybe…?

"Uh-uh." The Talon wagged his finger. "Don't even think about it."

Her last hopes evaporated. She looked around desperately, but there was no salvation in sight. She was alone and abandoned in a city of millions. A train whistle sounded in the distance.

"I'm not going to give Joanna up," she said. "I don't even know where she is," she added in a wail.

"Then I guess you're just going to have to burn for nothing."

He was halfway across the street when an engine roared out of darkness. A pair of blinding headlights flared to life, catching the Talon in their high-beams. He spun toward the lights as the Batmobile accelerated, its matte-black finish and tinted windows giving it the look of speeding shadow. The vehicle slammed into the Talon, knocking him through the chain-link fence that denied access to the train track, then stopped on a dime next to Claire. The passenger door slid open, revealing Batman at the wheel.

"Get in," he said.

She didn't need to be asked twice. Still shaking, she scrambled into the car beside him, not feeling truly safe until the door slid shut behind her. Déjà-vu struck her as she realized this was the second time she had sought shelter inside the Batmobile.

When did her life go insane?

"Nightwing?" Batman asked her. His eyes scanned the deserted scene around them, on the lookout for the Talon who had been flung into the shadows beyond the streetlights. Batman's tense body language scared and confused her. The Talon had just been hit by a speeding car. He couldn't still be a threat, could he?

"Inside," she answered. "He saved my life, told me to run, but I don't know what happened next, except the Talon came out of the house and Nightwing didn't…" Had the Talon killed him too, like he had killed the police?

Something flickered briefly behind Batman's stoic expression.

"I'm sorry—" she began.

"Don't be." His voice was decisive. "I'll see to Nightwing, after we get you safely away from here."

"But you hit the Talon at top speed. He's toast, right?"

"I wish." The driver's side door slid open and he stepped outside. "Buckle up. The car will take care of you."

"The car?"

The door slid shut, locking her inside.

•

"Alfred," Batman said into his cowl's built-in mike. "Engage remote navigation mode. Extract Claire to a secure location at once."

"Understood, sir," the butler replied. "And Master Richard...?"

"I'm on it."

There was no reason to worry Alfred before the facts were in. Batman stepped away from the car as the butler took control of the wheel from the cave. The Batmobile's engine went back into silent mode as the sleek black vehicle executed a rapid U-turn before zooming off into the night. Contingency plans already existed in case the safe house was compromised. Batman trusted Alfred to carry out those plans while he looked for Nightwing.

Hang on, Dick.

Finding Nightwing took priority over pursuing the Talon, but anxiety over his former ward's safety did not impede his vigilance. The assassin may or may not have retreated after being hit by the car. Batman remained on alert as he rushed into the violated safe house.

"Nightwing?"

Crimson footsteps, which appeared to belong to both Claire and the Talon, led him upstairs to the gym. His heart sank at the grisly tableau confronting him, which included at least two headless cops. For a moment he feared that Nightwing was past saving, as well, but then he heard a low moan coming from another corner of the gym. There he found the younger hero collapsed on the floor, bleeding from multiple wounds. One of the Talon's trademark throwing knives still jutted from Nightwing's chest. Anger flared. Batman wished he'd run the Talon over a few more times.

Stirring, Nightwing managed to lift his head.

"B—Batman?"

Even in distress, he knew better than to address his mentor by name in a house rigged for audio. He tried to sit up.

"Stay down." Batman gently prevented Nightwing from rising. As triage, he assessed and ranked the wounds by severity. First-aid supplies from his belt would help to staunch the bleeding, but Nightwing clearly needed more serious medical attention as soon as possible. Stitches and a blood transfusion at the very least, perhaps even surgery. For a moment, he regretted sending the Batmobile away, but he knew that had their situations been reversed, Nightwing would also have put Claire's safety first.

"Claire?" Nightwing said.

"Safe," Batman assured him. "You did good."

Nightwing coughed up blood. "And the Talon?"

"In the wind... for now." Batman hoped that getting hit head-on by the Batmobile had taken the Talon out of the picture, at least for the moment, but knew that he would be back at a hundred percent all too soon. Dick had to be under Alfred's care in the Batcave before that happened.

"Nightwing needs immediate medical assistance," he said into the mike. "Dispatch Batwing to this site, on the double."

"Medevac on the way, sir."

In theory, the aircraft would be here in a matter of minutes. As he treated Nightwing's wounds, Batman looked up to contemplate the two murdered police officers, slain by the Talon along with the cops outside—and probably a few more elsewhere in the building. He wasn't looking forward to informing Gordon of the losses. The GCPD wasn't perfect, but these officers had died in the line of duty. He mourned their deaths even as he silently vowed to stop this Talon sooner rather than later.

"I'm sorry," Nightwing murmured. "He got the better of me..."

"You protected Claire. That was job one and you got it done."

You've done your part, Batman thought. *Let me take care of the Talon.*

18

"Civic Spirit" was the largest statue in Gotham City. More than twenty feet tall, the gilded copper figure gazed out over the city from her perch atop the old municipal building. A crown graced her brow as she held a blazing torch aloft, not unlike Lady Liberty.

Lit by halogen spotlights, draped in sculpted Grecian robes, she posed barefoot atop a gleaming metal orb. Batman peered up at her from the base of the statue, his cape flapping in the night breeze, dozens of feet above the city streets.

Hello, Lydia, he thought, seeing her through new eyes.

The top of the building offered an expansive view of the city. In fact, Batman had often visited these heights during his night-time patrols, but as with the fountain back at the Manor, he had grown so accustomed to the towering figure that she'd become all but invisible to him. Tonight, however, he recognized Lydia Doyle's increasingly familiar features in the noble countenance. According to Barbara, Percy Wright had sculpted this statue in 1922, only four years after Lydia's disappearance. Since she would have not been available to model for "Civic Spirit," he must have worked from preexisting sketches or studies, or perhaps even from memory. Lydia certainly was memorable.

"I'm here," he said, seemingly to empty air. "It's her, all right— I'm beginning to think she's everywhere."

"Tell me about it," Barbara replied from the Clock Tower,

where she was continuing her historical deep dive. Her voice came through clearly, while the high-tech lenses in his cowl allowed her to view whatever he did. "The more I scour the past, the more I find her—or at least her image—immortalized everywhere. She really *was* Miss Gotham."

Until the city devoured her.

Or the Owls did.

Assuming they weren't one and the same.

"We already knew how ubiquitous she was," Barbara continued. "But, working from the notes and drafts you recovered from the cabin, I've been trying to reconstruct Joanna's theory—that Percy hid a message of some sort in his sculptures, and I think maybe I'm onto something. I'm not entirely sure what it means, though."

It was the night after the attack on the safe house. Claire was safely ensconced in Metropolis, with Nightwing serving as her escort. Dick had been reluctant to leave Gotham at this juncture, but the Talon had already gone after Claire twice, and clearly the GCPD lacked the ability to hide her from the all-seeing eyes of the Court. She would be in constant danger as long as she stayed in Gotham, and Dick needed time to recover from his wounds.

Thankfully, none of his injuries were irreversible—not even the severed tendons in his arm—but he wasn't going to be at full fighting strength for some time. Batman wanted them both safely out of Gotham for the duration. If anybody was going to take on this vicious new Talon, it was going to be him.

"Tell me," he said to Barbara.

"A few points of interest," she replied, sounding like a tour guide. "Note that her crown has four points, on each of which is inscribed the image of a winged creature: a robin, a bat, a crow, and an owl. Now, traditionally, these are believed to symbolize, respectively, dawn, dusk, the countryside, and the city, and that's always been the conventional interpretation, at least by anybody who's actually examined the crown in the last hundred years or so."

Batman nodded. He understood the symbolism. Owls, in particular, had long been associated with the goddess Athena, the patron goddess of a great city-state. They were symbols of wisdom as well as harbingers of death.

"But...?" he prompted.

"A Bat, an owl, a robin and a crow... as in Scarecrow? Kind of weirdly prophetic, don't you think?"

Batman thought on that. "From the perspective of today, yes, but in Percy's time?" he said. Nobody would make those associations back then."

"I know," she said. "That's the creepy part."

The symbols in question were barely visible from the rooftop, and too high up to be seen at all from the street, so it was small wonder they had gone unnoticed for years. Batman decided to get a closer look at that crown. Using a Batrope, he scaled the colossal statue until he was standing on its shoulder. What Barbara was suggesting seemed preposterous on the face of it, yet rather than reject it out of hand, he kept an open mind as he trained a high-powered flashlight on the four points of the crown, one at a time.

Exactly as Barbara had stated, the silhouettes of three birds and a bat were embossed on the gilded tines. He considered their placement.

"Interesting," he mused aloud.

"What is it?" she asked.

"The crow is facing west toward the rural farmlands across the river, while the robin is facing east toward the rising dawn. Both of which fit with the traditional interpretation, but in light of what you suggested, I can't help noticing that the bat faces north— toward the cave and the Manor, while the owl faces south toward Harbor House, the Court's old headquarters."

"Coincidence?" she said.

"One might think so," Batman said, "but this is the Court of

Owls we're talking about. They've pushed the boundaries of what's possible: rejuvenation, healing serums, cryogenics, and more. Still, genuine precognition seems like a stretch, even for them."

"Yet Joanna believes that Percy's statues hold a warning about the future," Barbara persisted. "About an inferno that awaits Gotham."

Batman lifted his gaze to contemplate the gleaming torch at the end of the figure's upraised right arm. To light the way to the future—or to burn everything down?

"And the Court seems to be taking Joanna's theories seriously," he noted, "as they search for Percy's mysterious elixir or formula." Descending to the rooftop, he summoned a drone that had been hovering nearby, waiting to be called into service. He directed it to scan and photograph the statue from all directions in order to construct a flawless 3D model of "Civic Spirit" that they could study more extensively. That would be far more complete than whatever isolated still photos and illustrations currently existed.

Laser beams, glowing ruby-red in the night, shot from the drone, mapping every inch of the mammoth sculpture while Batman waited patiently for them to complete the task. As a rule, he preferred to inspect evidence physically, whenever possible, but it would be useful to have a digital copy for future reference.

He still didn't know what this long-sought elixir was supposed to do, and that nagged at him. Certainly, given the incendiary side effects, he needed to get his hands on the formula before Vincent did. Yet given the condition of the Talon's recent victims, might it be that the Owls already possessed it?

No, the Grandmaster's own words indicated otherwise. Whatever Vincent had, it remained incomplete—though no less lethal.

Briefly he wondered if the formula might be hidden somewhere inside this particular statue, but the odds were against it. "Civic Spirit" was only one of many works by Percy Wright scattered throughout the city—and a "formula" could be hidden anywhere, in any number of ways. Nevertheless, he had the drone make an ultrasound scan, as well, for further examination.

"What else have you turned up?"

"How much time do you have?" she said wryly. "We're talking parks, gardens, bridges, courthouses, museums, memorials, friezes, pylons, postcards… you name it, and that's not even counting the art that's been moved, stolen, misplaced, destroyed, or simply forgotten over the decades." Her voice held a trace of fatigue, as though she had been burning the proverbial candle at both ends. "But we can start with some of the better-known public works. There are a few in particular that you might want to check out."

"Why is that?"

"Better that you see for yourself," she said. "I don't want to prejudice your findings."

Fair enough, Batman thought. "Tell me where."

•

The fountain in front of the Plaza Hotel dwarfed the one back at the Manor. A nude water-bearer, nearly eight feet tall and sculpted of polished marble, posed at the center of the wide circular display, bending slightly as though about to draw water into a large ceramic ewer. Her hair was neatly braided, her expression placid, and her face and figure were Lydia's. Not wanting to attract attention, Batman studied the figure from a shadowy ledge across the street. Binocular lenses allowed him to inspect it at a distance.

"The story is," Barbara said, "that this statue is based on an earlier, smaller figure that Lydia posed for not long before her disappearance. There are no owls or bats hidden anywhere, at least that I can see, but look at it closely. I want to know if you see it, too, just to be sure that I'm not letting my imagination get the better of me."

He scanned closely, starting with the looming figure itself before moving on to her setting. Decorative fish ringed the basin, sculpted in the act of leaping in and out of the water. Their faces and tails alternated in a static procession. Rising up to greet the open air, the fish heads sported exaggerated features that struck Batman as being at odds with the classical realism of the female figure. The smiles on the grinning fish were...

Grotesque. Like those of a death's-head.

Like Joker fish.

Years ago, the Joker had poisoned the water in Gotham harbor, resulting in a mass of hideous, toxic, mutated fish. The disfigured "Joker fish" had borne a distinct resemblance to the ones Percy Wright sculpted, many decades earlier.

"Joker fish," he finally said aloud.

"So it's not just me," Barbara responded. "You see it, too."

"Another coincidence?"

"That's what I thought," she said. "The Joker fish came almost a century after Percy's time. There's no *way* he could have known about it."

Commissioner Gordon liked to say that detectives weren't allowed to believe in coincidences. Batman was inclined to agree with him.

"Show me more."

•

Next stop, the City Courthouse downtown, where a relief sculpture of "Lady Justice," occupied the pediment above the front entrance. Accessorized with the traditional blindfold, scales, and sword, this depiction of Justice struck Batman as well-crafted but unremarkable, until he noted an odd element of the artwork.

Flanking Justice on each side were matching profiles of a bearded man, facing away from each other. Identical in every way except their orientation, the faces were divided by Lady Justice, but shared an obvious commonality. Batman recognized the deity they depicted.

"Janus. The Two-Faced God."

"Yep," Barbara chimed in. "Remind you of anyone?"

She didn't need to spell it out. It was in this very courthouse some years ago that District Attorney Harvey Dent lost half of his handsome face to acid thrown by a vengeful mobster. His disfigurement had driven Dent mad, transforming Batman's one-time friend and ally into a psychotic split personality.

"Two-Face."

Once again, Barbara felt obliged to play devil's advocate. "On the other hand, according to Roman mythology, Janus *is* the god of doorways, gates, and transitions, so one might expect to find him over the entrance to a courthouse, where lives undergo transitions every day—marriages, divorces, sentencing, and what not. There's a certain artistic logic to it, which is probably why nobody has ever wondered about it before now."

"Except that Janus is *not* traditionally associated with Lady Justice," Batman said. "That's an innovation on Percy's part, which, in light of later events, now seems eerily on the nose. Almost prophetic."

"*Much* later events," Barbara stressed.

"That nonetheless took place at this very location." Batman's mind boggled at the notion. Harvey would have passed beneath the twin profiles on the day of his undoing. "A two-faced god presiding over Two-Face's birthplace? Percy is batting a thousand so far."

"Hang onto your cowl," Barbara said. "We're not done yet."

•

"Eve" was found in a public garden in Grant Park, south of the courthouse. Given the hour and the season, the gardens were deserted when Batman arrived, its dormant blooms and skeletal bushes patiently awaiting the coming of spring. The life-sized bronze statue contemplated a sculpted apple, as one might expect, but instead of the traditional fig leaves, her modesty was protected by strategically placed vines of ivy, which played along her arms and trailed down her shapely legs before spreading out over the base of the statue.

Thorns sprouted from the vines as they extended beyond the figure's bare feet. Pointed, trifoliate leaves betrayed the true nature of the vines.

"Poison Ivy," Batman said.

"As portrayed by Lydia Doyle after her death, yet long before Pamela Isley was born," Barbara agreed. "I don't know about you, but I'm detecting a theme here."

"Dangers to Gotham City," Batman said. "Menaces somehow foreseen by Percy Wright, embodied by Lydia for reasons known only to him." It defied reason, but they were far beyond coincidence now.

"Still nothing that tells us anything about Percy's so-called elixir," Barbara said, "or that inferno he spoke of."

"Not *yet*," Batman stressed. "We know Percy sculpted Lydia many times, both before and after she vanished. Maybe we just haven't yet found the right artworks."

"That's always possible," Barbara said. "Especially given the sheer quantity. These are the easy-to-find ones. Some have ended up in private collections, been shipped cross-country or overseas, or been destroyed over the years. Remember the time Bane blew up City Hall? Well, that statue is long gone. In some cases, all that's left are reproductions or old illustrations. The originals didn't survive."

That complicated matters, Batman understood, but they could

still work with whatever statues remained. A jigsaw puzzle could be identified, even if a few pieces were missing. They just needed to assemble enough pieces to see the big picture.

"We should chart the statues on a map of Gotham, to see if their placement forms a pattern of any sort," he suggested, "taking into account both their past and present locations."

"Already working on it," she assured him, "although no obvious patterns are leaping out at me just yet." Batman trusted her powers of observation, but resolved to conduct his own analysis anyway.

"Let's narrow our focus to sculptures done after Lydia's disappearance in 1918," he said. "That's where all of this seems to have begun."

"Will do," she said. "To be honest, I was starting to feel a little overwhelmed." She sighed audibly. "Being a research junkie can be a double-edged sword sometimes. It can be too easy to lose the forest for the trees, especially in the age of the internet, when countless bits of obscure data are only a keystroke away."

He knew what she meant. When he'd first started investigating the Court of Owls, it had threatened to become an obsession. The more he'd looked, the more he seemed to find evidence of them lurking just out of sight, until he started seeing Owls everywhere—to the point of paranoia.

But was it just paranoia?

"We need to keep our heads clear and our eyes focused," he said. "Take nothing for granted. There are two fronts on this case: yesterday and today. We need to work both angles in hopes that one will illuminate the other... and keep Joanna from going the way of Lydia."

"In which case, there's probably another statue you need to see," Barbara said. "But I should warn you, you're not going to like it."

Batman was losing his patience with cryptic warnings. He

wanted answers, not more mysteries. He knew, however, that Barbara had her reasons to be concerned.

"Where?"

•

The sculpture was titled "Mother and Child" and it could be found on display, at least during visiting hours, at the Ellsworth Museum in Old Gotham. Bronze figures depicted a young mother balancing a cherubic male infant on her lap. The pudgy child tugged on a pearl necklace strung around his mother's graceful throat, which had been sculpted at the very moment it broke apart. A handful of fallen pearls littered the base of the statue, while the sad smile on the mother's face broke Batman's heart.

Falling pearls, he thought. He couldn't blame Barbara for wanting to prepare him. His throat tightened. A gunshot echoed in his memory.

She didn't need to ask if he'd made the connection. There was no way he could miss it, even if he wanted to. The possible involvement of the Court of Owls only made it worse. He wasn't just trying to solve a century-old mystery. It felt as if the Owls' constant presence throughout Gotham's history was being rubbed in his face.

"I'm sorry, Bruce," she said gently.

"Don't be," he said gruffly. "It's just a statue. Another piece of the puzzle."

"Are we sure of that?" she asked. "Tell me I'm crazy to think this has something to do with what happened to your parents. How could Percy Wright have *possibly* anticipated that?"

"He couldn't have," Batman said. "The same way he couldn't have anticipated the Scarecrow, or the Joker, or Two-Face, or Poison Ivy. And yet somehow he did. All these statues hint at horrors and tragedies awaiting Gotham, long after Percy's time. In our time.

Who knows what we're not seeing, that occurred before we were even born."

"So what does it mean regarding his rantings?" Barbara said. "What could his 'inferno' refer to? Another outbreak of the Burning Sickness, or something else altogether?"

Batman wished he knew. He didn't believe in fate, but he couldn't ignore what stood right before his eyes.

19

MacDougal Lane, Gotham City, 1918

Percy's private laboratory occupied the basement of his downtown row house, a full three floors beneath his studio in the attic. Only a few small windows at the top of each wall offered any light from outside. The majority of the illumination came from electric bulbs. He had been known to wryly observe that the floor plan placed Art closer to heaven, and Science closer to hell.

Never had that seemed truer than today.

"Explain again the theory behind your elixir," the Grandmaster demanded. Despite his advanced age, the geriatric Owl had chosen to pay a personal visit to the laboratory, which he had reached via a series of underground tunnels that connected the soundproof basement to hidden nests throughout the city. This unprecedented call was surely intended to impress upon Percy the urgency with which the Court desired a perfected version of his elixir.

A formula that, in theory, would grant human beings the ability to see the future.

"It sounds incredible, I know," Percy said, "but hear me out. We know already that certain exotic heavy metals and alloys—most notably electrum—possess unique properties of which we are only beginning to grasp the full potential. My own studies suggest that, properly administered, these metals can increase the superconductivity of the brain, speeding its electrical impulses to

163

an uncanny degree." He pointed to an elaborate chemical formula he had written on a scrap of paper.

"At the same time," he continued, "I have concluded that electrum, combined with certain other metals not yet found on the Periodic Table, can transmit and receive vibrations from across time and space, which current science holds to be one and the same. Taking advantage of these properties, my elixir allows the brain to receive signals from across the fourth dimension by way of ripples in the very fabric of what we now refer to as space-time."

"Fascinating," the Grandmaster said. Per tradition, or perhaps merely to conceal the ravages of age, he wore his gold-trimmed mask. He leaned heavily on a polished wooden cane topped by a silver owl's head. "And yet, receiving messages from the future, perceiving that which has not yet occurred—how is that even possible?"

"The basic theory is not new," Percy insisted. "Indeed, no lesser personage that Edgar Allan Poe proposed some seventy years ago that, and I quote, 'space and duration are one.' It has been commonly accepted by modern science that time is merely another dimension. It differs only from the other three—length, width, and height—in that our consciousness travels along it in a linear fashion. It therefore stands to reason that our consciousness, as generated by the brain, should be able to receive signals across time as well as distance. All that would be required is the proper stimulation."

"As provided by your elixir," Margaret stressed.

Like Percy, she was unmasked. This was the first time she had set foot in his downtown sanctuary. That she had done so testified to her ambitions. Only the opportunity to play host to the Grandmaster, and tout Percy's elixir, could have induced her to join him here. Her face bore a look of smug satisfaction.

"Astounding," the Grandmaster said, staring at the formula. "I must see this for myself."

Percy attempted to lower the old man's expectations.

"Soon, perhaps," he said. "As I've explained, the elixir in its current formulation cannot be consumed without loss of life. Its interaction with human physiology generates a tremendous amount of energy, and overheats the brain, resulting in a fever that ultimately leads the test subjects to spontaneously combust. I have every hope of eliminating this dire consequence, but that will take time."

"Nevertheless," the Grandmaster said, "I demand evidence of your claims."

A bell rang at the rear of the basement, indicating that someone desired admittance from the tunnels beyond. Startled, Percy turned toward the hidden door.

"What the devil?"

"Ah." The Grandmaster consulted his pocket watch. "Right on schedule."

Percy noted that Margaret also appeared to be considerably less than surprised. He looked to her for an explanation.

"Margaret?"

"Surely you didn't think that the Grandmaster came all this way just for a lecture," she said, smugness giving way to a smirk. "He has requested a demonstration, and he shall have it."

"Demonstration?"

"Open the door, Percy."

Growing increasingly apprehensive, he did as instructed. A concealed latch caused a section of the basement wall to swing open, admitting a Talon who bore a heavy bundle over his shoulder. Percy shuddered at the sight of the fearsome assassin in his ominous black regalia. A black leather trench coat, worn over a double-breasted leather tunic, distinguished this Talon from those of earlier generations. A hood and goggles rendered him faceless. He effortlessly toted a large burlap bag whose unseen contents appeared to be… squirming?

"What is this?" Percy demanded.

"Nothing anyone will miss," Margaret said.

"True enough, madam." The Talon dumped the contents of his bag onto the concrete floor in front of them. Percy was horrified to find a bound human captive lying at his feet. The man reeked of rum and his tattered, soiled clothing gave off a nauseating stench of urine and filth that made Percy's gorge rise. Bloodshot eyes and a bulbous red nose marked him as a likely dipsomaniac. His unshaven face and generally bedraggled appearance led Percy to suspect that he was some unfortunate sot plucked from the gutters of Gotham.

Panic showed in the man's eyes, although a gag muffled his anxious vocalizations. The conspicuous absence of a blindfold troubled Percy. The Talon seemed unconcerned with what his captive might witness.

"A fine selection, Frederick." The Grandmaster congratulated the Talon. "You have done well."

"Whatever pleases the Court," the hooded killer replied. In his youth Frederick Coolidge had been conscripted from a traveling carnival, and had served the Court faithfully for years. His loyalty ran deep. "Rest assured that I was unobserved."

"I never doubted it." The Grandmaster turned his masked face toward Percy. "You have your test subject, Wright. Let us proceed with the demonstration."

"But I just told you. The elixir is not ready to be tested on human beings!" The scientist could not contain his horror. His prior tests had been conducted on animals, employing an elegant experimental technique of his own conception, which had involved forcing mice and rabbits to choose between three empty boxes. Once injected with the elixir, the animals would invariably head straight for the box which would *soon* contain food.

Their accuracy was uncanny.

"If you insist," he said, "I can certainly arrange a demonstration employing a laboratory rat." He needed to regain control of the situation.

But no.

"I have no interest in animal tricks," the Grandmaster said. "If I wished to observe performing animals, I would attend a circus." He gestured with his cane at the kidnapped rummy. "Get on with it."

"But the side effect!" Percy protested. "This would be nothing short of murder!"

"We are the Court of Owls," the old man replied. "I fail to grasp your objection."

Unsurprisingly, the word "murder" only heightened the captive's fearful state. He thrashed violently upon the floor, struggling in vain against the ropes that bound his wrists and ankles. His muffled cries grew louder.

"No," Percy stated. "I won't be party to this."

"The Court demands otherwise," the Grandmaster decreed. "Do not test my patience."

Percy turned to his wife for support. "Margaret, please. Help me make him understand. You must see that how unconscionable this is."

"Must I?" she said coolly. "If this subject does not suit you, perhaps we can find another? Maybe one of those highly disposable young women who model for your art? Certainly such creatures are a dime a dozen."

"No!" Percy said. "You can't be serious..."

"Do not test me, Percy." She backed away from the panicked rummy, wrinkling her nose in distaste. "Are you truly prepared to take that risk... for the likes of this miserable specimen?"

He imagined Lydia in the drunkard's place.

His shoulders slumped in defeat.

No, he realized. *I'm not.*

"Very well, damn you." He gestured toward a large cast-iron

tub which he used to rinse his equipment and dispose of excess chemicals. "Place him over there… for our own safety's sake."

"As you wish." The Talon easily lifted the squirming man from the floor and deposited him in the tub. The man's thrashing became even more violent, yet the assassin showed no notice.

"Now you're seeing reason, Percy," Margaret said. "I must say I'm relieved. For a few moments there, I was starting to fear that something—or *someone*—had softened your heart… and your brain." Percy didn't dignify the insinuation with a reply. Under these nightmarish circumstances, his wife's sharp tongue was the very least of his concerns.

As she and the Grandmaster looked on, he extracted the most advanced version of his elixir from a refrigerated cabinet of the very latest design. He had yet to test this formula. Once mixed, it had to sit for at least seventy-two hours, and that time had just passed. It included an antipyretic agent, so it was at least *possible* that he had succeeded in neutralizing the incendiary effect. The challenge had been to somehow retain the heightened cerebral function while suppressing the violence of the reaction.

To date, this had proven a difficult balance to achieve.

I'm sorry, poor fellow, he said silently to their captive. *I wish I could do better by you.* Preparing the hypodermic, he approached the tub.

The Talon held the rummy in an iron grip as Percy rolled up the man's sleeve to expose the vein at the crook of his arm. A faded tattoo of a ship's anchor suggested that the man had once been a sailor. This biographical detail, reminding Percy that the rummy was an individual with his own unique history, made the task all the harder. His heart sank as he injected the sot as painlessly as he could.

May God have mercy on my soul.

The protestations continued, and he tried his best to ignore them. He tried to tell himself that this poor, pathetic wretch had already wasted his life, that the rummy's part in this experiment might well be his greatest contribution to mankind, but the rationalizations rang hollow. He knew what he was doing.

What would Lydia think if she saw him now?

"It's done," he announced.

"Excellent." The Grandmaster settled into a chair next to Percy's downstairs desk. "How long before we can expect results?"

"It would be difficult to say," Percy replied. "I administered a high dosage, so I anticipate a rapid reaction, but as noted I've never tested the elixir on a man before. The sheer bulk of the… test subject adds a factor that is difficult to assess."

His moral qualms aside, his scientific curiosity made him anxious to discover the results of the experiment. The man in the tub finally stopped struggling, perhaps from sheer exhaustion. When nothing incendiary occurred, Percy scurried upstairs to locate an ordinary deck of playing cards from the parlor. Returning to the basement, he offered the deck to the Grandmaster.

"Please shuffle these to your satisfaction."

The Grandmaster accepted the cards. Rheumy eyes peered out from behind his mask as he examined them dubiously. "I hope you have more to offer than card tricks."

"It's not trickery," Percy promised. "Science."

Would that we were only playing parlor games, he thought ruefully. The Grandmaster shuffled the cards repeatedly and returned them to Percy, who approached the tub. Percy nodded to the Talon.

"Remove the gag."

"Easily done." A flick of a blade caused the gag to fall away, unleashing a torrent of protests from the test subject, as Percy forced himself to think of the man. With the curses came the foulest breath he had ever experienced, and he took a step back.

"Let me go, you filthy bastards!" the man cried, his voice cracking with the effort. "What the hell do you want with me? What was that shite you just poked me with? You can't do this! You have no damned right!"

"Silence!" The Talon cuffed the man hard across the side of the head. "You'll speak when spoken to." The assassin's appearance seemed to cow the man as much as the blow.

"Lord help me," he whimpered.

"I suspect He has better things to do." Margaret snickered, and Percy cringed.

"We're simply conducting a scientific experiment," he said, doing his best to affect a soothing bedside manner. He was tempted to offer the man a drink to calm him, but feared that strong spirits might compromise the experiment. "How are you feeling?"

"Like my brain is buzzing," the rummy volunteered. "Like I'm thinking faster than I can think, if you know what I mean. I can't make it stop. Make it stop!"

"I want you to play a game with me," Percy said. "Can you do that?" When the man didn't answer, the Talon held up the knife he had employed on the gag, and waggled it back and forth.

"He'll play," the Talon said, touching the point. "Or he will regret it."

Staring wildly at the blade, rummy gulped. Percy considered asking the man his name, but decided he didn't want to know it. This was difficult enough as it was.

"I'll play along, sirs," the man croaked. "Just tell me what you want." Percy held up the deck of cards.

"Tell me what card I'm about to draw."

"How the devil should I know—?" the subject began; then he paused in surprise. His eyes lost focus, as though he was gazing inward instead. His voice emerged in a whisper. "The four of clubs?"

Percy drew a card from the top of the deck. Four black clovers greeted his eyes. He held the card up for the others to see before replacing it in the deck.

"Well, I'll be damned." The rummy gaped at the card in astonishment. "How on Earth did I do that?"

"Let's try again."

More trials followed. Thirty more cards were drawn, and thirty times the rummy predicted what they would be, with an accuracy rate of one hundred percent. Percy was thrilled by the results, even as he feared what was yet in store.

There's still a chance he will survive...

"I remain unconvinced," the Grandmaster said, his voice flat. "That fellow Houdini—and any number of other stage musicians—could pull off the same trick with ease. Stage theatrics, and nothing more."

"But you selected the test subject," Percy reminded him. "You forced the time and place upon me, without any warning." Despite his better judgment, he was beginning to feel anger. "I am no charlatan, sir. What you see is the future impinging on the present, by way of the liquefied, super-conductive metals now coursing through the subject's brain."

"What's that?" the rummy said, and he became agitated again. "What did you do to me?" His outburst earned him another cuff from the Talon. The man curbed his tongue, aside from a few anxious whimpers.

"Then stop wasting my time with *card tricks*," the Grandmaster roared, followed by a fit of coughing. When he recovered, he continued. "Ask him something of value. What will be the outcome of the Great War? Who will succeed Wilson as President? What awaits Gotham in the years to come?"

Percy frowned at the old man's impatience.

"I must remind you that we are in the early days when it comes to harnessing this new discovery," he said, choosing his words carefully. "The full extent of the abilities granted by the elixir has yet to be—"

Abruptly the subject moaned loudly.

"Excuse me, sirs, but I'm not feeling well." Beet-red now, and sweating profusely, he cringed in anticipation of another slap from the Talon, who held up a hand but refrained from delivering the blow. "I feel all hot and feverish-like, like I'm burning up."

Oh, no, Percy thought. *It's happening already.*

He placed his hand on the man's forehead, if only to confirm the truth, and found it too hot to touch. He yanked the hand back as though from a red-hot stove. Sweat poured off of the man, soaking his tattered and filthy clothing. His moans increased in intensity.

"Oh, dear Lord! Help me! I'm baking alive!" He stared in terror at empty air. "I can see it, feel it! I'm going to burn!"

"Blast it!" Percy shouted at his fellow Owls. "I told you it wasn't safe!"

He dashed to his chemical pantry in search of cyanide that would stop the man's heart before he suffered too much, but he was already too late. With a tremendous *whoosh,* the man burst into flames as though he had been drenched in gasoline. The Talon barely backed away in time to avoid being scorched by the sudden conflagration, which remained contained within the cast-iron tub.

Within moments, the nameless rummy was nothing but a blackened husk. Percy averted his eyes from the unspeakable sight. The prior incineration of assorted mice and rabbits had failed to prepare him for this horror.

"I told you!" he lamented. "Why didn't you listen to me?"

"It was… necessary," Margaret said weakly. Even she appeared shaken by the atrocity. Her face was pale. She placed a hand over her nose and mouth to shield herself from the smoke and smell. "The Grandmaster had to see."

"So I did," the old man agreed, and he alone had retained his composure. "Your elixir's side effect is as terrible as you said." He coughed hoarsely. "All the more reason then that you must devote every moment to eliminating it as expeditiously as possible. The Court of Owls *must* possess a perfect version of your elixir."

"You can still say that?" Percy said. "After what you just witnessed?"

"The advantages justify the cost," the Grandmaster declared. "Your elixir has the potential to become a powerful tool for controlling Gotham's destiny. We already dominate Gotham's past and present, but knowledge of future events will allow us to lay our plans with even greater certainty. Think of it! We would have prior warning of future wars, economic events, even scientific and technological innovations. With such power, the Court of Owls will truly be able to shape the future in our image."

"Well put," Margaret agreed, the color returning to her face. "You may count on my husband and me to bring that bold vision to fruition."

"I will hold you to that promise." The Grandmaster rose slowly from the chair and began to hobble toward the tunnels. "I have seen enough, I think. I will leave you to your work, which I trust shall be ongoing." He turned toward the Talon. "Come, Frederick. Let us depart from this place. The atmosphere does not agree with me."

"Yes, Grandmaster. Allow me to assist you." Together the men exited the laboratory, and Percy sealed the doorway behind them. The stench of burnt meat lingered in the chamber. He feared he would never be rid of it.

"What have I done?"

"Don't be so tender-hearted," Margaret scolded him, regaining her steely composure. "Did you think the Court of Owls was a benevolent society? Gaining knowledge of the future is worth any cost. This discovery will make us rich and powerful." He swore her eyes glittered. "You should be proud of your success."

"Proud?" He gestured at the smoking ruin in the tub. "Proud of that?"

"Proud of bending time to your will." She shook her head in exasperation. "I swear, Percy, that girl is making you soft. Life is not all pretty poses and sweet nothings. Power and influence are what truly matter in this world. I shouldn't have to remind you of that."

"And yet you do," he said bitterly. "More's the pity."

She turned her back on the smoldering remains and moved to the stairs.

"In any event, you heard the Grandmaster," she responded. "Perfect your elixir with all due speed, so that your next demonstration has a more positive outcome… for everyone."

20

Show no fear, Vincent thought.

Since the invasion at their last conclave, the Court had taken care to choose an even more secure venue for tonight's emergency meeting. Eschewing public venues entirely, they had gathered in a corporate boardroom in a skyscraper in midtown. Neither the corporation nor the building were officially owned by a member of the Court, but there were very few boardrooms in Gotham to which the Court did not have access.

Vincent had taken pains to travel to the site as covertly as possible, to avoid being tailed by the Dark Knight or his allies. The Talon, taking time out from the search for Joanna Lee, had personally shadowed Vincent's anonymous limo on the way here. Upon their arrival, the assassin remained outside, guarding the premises. Vincent had no intention of letting Batman spy on them again.

I'm already on thin ice.

"Thank you all for convening again so soon," the Grandmaster said to the group, "and for being courageous enough to do so after our last conclave was disrupted by the Batman. Rest assured we have taken every precaution to ensure that no such violation will happen again." Her gold-trimmed mask turned toward Vincent, who was once again seated at the opposite end of the table. "Assuming there is no further carelessness on the part of any members of this Court."

Bitch, Vincent thought. He bristled at her tone, even as his own mask concealed his vexation. The Grandmaster hadn't called him out by name, but she and others blamed him for Batman's unwanted presence at their last gathering. Vincent suspected they were right.

"Let me be blunt," the Grandmaster continued. "The matter of Joanna Lee grows ever more worrisome. We now have several dead police officers inviting attention, while we are no closer to finding the Lee girl or even her roommate. Thankfully, our informants within the police department have not been compromised, but there are still more risks than reward in this campaign. We should ask ourselves if it might have been ill-considered to begin with."

Her sycophantic supporters muttered in agreement, much to Vincent's annoyance. The Grandmaster represented the old guard, although not every Owl approved of her overly cautious approach. Among the younger generation, many favored a bolder, more aggressive strategy—as represented by Vincent and his faction.

They dared not openly defy the Grandmaster just yet, however. She was still shrewd, and possessed enough connections to wield considerable power in the Court. He knew better than to underestimate her.

"There have been delays," he conceded, "but our Talon remains on the case, as relentless and unstoppable as ever. Both Batman and Nightwing have tried to defeat him, and failed repeatedly. Despite their best efforts, they are fighting a losing battle. In the end, the Court of Owls always gets what it wants... including my great-grandfather's elixir."

His backers showed their support by nodding and hooting under their breaths. They had their own varied reasons for siding with him. Some truly shared his vision, while others had been bought with favors, bribes, and blackmail. A few simply saw him as a rising star within the Court, and had hitched their wagons to him accordingly. Vincent could respect that. Indeed, he admired their good judgment.

"Of course, the elixir," the Grandmaster scoffed openly. Vincent refused to let her bait him into losing his composure.

"Do I need to explain just what the elixir could do for the Court, once it's finally perfected?" he countered. "The advantages it would give us over our enemies and rivals? The ways in which it would help us shape Gotham's future?"

"Hardly," she replied, "since the Court has been hearing these same promises since before any of us were born."

Vincent ignored the jibe. "If it's Batman that concerns us, why not deal with him once and for all? We know who he is, we know where to find him. Why permit his interference for one day more?"

"We tried that, or have you forgotten?" the Grandmaster said. "Many once-prominent members of this Court had their secrets exposed, their lives and fortunes ruined. They were arrested, disgraced, or forced to become fugitives. Some even committed suicide, or had to be eliminated to protect the Court.

"We lost a large stockpile of Talons, as well," she continued, "some of whom had been kept in reserve for centuries. All in a reckless show of force of the sort that we have always avoided." She shook her head. "No, the Court of Owls operates from the shadows, shunning the light. The 'Night of Owls' exposed us to undue scrutiny, and there should no hurry to repeat that mistake... all for a mirage that remains forever out of reach." Again murmurs of assent, louder now.

Vincent felt himself losing ground. "But we can't give up now," he protested, focusing on holding his voice steady. "Not when we're so close to achieving success. My latest tests have shown promising results—"

"No more tests," the Grandmaster said, cutting him off abruptly. "No more experiments on the dregs of humanity. This entire affair is attracting too much unwelcome attention. The last thing we need is more vagrants bursting into flames."

That had been an unfortunate accident. A careless subordinate had allowed Joe Bava to escape into the streets. A shame, really, since the man hadn't yet displayed any signs of fever. Bava's fiery end had been discouraging, albeit convenient. At least he had ignited *before* he could reveal any of the Court's secrets.

"But my work," he protested. "My family's work. We're talking decades of labor and sacrifice... all for the good of the Court. These experiments—"

"Are a hazardous luxury we can ill afford at this time," she stated flatly. "Better safe than sorry."

Vincent started to sweat. The Grandmaster was actually going to shut down his life's work, the work of generations, just because Batman was getting in the way. He anxiously scanned the Owls seated around the table, trying to figure out where he stood, but the masks made it damned hard to get a read on the room. He couldn't be certain he had enough votes to challenge the ruling cadre over this issue. He needed to think fast, if he wanted to turn this situation around.

Apologizing for the Bava screw-up would do no good—he couldn't afford to show weakness or admit fault at this point. He had to flip the script somehow, make a negative into a positive...

Then it hit him.

"But don't you see?" he said, leaning in. "Random non-entities, bursting into flames for no discernible reason—that's *exactly* what we need right now... to distract Batman and throw him off the scent. Give him some victims who, unlike the professor or the boyfriend, have no apparent connection to Joanna Lee or her studies." Silence, as they waited for him to continue. "Let him chase dead ends, while we keep our eyes on the prize—the future of Gotham."

Murmurs of interest circulated around the table, encouraging him. His confidence returned as the Grandmaster heard the whispers, as well. He sat back and waited for her to respond.

"An... interesting strategy," she hedged, "although perhaps too flamboyant for comfort. The Court of Owls has prospered this long by maintaining a low profile, not by indulging in theatrical feats of terrorism of the sort practiced by psychopaths like the Joker. As the rhyme indicates, we rule Gotham from a *shadowed* perch."

"That old doggerel also speaks to chopping off the heads of our enemies," Vincent said. "The Court of Owls has relied on fear as well as discretion. There's a time for perching in the shadows, but there's also a time for boldly taking action. Our enemy knows this, even if we may be forgetting it." He pressed his point. "We've come too far to falter now. What are a few more smoking cadavers if it means distracting Batman long enough for us to get to Joanna Lee—and Percy's lost secrets?"

Still the Grandmaster remained silent.

"With all due respect to our venerable traditions," he said, "we might also consider a more modern saying, as well. Go big or go home."

A smattering of applause greeted his big finish. Vincent smirked behind his mask as he imagined the Grandmaster scowling behind hers. He wasn't ready to call for a vote of no confidence. Not just yet, but soon perhaps, after the elixir was his—and vindication, as well. Then they would see who was suited to lead the Court into the twenty-first century.

"Very well," she said sourly. "Burn up a few more pathetic test subjects if you must, but understand that we expect *results*. It will not go well for you, or your bloodline, if this proves to be another wild goose chase." The threat was unmistakable, raising the stakes in a very big way. Vincent exerted the effort needed to keep from swallowing hard.

Failure had just become unthinkable.

"Thank you, Grandmaster," he said. "It's reassuring to know

that the Court of Owls still dares reach for the future, no matter the risk."

"You're welcome," she said. "Now perhaps it's time to look to the past as well... for reinforcements. You and our new Talon may benefit from some assistance, and I believe I know just the right person to call upon."

21

MacDougal Lane, Gotham City, 1918

"I'm going to burn!"

The terrified rummy burst into flames. The iron tub turned into a funeral pyre. Percy's hand blistered from the brief contact. Holding it up before his eyes, he screamed as his fingers caught fire like a Hand of Glory…

•

Percy awoke abruptly in the dark, his heart pounding. The smell of burning flesh lingered in his nose and throat. It seemed to cling to him. He reached for his hand, just to assure himself that it wasn't actually ablaze.

"Percy!" Lydia said, her voice very close. "What is it? What's wrong?"

It took him a moment to shake off the nightmare and realize where he was, sitting up beside Lydia in the second-floor bedroom of the row house. Moonlight coming through the curtains provided the only illumination at this late hour. Tangled sheets covered his lower body, while his torso felt drenched in sweat. He took a deep breath to steady himself.

"It's nothing, darling," he dissembled. "Just a bad dream."

Would that it were so!

"Please, Percy, don't lie to me." She nestled closer to him in the dark. "Something terrible is troubling you, although you try to hide it. I can see it in your eyes, and in the dark circles beneath them. I can even see it in your recent letters to me. They're different somehow from the letters you once sent. You think you are putting on a happy face, holding back whatever is tormenting you, but your fear, your sorrow can be read between every line. Your words frighten me for what they try so hard not to say."

My letters? Panic gripped him. How much had he inadvertently revealed in his missives? He had been writing her near daily while cloistered away in his laboratory, slaving over his elixir. Had he been as circumspect as he should have been, about the situation that weighed down upon him?

"The letters!" he hissed. "Tell me they are safe. That no one can ever find them." That their love affair might be exposed was of no great concern to him. Margaret already knew. So likely did others of their set. Even Alan Wayne had already voiced his suspicions.

No, it was the ghastly possibility that he might have somehow betrayed the Court's secrets. That terrified him—for Lydia's sake. The Talons were nothing if not zealous when it came to guarding the Court's privacy.

Speak not a whispered word of them...

"I promise you, Percy, the letters are well hidden," she said reassuringly. "They are quite safe from prying eyes."

"Good, good." He prayed she was correct. "You have no idea of the possible repercussions should they fall into the wrong hands."

"Then tell me, Percy. Let there be no secrets between us. I can't bear to see you suffering without even knowing the reason why."

"You don't know what you're asking," he said. "If you knew what I've done..."

"I would still love you." She wrapped her arms around him and rested her head against his chest. "I have no illusions about the world, Percy. Be we rich or poor, man or woman, the world can be a cruel place that forces hard choices upon us all." That elicited a deep sigh. "I *know* you, Percy, so I know that whatever you've done, you surely felt you had no choice in the matter. You would not do evil unless you were compelled to do so. Please, share your troubles with me. Let me ease them if I can."

He looked down at her. As his eyes adjusted to the gloom, he could make out the lovely angel he knew so well. The temptation was overwhelming. His guilt was crushing him, consuming him from within, and he was desperate for relief. In truth, he should not even be with Lydia tonight. He should be working downstairs in his lab, except that he had needed the comfort of her arms to get him through another night.

"Talk to me, Percy. Don't lock me out."

Her pleas were irresistible.

"What do you know," he began, "about the Court of Owls?"

•

He told her everything, from his involvement with the Court to the nature of his experiments, to the fiery after-effects of his elixir and the horrific death of his ill-fated test subject. When he was done, he turned his face away from her, grateful for the darkness. He couldn't bear to face her.

"What you must think of me…"

She reached out for him.

"My poor Percy, I had no idea. How you have suffered." She grasped his chin and turned his face back toward hers. In the dim lighting, he saw nothing but sympathy in her divine countenance. Her eyes shimmered damply. "Don't you see? You are as much a victim of the Owls as that wretched soul in your basement. You didn't choose any of this."

Sobbing, he embraced her, profoundly grateful for her forgiveness and compassion, although uncertain if he deserved it. He had accepted his place in the Court for close to his entire life, turning a blind eye to its darker aspects. He had known about the Talons and their purpose, but had chosen to look the other way, assuming they had nothing to do with him personally. Indeed, he reflected with bitter irony, it was not too long ago that he had offered to dispatch a Talon on Lydia's behalf, to deal with that relentless playboy, Billy Draper.

Percy could not claim ignorance of the Court's true nature. He was complicit in its sinister workings.

"What am I to do, Lydia?" he asked. "I can't abide this anymore. I've changed. *You've* changed me, starting with the effect you had on my art. It's no coincidence that my career has thrived since you came into my life. Before I met you, my work was technically adept, but lacking in warmth and heart. Then you awakened my humanity. Raised by Owls, I had always accepted that life was essentially a harsh Darwinian competition between the haves and have-nots, predators and prey. That it was simply the natural order of things, but now…"

His voice trailed off. Margaret had been right when she'd accused Lydia of softening his heart. She was only mistaken in failing to see what a blessing it was.

"Let's flee, Percy," she said. "Run away from Gotham, from the Owls, *all* of this. We can build a new life somewhere else, together."

He shook his head. "It's an enticing dream, but it's impossible. The Court of Owls does not tolerate betrayal, or loose ends. The Talons would hunt us down wherever we went." He breathed deeply as he accepted the reality of their circumstances. "There is only one way forward. I must labor tirelessly to give the Court what they want—a perfected version of the elixir, free of its terrible side effects, so that no one else will have to suffer what that poor bastard endured. No more deaths, no more burnings."

"Can you do it, Percy? Find a solution?"

"I have to," he replied. "There's no other choice." His spirits rose slightly as he saw a light ahead. "Who knows? Perhaps I can use the formula as a bargaining chip to secure a divorce from Margaret, and my discreet retirement from the Court. Then we can buy our freedom, and be together at last!"

22

The van skidded to a halt in front of Gotham Central Terminal. It was the morning rush, and a flood of commuters poured out of the station onto the streets.

Rough hands seized Ronnie Kellogg, then shoved him out of the van onto the crowded sidewalk. The scruffy-looking teenager threw up his hands to break his fall, but he still hit the pavement hard, scraping his knees and palms. Startled pedestrians gasped or cursed at him, depending on how personally inconvenient they found his spill.

His abraded skin stung, but Ronnie barely noticed the pain. Scrapes and bruises were the very least of his worries. He didn't even look at his raw, red palms as he scrambled to his feet. He saw worse things ahead.

His worn and rumpled clothing had seen better days. A military-surplus jacket, fraying jeans, and a faded black tee featuring an obscure metal band he'd never heard of made him look like just another street kid, down on his luck. He was flushed and sweating, his soggy black bangs plastered to his brow as if he'd just had a bucket dumped over his head. The morning light hurt his throbbing, bloodshot eyes, but closing them was worse.

Then all he saw was what was coming next.

Steam rising from his skin. Filling his mouth and lungs...

His head felt like it was already on fire, deep inside his skull.

The searing pain was greater than any headache he had ever known. Was it just his imagination or could he already smell himself burning?

His brain boiling over inside his skull. His entire body lighting up like a torch...

Ronnie wanted to think he was just seeing things, that the serum was causing him to hallucinate, but he could see too clearly what was coming. Desperate to escape the nightmarish fate bearing down on him, he staggered into the train station. He pushed through the exiting crowds like a salmon fighting its way upstream. His ragged attire and obvious distress helped clear a path through the throng, which parted rather than come into contact with him. They had no idea what a smart idea that was.

His skin igniting.

His flesh turning to ash.

People screaming...

"Stay away from me!" he croaked, his throat and tongue drying up. "It's not safe!" Feverishly he stumbled down a flight of steps onto the main floor of the terminal, which resembled the interior of a particularly busy anthill, with streams of Gothamites flowing toward the exits with practiced precision—aside from the occasional tourist gumming up the works.

A mural on the domed ceiling depicted a dancing, toga-clad woman whose slender limbs aligned with the four points of the compass. Electronic signs displayed ever-changing lists of departure times and gates, but Ronnie didn't care about those. Boarding a train wouldn't save him. He only *wished* he had time to get as far from the city as possible.

It was too late for that.

Sweat dripped into his eyes. Compared to the chilly weather outside, the interior of the station felt like an oven. It was all he could do to keep from stripping his clothes off in search of relief. Panting, he scanned his surroundings, looking for... what? First aid? An infirmary? Police? No one could save him now, but maybe he could still point a finger at his killers while there was still time. Keep other folks from falling into the same hell.

The lab, he thought. *I need to warn people about the lab.*

He'd been blindfolded in the van, and had no idea where the lab was located, but the world needed to know that it existed. What was being done there. Those smirking sons of bitches had to be stopped. They couldn't get away with this, they couldn't keep destroying lives, burning up hopes and dreams and futures.

It wasn't supposed to be like this.

I'm only nineteen…

Agony stabbed through his brain like a red-hot poker. His eyes felt like burning coals. The images came faster and faster, superimposed over his regular sight, even when his eyes were wide open and bulging from their sockets. Hallucinatory flames licked at the periphery of his vision, obscuring his view. Peering through the blaze, he spotted a uniformed police officer keeping watching over the station floor.

Ronnie quickened his pace, cutting through the mob to reach the cop before—

A look of horror on the policewoman's face.

A flaming corpse lying at her feet.

The smell of burning flesh…

The cop looked bored, but not for much longer. Ronnie rushed toward her, running out of time. He waved his arms to get her attention. His hands looked dry and cracked already, like kindling.

"Please! I have to tell you something!"

His mouth was so dry he could barely get the words out. His hot breath burned its way up from his lungs, scalding his throat. The searing heat in his brain made it hard to think. Steam rose from his skin. It filled his mouth and nostrils.

Oh, crap, he thought. *It's happening.*

"Whoa, kid! Are you okay?" the cop said. Wariness warred

with concern on her face. *Horror contorted her face.* She reached instinctively for the baton at her belt. *She backed away from the burning corpse.* Anxious commuters glanced at Ronnie, clustering to see what was up. *Screams erupted and people ran in panic.* "Just take it easy and tell me what the matter is."

The gap between now and the next shrank at a terrifying rate, catching up with what he couldn't stop seeing. He wasn't going to make it, he realized. The future was now.

"They did this to me, they—"

He screamed in agony as his brain caught fire. His eyeballs melted and he thrashed wildly in the middle of the station, bursting into flames before the eyes of both the cop and commuters. The crackle cut off his screams as his hair and skin and clothing ignited. Ronnie's remains blazed brightly as they collapsed onto the scuffed, tile floor of Gotham Central Terminal. Smoke rose toward the dancing goddess on the ceiling, like a sacrificial offering. Horror contorted the police officer's face as she backed away from the burning corpse. Tourists and Gothamites alike screamed and ran in panic from the ghastly scene.

Just like Ronnie had seen.

23

Lower Gotham, Gotham City, 1918

...the work proceeds apace. There are many setbacks and disappointments, but I comfort myself with the certainty that each day brings us closer to freedom and happiness.

Take care, my eternal muse, and know that you are never far from my thoughts.

With love,
Percy

"As you are never far from mine," Lydia whispered to her lonely apartment as she reread Percy's latest letter, over and over again. Summer was approaching. Weeks had passed since his tearful confession, and she had seen little of him. Sequestered as he was in his laboratory, searching for the solution to their problems, she had only their correspondence to comfort her as she waited for the day they could be together again.

"I miss you terribly."

Her teddy bear, Percy the Second, kept her company as she occupied a couch in her modest apartment in Lower Gotham, only a short subway ride from the art studios and galleries that lay several blocks north. On this unusually warm day an open window let in a breeze, fluttering the curtains. The clip-clop of hoofbeats, mingling with honking horns and the rumbling of automobiles,

191

rose up from the street below. Gaslights fought back the night. The dazzling sparkle of the Exposition seemed very far away.

Sighing, she read the letter one last time before carefully folding it and placing it back into its envelope for safekeeping. Conscious of Percy's warnings, she added it to the growing treasure trove of correspondence hidden away where no one would ever look to find them—tucked inside the bulging belly of the teddy bear.

The bear's tawny mohair coat concealed the narrow slit she had cut in the toy's back. Taking no chances, she assiduously stitched the slit shut as she did every night before returning Percy the Second to his accustomed place on her bedspread.

"Guard my secrets well, brave bear," she told him. "I am relying on you."

Yawning, she decided to turn in for the evening. She changed into her night things and was turning off the lights, one by one, when a loose floorboard—of which she had often complained to the landlord—creaked behind her.

She spun around to see a dreadful apparition standing between her and the open window. His owlish goggles and terrifying array of knives left no doubt as to his identity. The Talon stalked toward her remorselessly.

"Lydia Doyle, the Court of Owls demands your presence."

24

"So the Burning Sickness is back in a big way," Barbara said. "That's, what, four victims so far?"

"That we know of," Bruce said from his command center in the Batcave. Barbara's worried visage occupied the central screen, while other monitors held grisly images of the latest fatality, who had combusted in Gotham Central Terminal earlier that morning.

Only a few hours had passed since the incident, so the full autopsy results weren't yet available, but Gordon had already confirmed that the body was in the same state as the previous victims. At this point Bruce was less interested in the forensic evidence—which was becoming all too familiar—than in the choice of victims. He knew who was responsible. Now he needed to get out ahead of them before any more charred bodies ended up in the morgue.

"But this is no sickness," he continued, thinking aloud. "We know that spontaneous combustion is an unwanted side effect of some mysterious elixir concocted by Percy Wright a century ago, and that Wright's heirs have been trying to eliminate that side effect ever since, occasionally experimenting on human subjects."

"Hence the periodic outbreaks of 'fever' over the years," Barbara agreed. "Which were actually nothing of the sort."

"So it appears," Bruce said. Bouncing ideas off Barbara helped him in his thought processes. A fresh point of view enabled him to approach a given problem from a different angle, often with positive results. "Those were failed experiments, generations of them."

"Picking back up again today." Barbara shook her head. "What do we know about this new victim?"

"Ronald Kellogg, age eighteen. Ran away from home a few years ago, been in and out of foster homes and youth shelters ever since, when not living on the streets." He scanned the data. "No current address—at least none on record. Some minor run-ins with the law, but nothing serious. He's the sort of marginalized individual who can easily fall through the cracks... like Joe Bava."

That meant both the homeless man and the street kid had been judged as disposable. Yet why did Vincent and his forebears conduct their experiments on human subjects? Perhaps the effects of the elixir couldn't be measured using test animals. That might imply an effect on cognition or speech.

"Any connection to Joanna or her studies?"

"Not that I can determine," he replied. "Kellogg never attended Gotham University, never took a class from Professor Morse, and doesn't seem to have been acquainted with Joanna or any of her associates. I even reached out to Claire Nesko, via Dick, and she didn't recognize the name—not as a friend of Joanna, or Dennis Lewton.

"My working theory," he continued, "is that we're dealing with two different categories of victim: people connected to Joanna— like the professor and her boyfriend, who are being targeted for that reason, and people like Kellogg and Bava, who were simply test subjects. Guinea pigs."

Barbara nodded. "Same MO, but different motives."

"Yet all four men, equally dead."

One innocent victim was too many as far as Bruce was concerned.

He had no intention of letting the Burning Sickness run unchecked through Gotham once again.

Not on my watch.

"So where does that leave us?" Barbara asked.

"Looking for a connection between Bava and Kellogg, beyond the fact that they both lived on the fringes of society, and therefore were vulnerable. We need to find how exactly they fell into the Court's hands, and then ended up back on the streets. Once we discover how they were selected, we can try to prevent any more innocents from becoming victims."

"Understood," Barbara said. "What do you need me to do?"

"Keep working the history angle. I want to know how exactly this all began... and why this damned elixir is worth so many lives."

"And you?" she asked.

"Joanna is still missing."

•

"I appreciate your concern for the young lady's safety, Master Bruce, but you should get some rest. You'll be in no shape to help Ms. Lee if you don't take care of yourself."

Alfred hovered in the background as Bruce remained rooted at his computer station. Barbara's image had been supplanted by multiple photos of Joanna Lee, culled from social media in hopes of finding some clue as to where she might be hiding, now that her late boyfriend's fishing cabin was no longer safe. He scrolled through the photos one after another, scanning the backgrounds and attempting to identify her various associates.

"Soon, Alfred," he said. "As long as Joanna is in the wind, she's in danger from the Talon and any other resources the Court— Hang on, what's *this*?"

His search had turned up an older photo of a teenage Joanna at what looked like a beach in summertime. She lacked her glasses, and had yet to adopt the henna color and bobbed hairdo she had sported more recently. Damp, curly brown hair framed her smiling face, which once again struck him as oddly familiar.

Where had he seen that face before?

Then it hit him.

"Of course," he muttered. "How could I have been so blind?"

Alfred raised an eyebrow. "Sir?"

"Look at this," Bruce said. He knew he was onto something, but he still needed to verify his discovery. He enlarged Joanna's adolescent face as much as he could without losing too much resolution, then called up a vintage photo of Lydia Doyle for comparison, deliberately selecting an old beachside postcard in which she wasn't too heavily made-up or becurled.

Although the photos had been taken close to a century apart, there was a distinct resemblance between the two bathing beauties—one he might have missed if he hadn't spent so much time scrutinizing Lydia's bronze and marbles likenesses.

"I say." Alfred saw the similarity as well. "They could be sisters."

Just to backstop their own impressions, Batman ran both photos through a sophisticated facial-comparison program that quickly established a match. According to the computer, there was at least a seventy-nine percent chance that Joanna and Lydia were related.

Closely related.

"I knew it," Bruce said.

"Ms. Lee and the tragic Miss Doyle share a family connection?" Alfred peered at the computer result. "Who could have imagined it?"

"I should have," Bruce said, frowning. "Long before now."

"In your defense, sir, you can be forgiven for not immediately seeing the features of an old-fashioned Gibson Girl behind the contemporary stylings of a modern college student, particularly as there was no reason to suspect a familial link."

"True enough," Bruce conceded, "but now we know why Joanna was so fascinated with the sad saga of Lydia Doyle."

"Indeed," Alfred said. "One can only hope her story ends more happily."

25

MacDougal Lane, Gotham City, 1918

"Welcome back, Percy. I was wondering where you'd gotten to."

He was startled to find his wife waiting in the foyer when he returned to the row house after posting a new letter to Lydia. A cruel smirk belied her cordial greeting.

"Margaret?"

"Don't just stand there gawking, dear," she said, beckoning. "We've been waiting for you."

Percy blinked in surprise. "We?"

"All will be made clear," she promised, enjoying his stupefaction. "Shall we join the others downstairs?"

With a growing sense of unease he followed her down to the laboratory, where he found the Talon—and Lydia. His lover was lodged in the iron tub, bound and gagged as the doomed rummy had been. Her anguished eyes entreated him as he froze in utter horror, abruptly confronted by the worst nightmare imaginable.

The Talon stood beside the tub, dutifully keeping watch over his latest acquisition. A cotton robe protected Lydia's modesty. Muffled pleas escaped the gag around her mouth.

"Quiet, girl," Margaret said. "I need to speak with my husband."

Percy had words for her, too. "My God, what have you done? Have you completely lost your mind?"

"I could ask you the same thing, Percy." She produced a folded

199

piece of stationery and began to read from it aloud:

"'My beloved muse, how I wish we were together in my studio as before…'"

Percy's blood ran cold. He recognized the opening of a letter which he'd dispatched only days ago.

"How…?" he gasped. "Where did you get that?"

"I believe you are acquainted with a rather peculiar young gentleman named Billy Draper? A tad parvenu for my tastes, and possibly touched in the head but, like you, he appears unduly enamored with the lissome Miss Doyle." Margaret spoke Lydia's name as if it left a bad taste. "Indeed, he is highly suspicious of your relations with her. He's quite convinced, in fact, that you are 'corrupting' her, and is rather desperate to remedy the situation. He even went so far as to intercept one of your letters to the lovely Lydia, in order to confirm his dire suspicions."

Draper? Percy could well imagine that jealous lunatic doing such a thing, but—

"From the dumbfounded expression on your face," Margaret continued, "you wonder how this incriminating document came into my hands. As it happens, Billy came to me with the letter, apparently in the hopes that I could put an end to your sordid little affair." She chuckled. "I believe he saw us both as the wounded parties in this drama, and therefore natural allies. In truth, he was not entirely mistaken."

Percy silently cursed the man. *I should have sent the Talon after him when I had the chance.*

"In the interest of time and taste," Margaret said, flaunting the stolen letter, "I shall spare us the bulk of your romantic drivel and proceed to the passage that most caught my interest. No doubt you will recall it."

He twisted in agony as she quoted his own words back to him:

"'The work goes slowly, too slowly. At times I despair of ever finding the solution, but the thought of you—and our future together—gives me the strength and will to soldier on. Let others yearn to conquer tomorrow. I wish only to live out my remaining years with you at my side. You are, as ever, my inspiration. With love, P.'"

She lifted her gaze from the note. "Well? What have you to say for yourself?"

"I… I have never seen that letter before. It's a fake, a forgery, manufactured by that reprobate Draper. You said yourself that the man is demented, and—"

"Stop it, Percy," she snapped. "You're embarrassing yourself. Do you think me a fool to fall for such feeble denials?"

"No," he admitted bleakly. Margaret was many things, including a monster, but she had never been a fool. *Alan warned me not to cross her.*

"You've gone too far this time, Percy. Dallying with a wanton demimondaine is one thing, but confiding in her concerning the business of the Court? That is another matter altogether." Her manner became less mocking and more severe. "You know our ways, Percy. Such a grievous indiscretion cannot go unpunished. There must be consequences."

"Then punish me!" he pleaded. "I'm at fault here, I'm the one who broke our code of silence. Don't make her pay for my indiscretions. Let her go, I beg of you."

"You know that's quite impossible," Margaret said. "You sealed her fate when you rashly shared our secrets with her." She paused to let her words sink in before continuing. "But perhaps there is a path to atonement, one that might even spare your paramour's life."

"What path?" Percy grasped for hope as a burning man ran toward water. "Tell me what it is!"

"The Court is most anxious to learn how your work is progressing. I trust you have developed an improved formula by now?"

"I am continuing to refine it, yes, but—"

"Excellent," Margaret said. "Then let us test your latest formula on Miss Doyle, so we can measure your progress and derive some benefit from these proceedings."

Percy wouldn't have thought it possible for him to be more afraid for Lydia's safety, but Margaret's proposal plunged him further toward absolute terror—to the extent that he could barely stand. He had to fight the urge to try to physically wrest Lydia from the basement, even knowing that he was no match for Talon. He couldn't even lunge at Margaret, for the Talon would surely strike him down before he could do her any harm.

All he could do was beg for mercy from the merciless.

"Margaret, please," he said, "if ever you cared me for at all, don't make me do this. You've seen what the elixir can do. The odds that I've succeeded in eliminating the fever—"

"Are Miss Doyle's only hope," Margaret said. "I'm offering her a chance, Percy. Her life is in your hands now. If you have indeed perfected your elixir, she will live. If not… well, science is a matter of trial and error, is it not?"

Her callous indifference infuriated him.

"No, damn it! You can't make me do this."

"Don't be ridiculous. Of course we can." She glanced Lydia's way. "What deters you? Is it the thought of marring her celebrated beauty? If so, that can be easily remedied… by the Talon's blades."

She nodded at the assassin, who drew a knife from his belt and placed it against Lydia's cheek, pressing but not yet drawing blood.

"It would be a pity to deface such loveliness," the Talon said with what sounded like genuine regret. "An act of vandalism, truly, but you should understand, sir, that I will do what is necessary to serve the interests of the Court."

"No, don't!" Percy appealed to him. "I'm as much a member of the Court as my wife. I order you to put that knife away!"

"You are a *traitor* to the Court," Margaret said acidly. "You have no privileges here."

"Madam is correct, sir," the Talon said. "My duty and loyalties are clear."

Percy realized he was bound as much as Lydia. He had no allies, no recourses. He stared bleakly into his love's fear-filled eyes.

"Just… let me speak to her, please."

The Talon looked at Margaret, who nodded in assent. He deftly removed Lydia's gag.

"Percy!" Her voice was hoarse from fighting to be heard through the gag. "The Talon… he came for me… I'm so frightened!"

He went to her, as close as the Talon would allow. "Please, forgive me, my love. I never meant this for you. I never intended any of this!"

"For pity's sake, Percy," his wife said impatiently, "I hope you're not going to subject us to too much cheap romantic melodrama. Don't make me regret having that gag taken off."

"Just a moment's decency, Margaret," he said. "That's all I ask. Is that completely beyond you?" He turned his back on her to concentrate on the captive. "I'm so sorry, Lydia. This is all my fault."

She shook her head. "I told you before, you did not choose this. If anything, it was I who persuaded you to share your secrets with me. We are not to blame here, only the monsters who have us at their mercy, as they always have."

He did not deserve her absolution, but was grateful for it anyway.

"But what are we to do, Lydia? I'm trapped. I don't know how to protect you."

She swallowed hard before answering.

"You must do it. Let me brave your elixir… for both our sakes."

"No! You can't mean that!"

She gazed at him, her pale face so full of sorrow and resignation that, even now, part of him ached to preserve it forever.

"There is no other choice. I must put my faith in your genius."

She smiled sadly. "Your hands have shaped and molded my likeness, making me immortal. If I must now trust my life to them… that's only fitting, isn't it?"

He wished he shared her confidence.

26

It begins as it always does. She's down by the lake, fetching water under the cover of night, when gunshots come from the direction of the cabin, shattering the nocturnal stillness. The plastic water container drops onto the shore, making a hollow clattering sound. Her heart races in terror.

The Talon has found them.

For a second she dares hope that Dennis has shot the Talon dead, but then shouting and the sounds of a violent struggle crush those hopes. Dennis yells in fear or anger, although she can't make out the words. She knows, however, what he would want her to do.

Run.

She freezes by the shore, paralyzed by indecision. It's her fault that he's trapped in this nightmare with her. She can't just abandon him.

Can she?

A shriek of pain cuts through the night and jolts her into action. She races onto the dilapidated wooden dock, where a small rowboat is tied. She clambers into the boat. Cold water pooling in the bottom soaks through her sneakers. With shaky fingers she struggles to undo the rope that moors the boat in place. She peers back at the shore, wanting desperately to see Dennis emerging along the wooded trail.

Please, she thinks, *don't make me leave without you...*

The Talon strides out of the woods.

Shoving off from the dock, she tugs frantically on the ignition cord. The motor surges to life, drowning out his words. Then the boat speeds away from the dock, heading out onto the lake and away from her pursuer.

Thunk!

She jumps, causing the boat to rock alarmingly. Moonlight glints off of the blade, lodged in the wooden hull.

•

Joanna woke up abruptly, finding herself alone in the morning hours. Her heart pounded and she was drenched in sweat. Sitting up, she took a deep breath to steady her nerves even as the nightmare echoed in her mind, pursuing her as relentlessly as the Talon had in real life.

A sob escaped her, the dream having ripped the scab off her wounds once again. It wasn't fair, damn it. How many times did she have to relive that awful night?

"Crap, crap, crap," she muttered. *I'm so sorry, Dennis. I hope it was quick.*

A glance at her wristwatch informed her that it was well past nine, but she was in no hurry to return to dreamland. She glanced around, orienting herself in the here and now as her pulse began to settle down. The domed roof of a weathered concrete rotunda soared high above her, supported by a ring of once-majestic archways.

The imposing structure was all that remained of the Temple of Fine Arts, which had drawn throngs of wide-eyed visitors during the great Gotham International Exposition of 1918. Desperate for company, Joanna risked aiming a flashlight beam at the fading mural adorning the interior of the dome. Lydia Doyle, cast as the Three Graces, gazed down at her in triplicate.

"I hope you're looking out for me, wherever you are," Joanna said, addressing the long-vanished model. "Least you can do, after getting me into this mess."

Like Joanna, the old world's fairgrounds had fallen on hard times. She had seen more than her fair share of vintage photos and newsreel footage of that bygone Exposition, when vast crowds had packed acres of ornate courtyards, boulevards, and pavilions, all aspiring to the grandeur and elegance of classical art and architecture. Constellations of electric lights had lit the night, while fireworks and colored spotlights added to the spectacle. Images of Lydia presided over the festivities in countless decorative pieces of art.

That was a century ago, however, and those glory days were long gone. The fairgrounds had endured as an amusement park for decades, under various changes of management, before finally closing their doors in 1965. A ruinous fire had cost the lives of dozens of visiting patrons, delivered the killing blow after years of inexorable decay and neglect.

There had been talk—on and off over the years—of restoring the grounds to their former glory, but a tangled crow's nest of bankruptcies and competing claims had kept the property tied up in litigation for longer than Joanna had been alive, making its revival more unlikely with each passing year. Time and vandalism had taken its toll on the abandoned facilities, reducing them to a crumbling, graffiti-covered, burned-out landscape inhabited only by the occasional arch-criminal in need of a colorful hide-out or a convenient place to dump a body.

Marshland had reclaimed the converted estate the fair had once occupied. Once the pride of Gotham, the former World's Fair was now its own cemetery and all but forgotten, except perhaps as a place nobody in their right mind would want to visit anymore.

Or so Joanna prayed.

She shivered in the cold. The towering walls of the rotunda

sheltered her from the elements, while a hoodie and sweatshirt helped her hang onto whatever body warmth she could muster, but she would have killed for a space heater or even the courage to light a small fire. She hugged herself to keep warm as she contemplated her dismal surroundings.

After the Talon's attack on the cabin, she hadn't been able to think of anywhere to hide until she'd remembered the old fairgrounds. This place had been important to Lydia and Percy, back in the day, so she'd already spent some time exploring the place, seeking inspiration. She knew her way in and around the ruins, which offered sanctuary of sorts—at least while she tried to figure out what to do next.

Fleeing seemed her best bet, but how to do that while the Court of Owls was surely watching every escape route? Her only hope was to wait them out, hunkering down long enough for them to let their attention slip. In the meantime, she had resorted to dumpster-diving to keep body and soul together, foraging for food and supplies whenever she worked up the nerve to cautiously venture out into the city after dark. This had been her life for days now...

That her best option and only hope was squatting in a deserted wreck of a forgotten tourist attraction for as long as she could manage was about as bleak a prospect as she could imagine. When she looked back at what her life had been like, only recently, it was hard not to despair. She gazed at the trio of Lydias on the ceiling.

"Is this how you felt at the end, when you lost everything?" she whispered. In a strange way, she felt closer to the woman than ever before. "Did you wonder how the hell your future had been stolen from you? Did it catch you by surprise... or did you see it coming?"

Joanna knew exactly when it all went wrong for her. That night was burned into her brain forever...

Several days earlier

The night started like any other. She was heading home from the campus library after a long and productive evening working on her thesis. A small notice in a long-extinct Gotham tabloid had given her a new lead on a lesser-known Percy Wright work that, based on its description, might well be another post-mortem evocation of Lydia. She couldn't wait to track it down in person.

For now, though, she was ready to call it a night. She trudged down the main drag of the University District past assorted pizza places, coffee shops, hip record stores stocked with vintage vinyl, and other student hang-outs. Even though it was past ten on a weeknight, the avenue was still buzzing with activity. Joanna made her way down the crowded sidewalk, an overstuffed backpack weighing her down, while keeping a wary eye on the weather, which was threatening to take a nasty turn.

Thunder rumbled in the distance, accompanied by brilliant flashes of lightning, which appeared to be drawing nearer at a worrisome pace. Black clouds rolled in from the east, heralding a storm. A few stray droplets sprinkled her ahead of the downpour.

And me without an umbrella, she thought. *Crap.*

She paused at the entrance to a murky alley dividing a used-bookstore from a vaping parlor. The shortcut would cut a block or two off her usual route, possibly giving her time to get indoors before any heavy rain arrived. This being Gotham, she preferred to stick to better-lit, more populated streets after dark, but she wasn't keen on getting drenched either, especially since she wasn't sure just how waterproof her backpack was. The thought of her laptop and notebooks getting soaked made the shortcut seriously tempting.

Maybe just this once...

This was the University District after all, as opposed to the Narrows or some equally seedy part of town. She peered into the alley, which looked empty enough aside from a few rusty metal dumpsters. Just a quick dash through and she'd be halfway home.

"What the heck," she muttered. "Let's do this."

Thunder boomed at her heels, spurring her on. Raindrops pelted her face with greater frequency. Fishing a keyring from her purse, she clutched the mini-canister of pepper spray clipped to the ring and hurried into the alley. She walked briskly, the sooner to reach the other end, while staying carefully aware of her surroundings. Rats scurried as she passed the first dumpster.

Ick.

Despite her street-smart vigilance, part of her was already anticipating settling in back at her apartment. Leftover chicken souvlaki was calling her name, along with a hot shower and maybe some TV to help her unwind. Claire would surely be home at this hour. Joanna wondered if her roommate would be up to a little binge-watching before bed.

The rain started coming down heavier as the storm caught up with her. A flash of lightning, followed almost immediately by a deafening thunderclap, lit up the alley, exposing a hooded figure lurking on a fire escape. The glare was gone in a blink, but not before the menacing apparition was impressed upon her mind. Clad in black leather body armor, he sported a small arsenal of wicked-looking knives and claws and swords while peering down at her through tinted yellow goggles. A bird-like metal beak jogged Joanna's memory to terrifying effect. Well-versed in Gotham lore and history, she recognized a Talon when she saw one.

But that's just an old story.

His presence revealed by the storm, the Talon made no further attempt to conceal himself. She saw him as a dim silhouette, except during fleeting flashes of lightning. He drew a knife from a belt that was slung across his chest. It caught the faint light coming from the street as he turned it back and forth to keep her attention.

"Joanna Lee," he said. "The Court of Owls has need of you."

His words made her crazy suspicions all too real. Trembling, she raised the tiny vial of pepper spray, which seemed woefully inadequate when faced with a legendary boogeyman armed to the teeth. A cruel chuckle suggested that the Talon was similarly unimpressed.

"Seriously?" he mocked her. "Do you have any clue who you're dealing with?"

Joanna gulped. She knew more than she wanted to.

"T-Talon…"

"On the money," he said, still sounding amused. "They said you were a bright one. Prove it by not giving me any trouble. I'm not out to hurt you. At least, not yet."

That didn't ease her mind a bit. She supposed she ought to be relieved that the Talon wasn't planning to divest her of her head, but she was still trembling like a leaf, and felt sick to her stomach. Her eyes darted from one end of the alley to another. The well-lit avenues at each end looked impossibly far away. There was no way she could make it before the Talon pounced on her or nailed her in the back with a knife, but what else could she do?

Joanna knew deep down that if she let the Talon take her, she would never be seen again.

Just like Lydia.

Her arm shook as she brandished the pepper spray. The rain soaked her, chilling her to the bone. The strobe-effect of the lightning made everything even more surreal. She couldn't believe this was happening to her.

"Toss away that toy," the Talon snarled, "before I take it from you." An edge in his voice made it clear that she didn't want that. Losing hope, she let the key ring and canister fall from her fingers. They splashed into a muddy puddle.

This ambush had to have something to do with her thesis. One of Percy's letters to Lydia had contained an allusion to a mythical court, but Lydia had been reluctant to read too much into it. As far as she'd known, the Court of Owls was just a durable part of Gotham folklore.

How did the old rhyme go again?

Speak not a whispered word of them,
Or they'll send the Talon for your head.

She stared up at the figure on his perch.

"Please, I won't tell anybody. Tell them that I won't talk, not a word or a whisper."

"Too late for that, college girl. You've rattled too many old skeletons already. You need to—"

Loud bangs, like firecrackers, came from the main drag she had left behind. At first Joanna thought it was just more thunder, but then she recognized the sharp report of gunshots. The Talon glanced quickly over his shoulder.

"What the hell?"

Screams and shouts accompanied the gunfire from the street. Panicked people, mostly college-age, poured into the alley, fleeing whatever violence had erupted behind them. Seeing her chance, Joanna let the frantic exodus carry her away from her pursuer. Another flash of lightning illuminated the alley. Looking back over her shoulder, she saw that the fire escape was empty.

The Talon was nowhere to be seen.

"What's happening?" she called to the strangers shoving past her, pushing her toward the far end of the alley. She couldn't slow down without being trampled. "What is it?"

Competing answers assailed her.

"A drive-by shooting, I think!"

"No, there was a cross-fire. I saw some guy get gunned down!"

"Some sort of gang thing for sure! This city is a war zone!"

The very thought of a gang war triggered bad memories, flashing her back to the night she became an orphan, but it seemed as if she owed her escape to Gotham's sky-high crime rate. The irony wasn't lost on her as the mob spilled out of the alley into the street. Police sirens wailed in the night, converging on the crime scene an avenue over. A loud whoosh came from above, competing with the thunder, as a bat-winged aircraft swooped down from the clouds, skimming the rooftops as it passed overhead. Gasps and cheers greeted the Batwing while Joanna felt an irrational urge to call out for help—even knowing there was no way he could hear her from the street.

Her heart sank as the aircraft sped out of sight.

Batman wasn't going to save her this time.

The agitated crowd dispersed in all directions, fleeing the shootings and the storm. Joanna stuck with the largest group, afraid to be alone, but still felt horribly exposed and vulnerable. She had no idea where the Talon had gone, but doubted he was far away. Hiding her face beneath her hoodie, she searched every shadowy nook and cranny as she hustled to keep up with the other freaked-out pedestrians. The rain came down in sheets, making it harder to watch her surroundings. For all she knew, he was spying on her right now, tracking her every move.

Just like he followed me into the alley.

A subway entrance beckoned to her, offering shelter beneath the city streets. Along with many others, she descended into the station and, after paying the fare, scrambled aboard the first train that pulled up to the platform. She sighed in relief as the doors slid shut and the train started moving toward... where exactly?

The reality of her situation sunk in.

The Court of Owls was real and the Talon was after her... because of *something* in Percy Wright's history? Her backpack, holding her laptop and notebooks, suddenly felt a hundred times heavier. She couldn't go home, could barely trust anyone, and had nowhere to turn. All thanks to a secret society that was supposed to be an urban legend.

Percy, Lydia... what have you gotten me into?

The present

Joanna Lee huddled under a ragged blanket in the crumbling rotunda. She had been on the run ever since she'd first glimpsed the Talon in that alley. Dennis had tried to hide her at his grandfather's old cabin, even emptying out his bank account so that they would have money to live on while they struggled to stay off the grid.

The Talon had found them anyway.

Then Professor Morse had been burned alive.

Her thesis had a body count.

What about Claire? By now, her roommate would have reported her missing, but Joanna was afraid to reach out to her for fear of putting her in danger. Better for Claire to agonize over her disappearance than be drawn into this horror.

At least she hasn't been in the headlines.

Yet.

A yawn reminded her that she hadn't had a good night's sleep for longer than she could remember. Exhaustion won out over anxiety as she clicked off the flashlight and tried to get in a few more hours of shut-eye, while praying she wouldn't again relive the attack on the cabin. That would be just too cruel.

Joanna nestled into the heap of torn sheets, towels and newspapers that formed her bed. A lumpy backpack, packed with dirty laundry, cushioned her head as best it could. She pulled her legs up to keep warm, only to find that sleep remained maddeningly out of reach. Even though she was so tired she felt more dead than alive, her brain couldn't stop. She kept trying to figure out what she might have done differently and what her options were going forward. Or maybe she was afraid of sliding back into the nightmare.

She wasn't sure what scared her more: bad dreams or a bleaker reality. *Bad enough that the Owls have me jumping at shadows. Does my own subconscious have to conspire against me, too?*

Something rustled in the dark outside, jolting her eyes open. She reached frantically for the knife she kept hidden under the makeshift pillow. It was the Talon's knife, the same one that had lodged in the side of the boat during her narrow escape at the lake. Adrenaline coursed through her veins, combating the exhaustion.

With a sweaty palm she gripped the hilt of the knife. It was embossed with what she recognized as the Athenian Owl, an ancient symbol of wealth and power... as well as, according to the Romans, an omen of death. The foreboding emblem pressed against her flesh as she peered through an open archway toward the ruins beyond.

Don't panic, she told herself uselessly. *It was just a random noise in the night.* Anything could have caused it: a stray cat or dog, a hungry gull foraging in the trash, a gust of wind blowing over some precariously stacked debris. She strained to penetrate the darkness outside the rotunda, where heaps of rubble and refuse had long ago replaced the majestic colonnade. A stagnant, scum-covered pool barely resembled the sparkling artificial lagoon of decades past.

A faint splash set her nerves further on edge.

Perhaps it was just another homeless person, searching for refuge? Such people came and went, though not often. The desolate fairgrounds had proven largely free of junkies or predators, but she had remained on guard the entire time she had been squatting here. Had her luck finally run out?

It can't be him, she thought. *He wouldn't make a sound.*

Joanna was tempted to call out, just to end the suspense, but knew that silence was her best defense. Gripping the knife in her right hand and the flashlight in her left, she didn't move a muscle, afraid to make a sound—not unlike Lydia back in the day, when she'd held the same pose for long sessions at a time. It dawned on her just how physically arduous Lydia's modeling career had been, now that her own safety might depend on staying as still as possible.

She held her breath, praying that whoever or whatever was out there would move on without ever knowing she was here. The darkness both shielded and frustrated her, making it impossible to know what lay beyond the nearest archway.

"I beg your pardon, miss, but you're looking in the wrong direction."

She let out a strangled shriek.

The voice came from directly overhead.

Gasping for air, she clicked on the flashlight and aimed it at the roof, where the Talon crouched on the ledge that circled the base of the dome. His gloved hands clutched a tangle of ropes as he peered down at her. The hilt of a sword could be glimpsed behind his right shoulder. Knives, identical to the one in Joanna's hand, were sheathed all over his black leather gear.

"Oh, God..."

No longer caring what was outside, she tried to scramble to her feet, but the Talon was way ahead of her. He flung the ropes, which turned out to be a sturdy net worthy of a big-game hunter. It fell over Joanna, tangling her and dragging her down. Panicking, she flailed about wildly, slashing at the thick knotted cables, but only succeeded in snaring herself even more. Heavy weights held down the corners of the net, making it harder to throw off. In time, she might have extricated herself, but the Talon didn't give her the chance.

Nimbly descending the wall of the rotunda, he crossed the floor to where she thrashed. The flashlight beam captured his approach. He drew his gleaming sword from behind his back, holding it ready.

"Stay down, miss, if you know what's good for you."

His voice sounded different than before, not as smug. Confused, Joanna stopped flailing and squinted at her captor. Peering through the ropes, it took her a few moments to realize that this wasn't the same man who had pursued her earlier.

His garb varied from the other one, possessing a distinctly more retro look. An open black trench coat, reminiscent of those worn by army officers during the First World War, hung on him like a cape. Brass buttons, matching his polished brass goggles, gleamed upon his double-breasted black tunic. Cloth wrappings bound each of his legs from ankle to knee, providing support and protection. The overall effect harkened back to the early twentieth century, or so Joanna judged. Not quite steampunk, but close enough.

Like the other Talon, he was armed to the teeth.

"Who... who are you?" she asked.

"My name doesn't matter anymore. It hasn't since before you were born, before your mother's mother was born, most likely. I serve the Court of Owls. That's all you need to know." He chuckled wryly. "And haven't you led us on quite the merry chase... until now."

Until now, her mind echoed. A horrible sense of inevitability fell over her like another net. She should have known she couldn't hide forever. "How did you find me?"

"Call it a hunch," he said. "I recalled this place of old. Hearing of your well-documented interest in such matters, I suspected its history would call to you." He examined her through his goggles, which seemed to allow him to see in the dark. "Yes, I can see the resemblance well enough. Take away the garishly dyed hair and unsightly adornments, along with the color of your eyes, and you're the spitting image of her, more or less."

Curiosity cut through the terror.

"Lydia?"

"None other." He paused to take in the rotunda. "Ah, you should have seen this place back when it was new. Glorious, it was, a tribute to the century's ingenuity and aspirations." He sighed wistfully. "But time takes its toll, I suppose, although some of us have cheated it longer than most."

She didn't understand. He was talking as though he actually remembered the Exposition, and Lydia as well—but that was impossible. Even if he'd attended that World's Fair as a child, he'd be over a hundred years old now.

"No," she whispered. "You can't have been alive then."

"Think again, miss." His sword remained steady in his grasp. His posture showed no sign of age or infirmity. "Mind you, I've been asleep for some time, like Rip Van Winkle, you might say. Do they still tell that old story in this day and age, I wonder, or has it faded from memory like so much else?"

Joanna tried to process what she was hearing.

"You're insane. Delusional."

"If you say so, but I suspect you'll change your tune soon enough." He raised the sword above her. "Now be a good girl and let go of that fine knife you're holding. We both know it doesn't belong to you."

Her shoulders sagged beneath the net as she surrendered the knife along with what was left of her hopes.

"Please," she begged. "Just kill me now or leave me alone. I can't take any more of this. I feel like I'm losing my mind."

"Sorry, miss." The Talon confiscated the stolen blade, adding it to his arsenal. "Nothing personal, I assure you. Just tidying up some old business, is all."

27

"The joker."

Percy turned over the playing card to reveal the leering countenance of a clown. "Precisely, my love. You are correct again."

Lydia shuddered at the card. She was nestled into a comfortable wingback chair in the upstairs bedroom of the row house, a wool blanket draped over her lower body. Her favorite robe from the studio clothed her as, trembling, she averted her eyes.

"Please, Percy, don't show me that card again. It… frightens me."

He leaned toward her, both fascinated and concerned. "Why, Lydia? Why does this card bother you?"

"It puts pictures in my eyes, in my head. Terrible pictures. Dead men and women, grinning like skulls. A clown in a padded cell, cackling like a maniac." She buried her face in her hands to try to keep the disturbing images out. "It's like a nightmare. A waking nightmare!"

Percy sought to calm her.

"It's all right, Lydia. Look." He tore up the card and let the pieces flutter to the floor, while resolving to remove the jokers from every deck of cards henceforth. "It's gone. You never need to see it again."

She peered out from behind her fingers. "Truly?"

"I promise," he said soothingly. "You're safe. You have nothing to fear."

He prayed to God it was so.

Miraculously, Lydia had yet to catch fire. Nearly two days had passed since the experiment, and she was still alive. Margaret had been thrilled—and perhaps also disappointed—by Lydia's survival, but Percy had warned her not to celebrate their "success" prematurely. Lydia needed to be monitored for a time to ensure that there was no delayed reaction to the elixir.

His wife and the Talon had left him to the task, but Percy had no doubt that the house was under observation, with every exit watched through the day and night. He felt unseen eyes upon him.

They watch you at your hearth, they watch you at your bed…

For her comfort, Percy had installed Lydia in the master bedroom. A brass fire extinguisher filled with liquid carbon tetrachloride rested discreetly in a corner, along with a neatly piled stack of heavy wool fire blankets. A third precaution waited in his breast pocket—a hypodermic syringe containing a compound designed to stop Lydia's heart in an instant, should the worst occur.

"Thank you, Percy. You take such good care of me."

"No more than you deserve. How are you feeling?"

"I'm not sure," she answered. "It's difficult to tell how I'm feeling *anything* now, since I'm no longer sure when *now* is. I feel… unrooted, as though I'm experiencing something that hasn't happened yet." She looked at him with a distraught expression that tore at his heart. "When *am* I, Percy?"

"Precisely where you belong, with me."

He placed his palm gently against her brow. She was running a slight fever, but nothing like the scorching heat the doomed sailor had radiated before bursting into flames. Percy realized he should be grateful that she was still alive at all, yet he couldn't help worrying. What if his new formula had simply postponed the inevitable?

"Are you warm, dear?" he asked. "Would you like some ice water?"

"No, thank you, Percy. I think I just want to…"

Her voice trailed off as she stared into space. Her eyes widened, twitching side to side at whatever prophetic vision had caught her attention. Violet smudges shadowed her eyes, testifying to uneasy slumber. Her lower lip trembled. Shaking hands clutched the blanket over her lap.

"Lydia? What is it? What do you see?"

"Fragments, flickers, like a moving-picture show." Haunted eyes stared past him into tomorrow. "They're coming toward us, Percy, or am I rushing toward them? I can't tell anymore."

"Speak to me, darling! What exactly do you see ahead?"

"Owls," she whispered, "and bats. A bat across the moon, striking fear into the hearts of the wicked and unjust. Owls and bats, hunting one another in the night."

Percy struggled to decipher the cryptic prophecy.

"What else?"

Her eyes locked onto his. Her voice was hollow.

"Flames," she said. "The future is on fire."

28

"Sure, I know him," the bum said. "Old Joe. Been around forever, until… you know." He spat chewing tobacco onto the trash-strewn shore beneath the southern end of the Sprang Bridge. The looming structure provided shelter from the light rain that drizzled down. "Damn shame what happened to him."

Bruce Wayne had numerous contacts among Gotham's A-list, but Batman had his own sources closer to the streets. Frank Dodge was a semi-homeless street peddler who had often provided him with valuable intel. A regular at Leslie Thompkins' free clinic near Crime Alley, Frank was short and squat and affected the look of an aging hippy. His thinning gray hair was tied up in a ponytail, while a huge poncho fell over him like a tent. Mismatched socks could be seen through his sandals. It had taken Batman a few nights to track Frank down, but he wasn't surprised that the man recognized the photo of Joe Bava. Frank swam in the same waters as the murdered vagrant.

"When was the last time you saw him?"

"Hmm. Gimme a minute to think on that."

Frank scratched his chin as he searched his memory, which Batman knew to be fairly reliable. Unlike many other unfortunate denizens of Gotham's underclass, Frank wasn't addled by mental illness or substance abuse. He had simply checked out of the rat race and its demands, for reasons of his own. Batman had come to trust his observations. Frank's eyes and ears worked just fine.

"Let's see. Seems to me I ran into Joe just recently, but where exactly?" He snapped his fingers as the answer came to him. "Got it! It was at the plasma center, over on Duke Street."

Batman knew the place. It was a commercial outfit that paid donors for fresh blood plasma, which was then used to produce vaccines and other pharmaceutical products. Gothamites in need of ready cash could donate as often as twice a week. There was a more upscale plasma center in the University District, attracting cash-strapped college kids, but the place on Duke Street mostly lured in poorer folks who were down on their luck. He could easily imagine Joe Bava in that establishment.

"Do you recall anything unusual about that last encounter?" he asked. "Did Joe do or say anything that might seem strange in hindsight?"

"Come to think of it," Frank said, "one of those lab-coated vampires asked Joe to stick around after donating. Wanted to talk to him about making a little extra money by taking part in some sort of study." Frank shrugged. "Didn't think much of it at the time."

"No reason you should." It wasn't uncommon, in fact, for selected plasma donors to receive targeted vaccinations in order to increase the antibody count in their plasma, which could then be harvested at a profit. Batman changed the image on his phone to a photo of Ronnie Kellogg, and showed the dead teenager's photo to Frank.

"What about this man? You know him?"

Frank squinted at the photo. "Face rings a bell. Ron something-or-other? Don't know him like I knew Joe, since he's just a kid, but, sure, I've seen him around."

"At the plasma center?"

"That's right." He looked up from the phone. "That mean something?"

"Hard to say, but you'll want to find a different place to sell your plasma."

Frank nodded gravely. "Message received."

Batman fished a hundred-dollar bill from a compartment on his belt. Paying informants wasn't his usual custom, but he figured Frank had earned a few good meals at Bruce Wayne's expense, and it did no good to steer Frank toward social services. Frank wasn't interested in that kind of assistance.

"Here." Batman handed him the bill. "Don't flash it in the wrong places."

"Not a chance." Frank glanced around warily before tucking the cash inside his jacket. "Always glad to help you make this rough old city a little safer." He started to head off, his windfall burning a hole in his pocket, then paused at looked back at Batman with a mournful expression on his weathered features.

"You'll fix this, right?" he said. "Deal with whatever did in Joe?"

"That's the plan."

Backing away into the shadows, Batman ascended to the rooftops to consider what he'd just learned. The connection with a pharmaceutical company pointed toward Vincent Wright, whose family fortune was tied up with that industry. He recalled the scientific books and journals he'd found in Vincent's penthouse, indicating a personal interest in biotech. Now he just needed to confirm a connection between the Owls and the plasma center. He had to do it quickly, too, before more of the homeless became human guinea pigs.

A water tower shielded him from the rain, which was already dying out. He peered out over the city, spying a certain clock tower in the distance. He activated the headset in his cowl.

"What is it?" Barbara replied.

"The Crown Point Plasma Collection Center on Duke," he said. "I need to know if and how it might be connected to Vincent Wright and his family's business interests."

"You have a lead?"

"Possibly." He explained how he'd linked the two "random" combustion victims to a common location, which just happened to involve pharmaceuticals.

"As in compounds and elixirs?" Barbara grasped it immediately. "All right. Let me see what I can dig up."

Signing off, Batman waited beneath the water tower. Barbara could have joined him in the field, but she was more valuable in the Clock Tower. It allowed him to continue the search without distraction. Joanna was still in the wind, as was the Talon, while another innocent victim could be facing death at any time.

•

"You called it," Barbara reported a few minutes later. "I had to wade through a maze of corporate branches and shell companies, but, sure enough, the Crown Point Plasma Collection Center is a fully owned subsidiary of the Pangeonics Health Consortium— which is owned lock, stock, and barrel by guess who?"

"Vincent Wright." He nodded in satisfaction, convinced that he was on the right track. "Good work."

"Any time," she said. "What are you going to do now?"

He was already sprinting across the rooftops toward Duke Street. The last of the rain sluiced off his waterproof cape and cowl. It was well past eleven, and a police blimp passed by overhead. He briefly considered hitching a ride.

"I'm going to pay a late-night call to Crown Point."

•

Joanna had no idea where in Gotham she was.

That steampunk Talon had drugged her, so she only blurrily recalled being hustled into a waiting car and driven across town.

226

By the time the drugs wore off, she found herself strapped into a padded chair or recliner in what appeared to be a medical facility of some kind. A faintly antiseptic smell, like that of a hospital or nursing home, unnerved her. Her left shoulder ached—she must have slammed into something at the fairgrounds.

A large amount of sophisticated laboratory equipment occupied the windowless chamber, while the recliner into which she was strapped reminded her of the ones used by chemotherapy patients or blood donors. The laboratory setting scared her more than a conventional prison might have. Images of scalpels and syringes forced their way into her head.

The Talon stood watch from a corner, silent as a statue.

"Please, where are we?" she asked. "What are we doing here? What are you planning to do to me?"

"That's not up to me, miss," the Talon said. "Just be patient. What comes will come."

"Easy for you to say." She strained at the leather straps and shouted. "Help! Somebody? Anybody? Help me!"

"Save your breath," he advised her. "There's no one to hear you, and you can save your strength as well. Unless you're the reincarnation of Harry Houdini, you're not escaping that chair or this place." He placed his arms across his chest to signal the end of the discussion. "Now hush and make your peace with the Almighty, if need be."

Joanna shouted herself hoarse before finally giving up. Time passed, measured only by her growing anxiety, thirst, and hunger, until it was practically a relief when the door opened to admit another Talon. He was accompanied by a bald man wearing a goatee, a tailored business suit, and a smug expression. Whatever was about to happen could not be good, she knew, but at least it was happening. She had no illusions that the newcomers were here to rescue her. If anything, they acted like they owned the place.

"Finally," Vincent Wright said, looking her over. "I was starting to think that you'd dropped off the face of the Earth."

She recognized Percy's descendant at once. Indeed, she had hoped to contact him at some point, in hopes of gaining access to whatever personal papers and memorabilia might still be in the family's possession. His appearance alongside the Talons startled her, but she couldn't help being intrigued, as well. What did this have to do with Percy and Lydia?

"I would have found her eventually," the newly arrived Talon grumbled. He glanced at his fellow assassin. Although his face was hidden, resentment could be heard in his voice. "On my own."

"Don't be too proud to accept help, lad," the older Talon said. "I'm sure you earned your station, just as we all did in our day, but it's never too late to learn from those who came before you."

"Says the old man who was put on ice how many decades ago?"

"Watch your tongue, boy. I was serving the Court before your father's father was conceived." Their hoods failed to conceal the tension between them, yet Joanna had no idea how she might use it to her benefit.

"That's enough, both of you," Wright said. "All that matters is what best serves the interests of the Court." He turned toward the retro Talon. "You've done well, Frederick. The Grandmaster will be pleased, I'm sure. No doubt she's waiting for your report."

"No doubt," the older Talon said a bit stiffly. "Unless you'd prefer me to remain?"

"I don't think that's necessary," Wright replied. "Your associate and I can handle matters from here. But thank you again for your invaluable service in locating our new guest."

"You're welcome, sir. I'll be on my way then."

Joanna wished she had a better sense of what was going on between her captors. She watched tensely as the older Talon exited the laboratory, brushing past the modern one—who made no effort to get out of his way.

"Stuck-up old relic," the younger Talon snarled after his

counterpart had gone. "Who does he think he is?" He swung his gaze toward Joanna. "He just got lucky, that's all, going back to that broken-down old fairground."

"Let it go, Carson." Wright checked to make sure the door had locked. "I'm no happier than you are that the Grandmaster thawed him out to babysit us. His first loyalty is to the Court, not our grand objectives." He turned to face Joanna. "Still, I can't deny that it yielded valuable results."

The Talon muttered behind his hood.

"Hello, Joanna," Wright said. "It's past time we talked."

Taking his time, he hung his jacket on a hook by the door and put on a white lab coat instead. Next he pulled on a pair of sterile latex gloves.

"Do you know who I am?" he asked.

Joanna didn't see any point in pretending otherwise.

"Vincent Wright."

"Good. That makes things simpler." He approached her. "Here's how it's going to work. You're going to tell me everything you've learned about my distinguished ancestor and his work."

"Everything?" She tried to put on a brave face. "That could take a while."

"The night is young," he said with a smirk, "and I've got as much time as it takes. Don't even think about holding anything back, not unless you want to go the way of your boyfriend or professor."

His threat amounted to a confession. Dennis's screams echoed in her mind as she suddenly hated Vincent Wright with all her heart.

"You son of a bitch!"

"I'm also a busy man," he said glibly. "Can we save the histrionics for later?"

You wish, she thought angrily. "You had him killed, didn't you? And Professor Morse?"

"I think there's a lot of guilt to go around here," Wright said. "You're the one who started this by digging into my family's past.

Your associates were just… collateral damage."

Guilt stabbed her again, but not enough to let Wright and the Talons off the hook. She strained again to break free, wanting to lash out regardless of the consequences, but her fury didn't make her bonds any less secure.

"I was just studying history," she protested. "That's no excuse for murder or any of this."

"You see, that's where we must agree to disagree," Wright responded. "And if I were you, I'd focus more on my own situation right now than on any past grievances." He beckoned to the Talon, who stepped closer. She froze in her struggles. "Perhaps you'd like my lethal friend to describe in detail *exactly* how your friends met their ends… and what's waiting for you if you don't cooperate."

"Works for me," the Talon said. "I can give you a play-by-play, right up to the moment your boyfriend died screaming…"

"No!" she said. "Don't, please." The ghastly prospect was enough to mute her rage for the moment. Despite her anger at coming face-to-face with Dennis's killers, she needed to keep her wits about her if she wanted to survive this ordeal. Dennis had died to save her from the Talon. She couldn't let that sacrifice go to waste.

"Fine," she said bitterly. "Let's talk."

"That's more like it." Vincent gestured for the Talon to back off. "We've seen your notes, what you shared with others. But there are gaps—details to which you allude, but don't follow up. What do you know that *isn't* there, in black-and-white?" He leaned in. "What do you know about my ancestor's work?"

She still didn't know what he was after, but talking about Percy Wright enabled her to focus, no matter how scared or angry she was. It was almost comforting to think about her work, instead of her own uncertain future.

"It's not so much what I know as what I suspect," she hedged. Joanna's mouth was dry. She considered asking for a glass of water, but feared that would be pushing her luck. "I know that Percy and Lydia had a secret affair, that he remained obsessed with her after her disappearance, immortalizing her in his art, over and over. It was as if he blamed himself for her death…"

"All of which is hardly revelatory," Wright said impatiently. "What else?"

Aside from the fact that Percy was mixed up with the Court of Owls? She was only just now figuring that out. Bitter experience had led her to that particular realization. "Well, I have a theory that Percy hid something in his depictions of Lydia. There's imagery that suggests Gotham's future, warnings of days to come, even though they were sculpted a century ago." She expected him to scoff… or worse. "I know it sounds crazy, but—"

"Hardly," Vincent said, smirking. "Your 'crazy' theory is why you are here, so let's skip the generalities. What do you know about Percy's elixir?"

"Elixir?" she said. "What elixir?"

Wright looked angry at that, and she wondered if he might strike her—or have his muscle so do. Instead he stepped back.

"The elixir that enabled his subjects to perceive the future," he said, and he began to pace. "Where else do you think those coded 'warnings' came from?"

"Percy could see the future…" Joanna was confused by what he was saying, and yet it also made a certain amount of sense. She needed to know more. "Because of this elixir?"

"Not Percy," he said. "Lydia… before her unfortunate demise. She was his test subject; it stands to reason that he learned of the future from her. Are you saying you knew nothing of his formula?"

"I knew he was a scientist as well as a sculptor," she responded, "but that's all. And I've never read anything about him devising any… elixir."

Wright frowned and stopped pacing. "That's both comforting and discouraging. Comforting in that the secret remains hidden—

no one else has located it, to use it against us. Discouraging, however, in that it makes me wonder if you were worth all this trouble."

Joanna heard herself becoming expendable.

"Just tell me what you want to know, what you're looking for," she insisted. "Maybe I know more than I realize."

"Let's hope so," Wright said. "Tell me, have you heard of the Burning Sickness?" The phrase sounded familiar, but it took Joanna a few long moments to place it from some of the old newspapers she'd prowled through in her research.

"It was some kind of epidemic or fever," she said. "Beginning in Percy's time, and continuing after his death."

"It's more like a recurrent ailment, actually," Wright said, "but give yourself a gold star. A particularly nasty 'fever' that literally turned its victims into human bonfires, igniting their brains before baking them entirely."

"I don't understand." Joanna shuddered, remembering the description of Professor Morse's death. "What does this have to do with Percy and Lydia?"

"It seems as if Percy's elixir had an unfortunate side effect—spontaneous combustion." He started pacing again, and she wished he would stop. "My family and I have been trying to eliminate this drawback for generations, but have hit roadblock after roadblock. It's been maddening."

Spontaneous combustion? Joanna's mind reeled. She'd always thought that was just an antiquated notion—something nobody took seriously anymore. Then again, she used to think that about the Court of Owls, too.

"I don't know," the Talon commented. "It isn't entirely 'unfortunate'—especially if you like watching people go up like fireworks. Trust me, it's quite impressive, and comes in handy if you don't want to leave any evidence." A sadistic chuckle emerged from his hood.

Oh, God… Was that how Dennis had died—engulfed in flames? Burnt alive? She tried to force the image out of her brain, but failed miserably, choking back a sob.

"I'm glad you find it so entertaining," Wright said dryly, wrinkling his nose in disgust. "Your sadistic enthusiasm aside, however, the elixir is of little value if all it gives us is human torches. We need more." He turned back to face Joanna. "That's where you come in."

"I still don't understand." She felt frustrated, angry, and grief-stricken in equal measures. "Exactly what is it you *want* from me?"

"Near the end, relations between Percy and the Court were… strained. He insisted to his dying day that he had never overcome the problem, yet when he died, he left behind a letter. In it, he claimed to have secretly *perfected* the serum, but he left no details." Vincent looked angry, as if he had been the person betrayed. "It was his final revenge, all because of what happened to Lydia."

"What *did* happen to Lydia?"

"Like you, she learned more about the Court's affairs than was healthy for her," he explained, "which is why she went from model to guinea pig."

"Oh, no." Joanna put the pieces together. "For the elixir."

"Another gold star," he said. "Without going into the messy details, let's just say it didn't end well for Lydia—much to Percy's chagrin. As a result, he had more than enough reason to hide the formula from the Court. I suppose I can't blame him, really, but that brings me no closer to the answers I want. Answers I *need*.

"You, however, have fresh insights into my great-grandfather and his work," he continued. "You've seen patterns where others have missed them. If there are secrets to be found—in his works, in the messages to his beloved Lydia—you will know where to find them. Do you understand?"

"I think so," she said, fascinated in spite of everything. "But I'm an art history major, not a chemist. I don't know anything about elixirs or formulas."

"So you say," Wright said, "but I'm not certain I believe you. I'm not entirely convinced that, like Percy, you aren't holding something back. If you wish to survive this, however, you would do well to cooperate." He gave her a smug smile. "I'm a scientist, you're an art expert. Think of it as a collaboration."

His arrogance infuriated her. "You call this a collaboration? You've threatened me, killed my friends, taken me prisoner. Why the hell would I want to help you get your hands on this 'elixir'? It sounds to me like Percy had the right idea, keeping it from the Owls."

The smile disappeared. "I was being polite," Wright replied. "But if you insist on making this unpleasant, allow me to oblige you." He crossed the lab to open a small refrigerator, from which he extracted a vial containing a shimmering, metallic silver liquid. "This is my latest variant on Percy's elixir. I have yet to test it on a human subject, so it's entirely possible that this version won't set anyone on fire." He carried it closer, for her to see. "Maybe it's safe, maybe it's not. Would you like to help me find out... or would you prefer to assist me in a less risky fashion?"

Joanna actually hesitated. The idea of cooperating with Dennis's killers made her sick to her stomach, especially since she knew damn well that Wright intended to dispose of her once she'd outlived her usefulness. He hadn't even attempted to conceal his identity.

And yet...

"It's far from a pleasant way to go," he said. "Burning alive from the inside out." He loaded the vial's contents into a syringe.

Joanna stared at it in fear and fascination.

"So," he asked, "what do you say?"

29

The Crown Point Plasma Collection Center looked as dull and institutional as its name implied. The two-story, white-washed cinderblock structure squatted on a rundown city block around the corner from the municipal bus station, in the vicinity of a soup kitchen, a condemned church, a liquor store, and a bail bondsman's office.

A helicopter parked atop the plasma center's flat roof looked out-of-place in the low-rent neighborhood. Studying the site from the church's dilapidated steeple, Batman could only assume that somebody really didn't want to rub shoulders with the folks down at street-level.

Vincent Wright.

It was well after midnight, and the center had been closed for hours, but lights on upstairs suggested that the building wasn't sitting empty. His infrared binoculars detected three human-sized heat signatures in an interior room on the second floor. One of the figures was seated and unmoving; the others were standing. Lowering the binoculars he spotted a fourth figure on the roof, smoking a cigarette—presumably the pilot.

When in doubt, ask.

•

The pilot was still working on the cigarette minutes later when Batman came up behind him as silently as a ninja. He clapped his hand over the man's mouth to keep him from raising a racket while twisting his arm behind his back.

Caught off-guard, the pilot reached back and tried to jab the lit end of the cigarette into his attacker's face, but Batman turned his head so that the glowing red tip was crushed against the heavy-duty casing of his cowl.

"Nasty habit," he growled. "You should get some air." He shoved the man to the brink of the roof, overlooking a back alley two stories below. The man squirmed, but could not escape. Batman let his black cape billow out where the pilot could see it.

"You know who I am?"

The man nodded.

"Good. Keep your voice low, or we'll see how well you can fly without a chopper." He took his hand away from the man's mouth, ready to cover it again the instant the pilot tried to sound an alarm. To his annoyance, however, the man mustered a show of defiance.

"Y-you can't scare me," he stammered. "You're bluffing. I've heard about this stunt of yours. You never actually kill anybody!"

Batman scowled. He didn't have time to waste.

"That's because they all talked… eventually," he growled. "You want to be one who didn't?" With that he kicked the pilot's legs out from under him, so that the man tumbled forward over the brink. He gasped as Batman seized him by the collar. Leaning out over the edge, gazing at the pavement below, the man was kept from falling by Batman's strong right arm. The pilot's bravado shattered along with his nerves.

"Okay, okay," he said quickly. "Wright isn't paying me enough for this!"

Batman didn't draw the man back. *Let him sweat.*

"Keep it down," he said. "So Wright is here?"

"Yeah, downstairs," the man replied. "I didn't do nothing, I swear to God. I just flew him here."

There had been three heat signatures. "Who's with him?"

"This creepy enforcer type, decked out like one of you costumed freaks. Calls himself the Talon, like in the old rhyme."

Batman's stern expression darkened further. Butchered cops and burnt corpses demanded justice. His voice took on an even harder edge.

"Who else?"

"I don't know. I just flew the two of them here. That's all I got."

"Not good enough." He shook the pilot roughly by the collar.

"A girl! I heard them say something about a girl, who they've got holed up inside," he said.

"What girl?" Batman stopped shaking him for a moment.

"I don't know. Cross my heart. I don't know anything else. I don't *want* to know anything else!"

"Joanna?" Batman asked. "Is her name Joanna?"

"Beats me! I'm telling you, man, I just fly the chopper." He sounded too scared to be holding anything back, and Batman grudgingly conceded that he'd probably gotten as much as he was going to get from the dangling pilot. He swung the man back onto the roof, then rendered him unconscious with a chop to a pressure point on his neck. The pilot collapsed onto the tar-covered surface.

It seemed likely that the woman was Joanna. Batman frowned. He'd hoped to locate the missing student before the Owls could, but they had found her first. What had been a fact-finding expedition was now a rescue mission. The Talon's presence wasn't going to make liberating their prisoner any easier.

He surveyed his surroundings. A roof exit resembling a tool shed led down into the building. A ventilation fan hummed in its casing. There was a conspicuous lack of skylights, thus limiting his options. He was tempted to charge in, counting on the element of surprise to give him an advantage over the Talon, but that was too risky. If he wanted to beat his opponent and get Joanna out of the hands of the Owls, he needed to arrange the chessboard in his favor.

I'll choose the battlefield this time.

Returning his attention to the ventilation fan, he plucked a smoke-capsule from his belt.

●

"Maybe if you tell me more about this elixir, I can figure out something that will help."

Joanna was stalling to a degree, but she was also curious as hell. This was more about Percy and Lydia than she ever dreamed of learning. She just prayed it wouldn't cost her life.

"I doubt you'd understand the biochemistry that's involved," Wright said. "Few people can. Let's just say the elixir stimulates the brain in ways unknown to conventional science. At the same time the chemical reaction produces unprecedented amounts of heat—with spectacularly incendiary results."

The Talon grunted. "That's one way to put it."

She glared angrily. "But precognition... how is that even possible?" she asked. "I mean, I knew there had to be *something* that caused Percy to incorporate that imagery in his sculptures, but some sort of chemical potion?"

"Don't underestimate my ancestor's genius," Wright said. To her relief, he placed the syringe down on a counter. It still lay within easy reach, but wasn't quite so immediate a threat. "Tell me, are you familiar with a substance called electrum?"

Before she could respond, a fire alarm went off, blaring loudly throughout the building. The sprinkler system activated, drenching the lab and everyone in it.

"Oh, for God's sake!" Wright exclaimed. "What the devil—?"

"Can't be a coincidence," the Talon replied. "It must be an

intruder." The spray ran down his skintight suit, leaving him considerably dryer than Wright or Joanna.

As the first hint of smoke appeared in the air, Joanna tugged futilely at her restraints, alarmed at the prospect of being tied up inside a burning building. The irony of her situation didn't escape her, either. She was going to go up in flames like Dennis and the others—just not as spontaneously.

"Damn it all!" Wright hastily capped the hypodermic and tucked it into a pocket on his lab coat, which was now soaked and clinging to him. "We have to go. I can't be caught here—with her—so soon after that break-in at the penthouse. The Grandmaster would have my head." He nodded toward Joanna. "Bring her."

The Talon quickly and efficiently released her from the recliner, yanked her to her feet, and took hold of her wrist. "Don't give me any trouble," he warned her. "You can leave here under your own power or not. Got it?"

She nodded, perversely grateful not to be forgotten, then hating herself for feeling any gratitude toward her captors. The Talon dragged her toward the door, which Wright held open.

"Hurry!" he said. "We need to head for the roof."

Abandoning the lab, they scrambled into the hall, which was filling up with thick, black smoke. The acrid fumes had a faintly chemical odor. Coughing, she held her free hand over her mouth as they made their way to a stairway at the end of a corridor. There weren't any flames, just the choking smoke, but her heart was pounding anyway. She hoped there was a safe way off the roof.

"I don't like this," the Talon said. His hood seemed to protect him from the fumes. "Something's up."

"All the more reason to depart," Wright said, "with all deliberate speed."

A short flight of stairs brought them onto the rooftop, where the cool night air came as a relief after navigating the smoky hallway. A helicopter was parked on a concrete pad, revealing how Wright planned to flee the scene. Its pilot was seated in the cockpit.

"Quickly," he insisted again. He shouted at the chopper. "We're coming aboard. Prepare for immediate departure!"

"Hold on." The Talon paused to look around. "I smell a Bat—" Before he could finish a razor-sharp object sank into his wrist, causing him to hiss in pain. His grip loosened. Joanna pulled her arm free and backed away from him.

"Not so fast!"

Despite the injury, he lunged after her, only to be tackled to the ground by a cloaked figure springing from atop the shed-like structure housing the stairway. Without hesitation Batman delivered one solid blow after another to the hooded assassin. In spite of herself, Joanna felt a wave of elation.

"Run!" he shouted. "Leave him to me!"

She glanced at the exit. "But the fire?"

"No fire. Just smoke." He grappled with the Talon as they rolled across the tar paper. He twisted the Batarang that was lodged in the killer's wrist, causing the assassin to howl in fury. "Now go!"

Over by the helicopter, Wright yelled frantically at the pilot, who seemed oblivious. "Answer me, damn you! What's the matter with you?" He pulled open the hatch and shoved the man, who lolled over in his seat and fell out of the cockpit. Wright reacted in shock. "No, no, no. This can't be happening…"

Joanna took a moment to enjoy his discomfort.

Now you know how I felt, jerk.

•

Batman had the Talon pinned to roof, but only for a moment. Breaking the hold, the assassin flung his adversary off him and sprang to his feet. Wrenching the Batarang from his wrist, he angrily flung it away, then swiftly drew a sword from one of the scabbards on his back.

Gripping the sword with both hands, he swung it down on Batman's head with enough force to crack the top of the cowl. The impact sent the hero reeling. The cowl was still intact, but another such blow and the sword might shatter both it and his skull. Staggering backward, he raised his gauntlets defensively as the Talon came at him again.

"Nice ambush," the assassin said, "but let's see how clever you are once your brains are splattered all over the—"

He let out a surprised shriek as Joanna jabbed the discarded Batarang into his back. Wheeling about, he backhanded her and sent her sprawling onto the surface of the roof. The blow sent her glasses flying, and she landed face-first with a grunt of pain.

"Not smart, college girl," the Talon raged. "You're pushing your luck."

Thanks to the distraction, Batman was no longer on the defensive. Cracked cowl or not, he delivered a flying kick that drove his opponent away from Joanna. Then he darted between her and her attacker, determined not to let the Talon lay hands on her again. She had been through too much already.

"Why didn't you run?" he asked.

"I'm tired of running," she replied. "Figure I'm safer with you."

The Talon snorted. "That's what you think." Reaching back with his free hand, he yanked the Batarang from his back.

"Forget them," Vincent shouted across the roof. "I can't rouse the pilot. I need you to fly the helicopter!"

"You're not going anywhere, Wright," Batman stated. "The chopper has been disabled." The look of chagrin that crossed the man's face was worth its weight in blue-chip stocks. With any luck, Joanna's testimony would convict Vincent of kidnapping and connect him to several murders, as well. He wondered what other evidence was waiting inside the building.

Sirens blared in the night.

"You hear that?" Vincent bellowed. "Get me away from here. That's an order!"

"I hear you," the Talon said sourly. Keeping his eyes on Batman, he backed toward the aircraft. "Another time, Dark Knight. Looks like you get off easy tonight."

"You think I'm going to let you get away so easily?" Batman said. His raised fists were clenched and ready. "Think again."

"If you say so."

Without warning the Talon hurled the bloody Batarang at the grounded copter. The blade punctured the fuselage and sliced through an internal fuel line. Gasoline spurted from the rupture and spilled onto the rooftop, where it streamed across the flat surface between Batman and his foes. The Talon scraped his sword against the roof to generate a spark, which ignited the flowing gas like the business end of a fuse. Instantly a trickle of flame sped toward the copter and its fuel tank. The pilot still lay where he had fallen.

"Think fast!" the Talon said.

Responding instantly, Batman whipped off his cloak and used it to beat out the flaming stream before it could reach the chopper. As he did, the Talon snatched up Wright, flinging the man over his shoulder, and leapt over the edge of the roof. Metal claws scraped loudly against the side of the building.

"Get back!" Batman shouted to Joanna. He smacked the fireproof cape against the burning fuel until he was certain the fire had been extinguished completely. Just to be safe, he pulled a canister of flame-retardant foam from his belt, and sprayed it over the fuel.

The smell of gas filled the air.

But where had the Talon and Vincent gone?

Confident that the copter wasn't going to blow up, Batman rushed to the edge of the roof and peered at the pavement below. The Owl and the Talon were nowhere to be seen, although deep gouges in the cinderblocks tracked the path they had taken in their rapid descent to the street.

Another time, the Talon had said.

Batman let out a growl of exasperation. It seemed his final clash with the Talon would have to wait. He took solace in the fact that he had rescued Joanna from the Court. That was, perhaps, victory enough for one night. Turning, he crossed the roof to join her by the exit, where she had taken shelter from the impending blast.

"Are you all right?"

"I think so... for now." She winced as she probed her injured nose. "Are they gone?"

"For now," he echoed. "Joanna Lee, I presume?"

She nodded.

"Pleased to meet you," Batman said. "We have a lot to discuss."

30

MacDougal Lane, Gotham City, 1918

"Bats, cats, robins, owls…"

Lydia babbled deliriously as she crouched over her chair, scribbling frantically in yet another journal, feverishly filling the pages as though she couldn't keep pace with the visions flooding her overheated brain. Her eyes were wild, her hair a tangle, so that she resembled a madwoman more than a model. An uneaten meal went ignored, like so many others before it. Percy looked on in dismay.

"Please, darling, you must try to calm yourself," he pleaded. "You're frightening me."

Despite her many dire prophecies, Percy had not yet lost Lydia to the flames. Yet that did little to relieve his guilt as he watched her sanity burn away before his eyes. At first the journals had seemed to help her, giving her an outlet for the visions which seemed to be coming faster and faster, consuming her every waking moment.

However, that had proved only a temporary cure. She was hardly eating, barely sleeping, and found no escape from the visions even in whatever fitful slumber she managed. He had tried sedating her, just to grant her a modicum of peace, only to watch her toss and turn restlessly, muttering constantly just as she was rambling incoherently now.

"Dark night rising, birds of prey, a league of shadows, a league of justice…"

Desperate, he snatched the journal from her hands.

"Stop it, Lydia," he demanded. "This can't go on. You need to rest…"

"…man of steel, daughter of the demon, contract with Judas, riddle me this…"

Heedless of his entreaties, she dropped from the chair onto the floor, where she began scribbling on the floorboards. The sight of her, down on her knees like a lunatic in Arkham Hospital, shredded Percy's heart and spirit. At a loss for what else to do, in search of something—*anything*—that might help him ease her pain, he began leafing through the confiscated journal.

As with previous volumes, the pages were filled with cryptic, disordered ravings, barely decipherable annotations, and, worst of all, countless sketches and drawings, each seemingly more grotesque and disturbing than the last. Freaks and monsters capered across the page. A menacing scarecrow with steaming test tubes. A scaly-skinned ogre, as much reptile as man, gnawing on human bones. A woman, alluring yet sinister, clad only in vines and thorns. A man whose face was hideously scarred on one side. Winged demons. Clay golems…

And—over and over—bats and owls and one thing more.

A woman on fire, burning alive.

Lydia's future? He dropped to the floor and clutched her wrists. "Look at me, Lydia! You must fight this. Gain control over your visions!"

For the briefest instant his entreaties penetrated the delirium. She looked up from the floorboards. Her eyes found him, clearing so that she could actually *see* him through the cascade of prophecies that were driving her mad.

"I can't help it, Percy," she said, her voice cracked and dry. "There's too much future to see, so much more than I can ever hold back. A darkness awaiting Gotham, sweeping over me, filling my mind. Bleak days, plagues and disasters, crisis after crisis…"

Tears streamed from her eyes. "It's too much for me, Percy. I can't bear it." She clutched at him. "Make it stop, please, I beg you!"

"Hush, darling." He let go of her wrists. "It will be all right. You just need to sleep."

"Sleep?" Her eyes lost focus again, looking beyond him, yet a peculiar calm came over her. "Yes, I see it now," she said dreamily. "Sleep will come soon. You're going to help me sleep, aren't you, Percy? Make the future go away?"

He knew what she meant. What she had foreseen. His throat tightened as he realized what he needed to do. He removed the syringe from his pocket.

"Of course, dearest. You will rest soon. I promise."

31

"What did I miss?"

Batgirl rendezvoused with them in a secure location not far from the Clock Tower. Batman had taken Joanna there for safekeeping. Batgirl's crime-fighting uniform hid her true identity behind a durable dark purple suit, cape, and cowl similar in design to his. The gold lining of the cloak, gloves, boots, and other accessories gave her a distinctive look, while long red hair escaped the back of her cowl.

The bunker was one of several satellite bases Batman had installed throughout the city under the cover of various urban-renewal projects funded by the Wayne Foundation. This particular one was located beneath the basement of a storefront in the East End. It lacked the full resources of the Batcave or even the Clock Tower, but was sufficiently stocked with computers, first-aid supplies, a small armory, and other gear that might be needed in a pinch. He took the opportunity to replace his cracked cowl and refill his belt.

"Tell my associate what you learned from Vincent Wright while you were held captive," he said to Joanna.

"Batgirl?" Joanna gaped at the other woman.

"That's what they call me." She came forward to shake Joanna's hand, then paused to examine Joanna's bandaged nose. "Ouch. Looks like you've had a rough go of it."

Batman had tended to Joanna's injuries after they departed the rooftop of the plasma center. As it had turned out, her nose wasn't actually broken, but needed some patching up. They would have to replace her glasses at some point, as well.

"Could be worse." She looked over at Batman. "You probably don't remember, but this is the second time you've saved me."

"I remember," he said gravely. "Now please go over the details again, and don't omit anything."

"Right." She sat down on a couch and took a deep breath before briefing Batgirl on her experience as the Court's prisoner. The masked heroes listened attentively until she was finished. "And here I am, bruised and battered, but not reduced to ashes."

"A second Talon," Batgirl said, "and an elixir that incites precognition... That's a new one."

"As improbable as it may seem," Batman replied, "it's not beyond the realm of possibility. Clearly the Court believes in this elixir, so for the moment we do, as well." He let that sink in for a moment. "As for the new Talon, it sounds as though he may be an old one, kept in a state of suspended animation since Percy's time. Perhaps he's been brought out of hibernation because of his prior experience."

"Suspended animation?" Joanna stared. "That's actually a thing?"

"It is," Batman said. "Which means we now have at least two assassins hunting you."

"Oh Lord, this just keeps getting better and better." Joanna buried her face in her hands. "I wish I'd never dug into Lydia's past. Dennis and Professor Morse would still be alive..."

"Don't blame yourself," Batman said. "The Owls are responsible for their crimes, no one else. You just wanted to learn more about your own roots."

She raised her head. "So you know?"

"That you're related to Lydia Doyle? Yes." He leaned forward to take a closer look at her. Up close, the family resemblance was even more apparent. "Was that what motivated your research in the first place?"

"It was," she said, nodding. "Growing up in Gotham, I began to notice my face all over the city—on monuments and buildings constructed long before I was born. It got to the point that I couldn't ignore it, so I did some digging, and found out about a long-forgotten model named Lydia Doyle, who turned out to be a great-aunt no one ever mentioned." Joanna chuckled bitterly. "Seems she was a deep-dark family secret, at least back in the day: the black-sheep relation who ran off to the big city to pursue a life of sin and scandal. The whole thing had been hushed up until I finally pried the truth out of my maternal grandmother."

Batman could believe that. The Waynes had skeletons in their closets, as well. He wondered if the Owls were aware that Lydia still had living relatives. Perhaps her estrangement from her family caused them to fly under the Court's radar.

"Had Lydia changed her surname, as well?"

"Yes, to avoid embarrassing her more uptight relatives," Joanna said. "Her birth name was Lydia Gresham. No idea where she plucked 'Doyle' from."

"So why didn't your roommate know that you were related to Lydia?" Batgirl asked.

"Because I never told her that part." Joanna shrugged. "What can I say? I was saving it for my thesis."

Secrets within secrets, Batman thought. "So this all began when you discovered the truth of your connection to Lydia."

"More or less," Joanna said, "but that wasn't all I found out. After Lydia disappeared, and Billy Draper confessed to her murder, the police boxed her personal effects and shipped them off to her next of kin—they were still tucked away in my grandmother's attic, where nobody had looked at them for nearly a century." A sad smile lifted her lips. "I can't tell you how excited I was when I found the box buried under miscellaneous old junk and cobwebs."

Batgirl's eyes lit up. "What was in the box?"

"Mostly souvenirs and memorabilia. Old playbills, a scrapbook of news clippings regarding Percy, a map of the 1918 Gotham Exposition fairgrounds, an old parasol, some mildly risqué postcards she posed for back in the day, and a battered old teddy bear that was literally coming apart at the seams. That's where I found the letters."

"Letters?" Batman asked.

"Love letters from Percy to Lydia, hidden away inside the teddy bear all this time. Honestly, the only reason I found them was because the bear's arms and legs were coming off, so I caught a glimpse of them, all tied up neatly with a silk ribbon." Joanna sighed. "Guess she couldn't bear to part with them."

"Was there anything of use in the letters?" Batgirl asked.

"Confirmation that Percy and Lydia were having a clandestine affair," Joanna answered, "and what seems to be a growing sense of paranoia on Percy's part. He gets quite insistent that Lydia take every precaution to hide the letters."

"She obviously listened to him," Batman said, "since the letters weren't found or destroyed by the Owls in the aftermath of her disappearance. The Talon of the day must have overlooked the bear, treating it as nothing but a harmless toy. That's the only way it could have ended up in the hands of your family instead. He left it behind with Lydia's other personal effects."

"Big mistake," Batgirl said. "What became of the letters?"

"I have no idea," Joanna said. "As far as I know, they're still tucked away back at my apartment. I haven't had the nerve to go back for them since I first caught sight of the Talon." She described the lucky break that allowed her to escape the first time.

"I doubt they're still there," Batman said. "Chances are, the Talon took everything of value from your apartment, the same way he removed any trace of your work from Professor Morse's office and from the cabin by the lake… except for the flash drive you hid in the woodpile."

"You found that?" she asked.

He nodded. "We've been trying to reconstruct your work, and can use your help." The puzzle was all but complete. Their mission was both clear and urgent. The Owls had done enough damage in the past and present—he'd be damned if they'd take control of the future, as well.

"Of course," Joanna said. "Count me in."

"We have to assume that Vincent is correct, and that Percy hid a formula for the perfected elixir. Even without your assistance, Vincent's going to keep looking for it, and we have to get out in front of him. Our job now is to follow Percy's clues and find the formula before the Owls do."

"What about the cataclysmic 'inferno' Percy claimed was coming?" Batgirl asked.

"It's a missing piece of the puzzle, and one we can't allow to distract us," Batman said. "For now we focus on the tangibles. Once we know what we're facing, we find a way to stop it."

"But is that even possible?" Joanna asked. "So many of the predictions have already come true. If the future is there to be seen, how can we affect it?"

"I refuse to accept that the future is set in stone," he replied grimly. "Percy's elixir may offer glimpses of a possible future, maybe even the most probable future, but as far as I'm concerned, we hold our fates in our own hands.

"The Owls must agree," he continued. "If the future can't be changed, then why go to such lengths to obtain the elixir? There's no telling how much power they could wield, how much damage they might cause, armed with knowledge like that.

"We have to get there first."

32

Harbor House, Gotham City, 1918

"So, the girl is gone?"

"Sadly, yes, Grandmaster."

The meeting at Harbor House was a private one. Only Percy, Margaret, the Grandmaster, and the Talon were in attendance. As before, Percy and Margaret had abstained from donning their ceremonial masks, so that only the Grandmaster and the assassin concealed their faces. Candlelight illuminated the secret room in the musty turret, lit by windows set high in the wall.

"The incendiary effect was significantly delayed in this subject's case," Percy reported, masking his grief behind a façade of scientific abstraction, "but, alas, the ultimate result was the same."

"I see," the Grandmaster wheezed. He glanced at the Talon, who stood at attention by his side. "Frederick?"

"I have examined the remains, Grandmaster. The young lady was indeed incinerated."

In truth, Lydia had died painlessly from the injection. Carefully preparing the body in his laboratory, Percy had set fire to it postmortem. He had counted on the fact that the Talon was an assassin, not a scientist. It was doubtful that the man had the expertise to grasp what had truly occurred.

"Where are her remains now?" the Grandmaster asked. "Have they been disposed of properly?"

"Not yet," Percy said. "With your permission, I have retained the remains for further examination, in order to better study the effects of the formula on her tissues."

"Very well," the Grandmaster said. "And what of her... disappearance? Is that being accounted for as well?"

"We are dealing with it appropriately," Margaret assured him. "A suitable scapegoat has been selected. There will be no hint of the Court's involvement."

"See that there isn't." The Grandmaster fixed his rheumy eyes on Percy. "I shall speak frankly, Wright. This news is most disappointing. I believe I made it quite clear exactly how desirous the Court is to possess a perfected version of your elixir."

"But the—" Percy began.

"You did indeed, Grandmaster," Margaret said, "but let me observe that the news is not entirely bleak. The fatal reaction was delayed for several days, instead of occurring immediately, as before. That very fact suggests that Percy is on course to eliminate this unwanted side effect. Don't you agree, husband?"

Percy was surprised to hear Margaret speaking up on his behalf. He could only assume that she sought to protect her own position within the Court.

"Just so," he agreed. "As you have had occasion to remind me, science is a matter of trial and error. We can take comfort in knowing that this poor woman's sacrifice may have brought us one step closer to success."

The Grandmaster harrumphed loudly. He seemed disinclined to wax sentimental about Lydia's tragic fate.

"Better sooner than later, Wright," he growled. "Keep at your work. The Court of Owls *demands* your elixir."

Percy nodded. "Understood, Grandmaster."

The old man stood, leaning heavily on a polished-wood cane. Together he and the Talon departed, leaving Percy and Margaret alone in the turret.

"I suppose I should thank you," he said grudgingly, "for taking my side."

"Do not delude yourself, Percy, that I did so for your benefit." She gazed at him with icy hauteur. "Any failure—or deceit—on your part would reflect poorly on me as well. I was merely acting in the best interests of our family." Her cold eyes narrowed in suspicion. "The girl *did* die as you said, did she not?"

"Yes," he said honestly. "My elixir destroyed her."

"Good riddance." Her lip curled in contempt. "I trust that you understand, Percy, the sole reason you are still alive—despite your grievous indiscretions—is that the Court still has hopes that you will perfect your elixir in due time. Never forget that."

"You needn't worry on that account, Margaret," he replied. "I could not forget if I tried."

Some things could never be forgotten.

Or forgiven.

33

The letters were nowhere to be found.

A quick solo excursion to Joanna's apartment, now sitting empty while Claire remained in Metropolis, confirmed that Percy's long-lost letters to Lydia had been stolen. Yet the damage was likely to be minimal. Some of the documents had been scanned and were on the thumb drive from the cabin. The rest of the data resided with the one asset the Court had *not* been able to acquire.

The Court had the letters, but Batman had Joanna.

"So the Owls tested a version of Percy's elixir on Lydia, who vanished around the same time," Batman said, reviewing the case with Batgirl and Joanna back in the auxiliary bunker. "Billy Draper was blamed, but there's nothing to connect him with the Court. So he was just a patsy who took the fall for her disappearance.

"Percy knew the truth, and never got over it," he continued. "He also hid imagery from Lydia's visions in his tributes to her, while overtly alluding to an 'inferno' that awaited the city."

"Could that have been the outbreaks of Burning Sickness?" Joanna asked, pacing restlessly. "Maybe Lydia foresaw the fact that the Court would continue Percy's experiments. It certainly qualifies as serial murder."

Batman's mood darkened as he recalled the four charred corpses for which the Owls had been responsible.

"And it's certain to continue," Batgirl added. "Vincent thinks

Percy somehow hid the formula, and he's not going to stop until he finds it." She glanced at Joanna, who was wearing a spare pair of glasses that Batman had procured during his visit to her apartment. A shower and a change of clothes had her looking less like a homeless fugitive. "He thinks your research will lead him to it."

"That's just insane," Joanna said. "I'd never even *heard* of this 'elixir' until Vincent told me about it. Percy never mentioned it in his letters, and I'd never made a connection between Lydia's disappearance and the Burning Sickness. I'm as much in the dark as the rest of you."

"Nevertheless," Batman said, "he thinks you have something he wants, and that gives us an advantage. It may be there's a pattern of some sort in the posthumous tributes to Lydia, and the warnings Percy snuck into them. They seem to prove that the elixir worked, at least to some degree, but they don't tell us where the final formula is hidden—if it exists at all."

"You think there's a chance it's all a hoax?" Batgirl asked.

"We have no way of telling," he admitted, "but given the threat it would pose, we can't take any chances. And regardless, the Burning Sickness experiments have to be stopped." He moved to a workstation boasting a modest array of screens, and Batgirl followed suit. Joanna stood just behind them. She kept nervously checking out the entrances and exits, as if she expected one or more of the Talons to charge into their safe haven.

"I can help with the search," she volunteered. "I know more than any one person should about the figures Percy sculpted after her disappearance." She laughed bitterly. "Serves me right, I guess. Curiosity killed the cat."

Selina might disagree, Batman thought. "Show us the sculptures we know about so far."

"Coming right up," Batgirl said.

She downloaded the files from a dedicated server at the Clock Tower. Thumbnails of the now-familiar monuments, museum

pieces, and architectural adornments spread out across the screen like playing cards dealt from a deck. Separate attachments contained links to the 3D scans their drones had conducted earlier, waiting to be called up as needed. She glanced over at Joanna.

"These figures were all done after Lydia's disappearance, right?"

"That's right," Joanna said confidently. "He'd sculpted her dozens of times before, to be sure, but the hidden prophecies didn't start showing up until after she was supposedly killed by Billy Draper."

"Who then burned her body," Batman said. "Allegedly. Can you help us place these figures in order of their creation or installation?"

She chuckled, far less bitterly than before. "After all those long hours slaving away on my thesis? I can do it in my sleep."

She squeezed past Batgirl to get at a keyboard. True to her word, she swiftly placed the thumbnails in chronological order. Batman sat back to survey them as a whole. It took him only a moment to spot a pattern.

"The hidden warnings," he observed. "They're in chronological order, too, when it comes to the events they seem to be predicting: Martha Wayne's murder in Crime Alley, Harvey Dent's mutilation at the Gotham courthouse, the Joker's toxin in the harbor, Poison Ivy's first assault on the Botanical Garden, the advent of the Scarecrow… they're all in sequence here. Each figure advances the timeline, as foreseen a century in advance."

Joanna gaped at the screen. "I never realized that before."

"You're less familiar with the criminal history of Gotham City," Batman observed. "Consider yourself lucky."

"Not *that* lucky," she replied, bristling a little.

Batman recalled the tragic deaths of her parents. "You're right," he said. "I apologize. I simply meant that you can be forgiven for not memorizing the Joker's rap sheet."

"Got it," she said, and she looked down. "Sorry. Just a bit on edge, you know."

"Anyone would be, after what you've been through," he said.

The case had him on edge, too. The Court of Owls had that effect on him.

"Sorry to interrupt, but I'm not seeing any warning of an inferno, or even of the Burning Sickness," Batgirl said, scanning the rearranged thumbnails. "If each statue points further ahead, and most of these prophecies have already come true, maybe we should just skip ahead to the very last statue?" She clicked on the final thumbnail, expanding it.

The image showed a bronze door on a mausoleum, where a life-sized female figure was posed in mourning, her bare back and shoulders to the viewer, her downcast face turned toward the door. Batman recognized the pose from the framed sketch in Vincent Wright's office.

"Whose crypt is that?" he asked, suspecting he already knew the answer.

"Percy's," Joanna confirmed. "His will stipulated that he be interred behind the door, regardless of any objections from his survivors."

"I can't imagine Mrs. Wright was in love with that arrangement," Batgirl said, "even if Lydia's face is tactfully concealed. Got to sting to have your husband's dead mistress eternally posed at the door to his resting-place."

"That may have been the intent," Batman guessed. "Is that the last of the Lydias?"

"As far as I know," Joanna replied. "There could be others out there, but none that I've found. He died very suddenly of natural causes."

Batman had his suspicions regarding the circumstances of Percy's passing.

Alan Wayne had died of an "accident."

"So that was the end of Percy's career, and his obsession with Lydia," Batgirl said. "Maybe he never got around to memorializing his final prophecy? If he died suddenly, he might never have

committed the formula to paper, or hidden it where he intended."

"'My muse is a muse of fire.'" Batman scratched his chin. "'A deathless inferno that consumes my soul, as it will someday consume all of Gotham.'" Percy said that *after* Lydia had died, and it sounded like something he was certain would come to pass. How far ahead would Percy have planned his predictions? He was a man of science, an artist who took mounds of clay and gave them form, definition... purpose. How could he have left his greatest work— his masterpiece—to chance?

He couldn't.

"We're looking at this from the wrong direction," he said. "What if the answers we're looking for can be found by looking *backward* through time to when this puzzle began?" He moved his gaze back to the beginning of the sequence. "What's the *first* sculpture Percy completed after Lydia's disappearance?"

Joanna didn't even need to look at the screen.

"The statue of 'Wisdom' at Gotham University."

Batman located the image, and enlarged it. A robed figure was seated on a throne. Behind her, the wide stone steps led up to the front entrance of the university's main building. A tiara crowned the imposing bronze goddess's brow. Her left hand held aloft a scepter, while her right hand beckoned to students in search of knowledge. Her face was Lydia's, which meant she looked like Joanna, as well.

The university, Batman thought. He recalled the scorched remains in Professor Morse's office. It seemed strangely fitting that the clues led them back there.

"What's the hidden message in that one?"

"That's the thing," Joanna replied. "I hadn't found one yet. I was still investigating when the Talon first came for me." She peered at the image. "Maybe something to do with the crown, or the scepter?"

"Batgirl?" he asked.

"Beats me." She threw up her hands. "Sorry to disappoint you, but nothing leapt out at me, either. If Percy hid a warning in this one, he was much craftier about it... and went to much greater lengths to hide it."

"Which makes this statue all the more interesting." Batman leaned forward in his seat. His gut told him they were getting warmer. "Maybe this will help." He opened the attached scan and a three-dimensional holographic rendition of "Wisdom" appeared in the empty air above an adjacent console, based on the scans Batman had taken at the site. Every detail had been captured in perfect detail.

Joanna gaped. "Whoa," she said. "I thought this stuff was only possible in the movies."

"Maybe I'll share the files with you once this is over," Batman responded wryly. The trio gathered around the glowing model to examine it from every angle. The weightless image was certainly easier to manipulate than the massive original. Working the controls, Batman was able to rotate it in every direction, enlarging and highlighting individual areas one after another. A separate control bar allowed him to control the lighting, so that he could heighten or lessen the contrast and the shadows defining the planes and edges on the statue. It was as if he could examine the statue with several different kinds of vision.

This must be the way Clark sees things every day.

In the macro view nothing appeared to be unusual, so he turned his attention to less prominent portions of the statue. Forget the tiara or the scepter or the throne—those were too obvious. His gaze prowled the contours and crevices of the sculpture as it might a crime scene, looking for something, *anything*, that seemed out of place or inexplicable. Something that didn't add up...

"There," he said after a few minutes. "What's that?"

Tucked away in the billowing folds of Wisdom's robes, just to one side of her draped left leg, there appeared to be something sculpted deep inside a shadowy recess. Batman highlighted the depression, then banished the rest of the 3D model with a single keystroke. All that remained, suspended above the projector, was a single object.

An owl.

"Wow," Joanna said. "I've admired that statue a zillion times, looked at it from every angle, and never spotted this before."

"Probably because it's not meant to be seen," Batgirl said, "unless you're *really* looking for it."

"A confession perhaps?" Joanna speculated. "Or an accusation?"

"Possibly." Batgirl studied the holographic raptor, which resembled an ordinary barn owl with its beady opaque eyes, long beak, and blank, moon-like expression. "Then again, owls *are* symbols of wisdom, associated with both Athena and Minerva, so we can't be sure that—"

"No," Batman growled. "That's *the* Owl. Their Owl."

The owl hidden within the folds of the statue was a miniature replica of the immense marble figure at the heart of the Court's subterranean Labyrinth. The Owl that had watched silently over the ordeal that had almost broken him. The Owl that still haunted his nightmares.

I should have known, he thought, *that it would come to this.*

"The Labyrinth," he told them. "The Great Owl of the Labyrinth. That's the very first clue Percy left for the future generations, pointing to their underground nest. If there are any further answers to be found, I'll lay odds that's where they've been waiting—for at least a century."

Joanna shot him a puzzled look, but Batgirl looked aghast. She understood what this meant. To stop the Owls from locating the formula, Batman would have to go back to the last place in Gotham he wanted to see again.

34

The Gotham Towers Hotel, Gotham City, 1918

"Billy Draper, the Court of Owls demands your obedience."

What? Billy woke from a groggy, whiskey-soaked slumber to find an ominous figure dressed in black standing by his bed in the penthouse suite of the Gotham Towers Hotel. Despite his hangover, he was immediately jolted to attention by the sight of the hooded intruder, who peered at him through tinted brass goggles that betrayed no hint of emotion.

"Who—? How did you get in here?"

He opened his mouth to scream for help, only to suddenly feel the point of a sword at his throat.

"Keep your voice down," the intruder advised. "It will go better for you."

Billy gulped, afraid to even nod with the blade at his throat.

"I have money," he croaked. "My family has money."

The intruder shook his head. "I'm not here for your money, Billy."

"Then what do you want?" he asked, teetering on the brink of hysteria. "Who are you?"

"Beware the Court of Owls," the man recited, "that watches all the time…"

Realization dawned on Billy. His eyes bulged as he identified the figure by his bed.

"The Talon."

"Good," the boogeyman said. "You know your nursery rhymes."

The sword at Billy's throat became even more frightening. He struggled to maintain control of his bladder.

"Are… you here t-to take my h-head?"

"Not if you do as you're told, Billy."

Billy seized on that shred of hope. "What do you want me to do?"

"You're going to get up and get dressed. Then you're going to walk down to the police station and confess to the murder of Lydia Doyle."

"What?" He couldn't believe his ears. "I didn't… I would *never*…"

"Nevertheless, that's what you're going to do." As he spoke, he gave the blade a slight nudge, almost breaking skin. Billy struggled to make sense of what was happening. Then the implications of the Talon's demand struck him.

"Hang on there," he said. "Did something happen to Lydia?"

"No questions," the man growled.

Billy didn't understand. Self-preservation won out over grief. He promised himself that he would mourn Lydia later.

"It wasn't me." His mind raced. "It must have been Percy Wright, that lecherous old bastard. He corrupted Lydia. Whatever has happened to her, he's the one you want!"

"Think about it, Billy," the masked man said. "Think about Lydia's reputation. Do you want the truth about her to be made public, to be splashed all over the front pages?"

Billy cringed at the notion. That was the reason he had taken Wright's letter to his wife, and not to the press. He'd had no desire to bring shame to Lydia. He just wanted that pervert Wright out of the way. Lydia was meant for him—of that he was certain.

"No, of course not, but—"

"Do you want her to be remembered as Wright's mistress, or as an innocent victim who perished through no fault of her own?"

The Talon eased the pressure of the sword, ever so slightly. "Lydia needs you, Billy. She counts on you to keep her name from being dragged through the mud.

"You loved Lydia, didn't you, Billy?"

"Yes," he said. "More than anything."

"This is your chance to be her hero, Billy. Do it for Lydia."

Billy wavered. He grasped what the Talon was saying. The idea of rescuing Lydia's reputation after Percy Wright had defiled her appealed to him. He would indeed be a hero, a martyr for love. It would be the ultimate sacrifice...

"No," he shouted. "I'll go to the electric chair!" A fresh wave of panic swept over him, and it was all he could do not to bolt for the door. *I can never reach it,* he thought wildly. *The Talon will take my head.*

"You can't ask me to do this," he whimpered, and tears began to flow down his cheeks. "Please..."

"That's good," the masked man said. "Contrition—it will make your story so much more believable. Yet perhaps you require more incentive. Something that will ensure that you won't betray us at the last minute." The Talon pulled an object from a pouch, a slip of cloth. He held it up, and Billy recognized it instantly as a woman's blouse.

His mother's blouse. She had worn it just yesterday.

Oh dear Lord...

"If you don't care about your own head, what about your mother's?" the Talon said, a new edge creeping into his voice. "She still lives in that big house outside Blüdhaven, am I correct?"

"Momma?"

"And your sister," the man continued. "She married that nice fellow—a lawyer, I believe. They have a lovely daughter, Rose..."

"No, please, don't!" He sobbed openly. "You win! I'll do it. I'll do whatever you say."

"For Lydia?" the Talon prompted.

"Yes, yes!"

"Very good, Billy. Now you're being reasonable." The Talon withdrew his sword, but kept it at his side. "Now get up and get dressed. I'll tell you exactly what to say…"

35

The Great Owl loomed above them.

At least fifty feet tall, the mammoth white marble statue dominated the otherwise barren chamber at the heart of the underground Labyrinth. Its vast, folded wings were the size of drawn sails, while its legs served as huge stone pillars.

The Owl perched atop a pedestal fashioned to resemble a large craggy boulder rising out of a ring-shaped fountain. High walls made of cruder, less expensive marble—too sheer to scale by hand—defined the chamber, with narrow gaps permitting access to the rest of the vast subterranean maze where the Court of Owls had tormented prisoners for generations.

To all appearances, the Labyrinth had been abandoned ever since Batman had escaped from it months ago. With its existence and location exposed, the place was no longer safe for its former inhabitants. The days when they could trap their enemies for weeks at a time, watching sadistically as the starving prisoners broke down, were past.

As they should be, Batman thought.

Strategically placed light sticks illuminated the chamber. He, Batgirl, and Joanna had reached the Labyrinth the same way he'd escaped it—via a gaping hole in the floor that led down into the filthy sewers below. Reversing his escape route, they'd climbed a Batrope up into the chamber. The stench from the sewers rose up through the breached floor.

"Ugh," Joanna said, wrinkling her nose. She was dressed for field work in a jacket, jeans, work gloves, and rubber boots. "Just when I was starting to feel clean again."

Batman peered up at the towering white bird. When last he'd seen it, sparkling water had cascaded down from the bird's beak to splash against its craggy perch before flowing into the fountain to tempt dehydrated prisoners. Against his better judgment he had succumbed to that temptation and drunk from the fountain. The clear, tantalizing liquid had been laced with a powerful hallucinogen that had made his ordeal in the Labyrinth even more nightmarish.

Lifting his gaze, he sought out the walkways atop the high stone walls, where the Court had flocked to witness his suffering. Blinding white lights had exposed him to their scrutiny while depriving him of any shadows in which to hide. His drug-induced delirium had transformed the masked Owls into monsters—inhuman, half-avian creatures sporting beaks and feathers and talons, hooting shrilly for his death as they hungered to consume him the way owls in nature ate bats, bones and all.

"You okay?" Batgirl asked quietly.

She came up beside him, but tactfully refrained from placing a comforting hand on his shoulder. Barbara had insisted on joining him on this expedition in large part, he suspected, because she hadn't wanted him to face these memories alone. He appreciated her concern, even if he didn't want to admit just how harrowing the memories were.

Deprived of his belt, his ropes, and his weapons, he'd had no way to strike back at them. He could only waste away in the maze the way his great-great-grandfather had done—before a Talon had put Alan Wayne out of his misery.

"I'm fine," he said.

Drawing a deep breath into his lungs, he pushed the memories back where they belonged, in the past, and inspected the Labyrinth as it was now. The chamber had seen better days. Beside the gaping hole he'd blasted in the floor, scattered debris littered the area both from the explosion and from his savage battle with a Talon. Cracks and craters testified to the force with which they had slammed each other into the stone walls and floor. Dried brown bloodstains could still be seen on what was left of the floor, looking like shadows with no source. The fountain had stopped flowing, so the water that remained in the pool was stagnant and coated with greenish scum.

He wasn't tempted to take a sip.

Batman looked around. Alan Wayne had died here, in fear and anguish. It was satisfying to see it fall into ruin.

Let it rot.

"You sure?" Batgirl pressed gently.

"Yes," he told her. "Let's get on with this."

Meanwhile Joanna circled the huge marble owl, studying it from every angle, an amazed expression planted on her face.

"Yes, yes," she said, talking as much to herself as to her caped companions, "you can definitely see Percy's style and technique here. The rocky pedestal, in particular, is reminiscent of his 'Andromeda' and 'Prometheus Tormented.' The stylization of the feathers, for that matter, echoes the feathers of the devouring eagle in 'Prometheus.'" She stepped back to take in the entire massive installation. "It belongs in a museum, not buried beneath Gotham."

"We'll have to see about that," Batman said. Unlike Joanna, he didn't see a magnificent work of art. He saw a monument to generations of fear, cruelty, and terror. Then again, as much as he wanted to deny it, the Owl *was* a part of Gotham's history. Perhaps it *should* be dragged into the light.

"The Court of Owls precedes Percy by generations," he observed, "dating back to the colonial era at least. I suspect that this isn't the first such idol, more likely a replacement or restoration undertaken during Percy's time. It's probable the Court would take advantage of having a celebrated sculptor among their number."

"There's no trace of Lydia anywhere," Batgirl observed, "although I suppose Percy would have to be pretty nervy to memorialize his mistress—no offense, Joanna—at the very heart of the Court's secret dungeons."

"Then again," Batman said, "we found an owl cleverly hidden with that last Lydia. I wouldn't put it past him to hide a Lydia amidst the Owls, particularly if he blamed them for her death." Stepping over the edge of the fountain, he waded through the scummy water to take a closer look at the immense sculpture, seeking out shadowy clefts and crevices that might hide another century-old clue. If necessary, he could dispatch a drone to conduct another 3D scan for analysis back in the bunker or the Batcave, but he hoped to avoid that.

I'm not coming back here if I can help it.

He recalled the harsh white light that had shone down on him before. The glare had come from high-intensity lights suspended high above the chamber. The Owls, too, had peered down at him from their lofty perches atop the walls. Thus, if there was anything Percy wanted to hide, he'd have made certain it couldn't be spotted from *above*. Tapping into the barbed memories of his captivity, Batman visualized the light pouring down, illuminating the finely sculpted surface of the idol while creating contrasting shadows…

Where?

Climbing onto the rough-hewn pedestal, he squinted into the negative space beneath the Owl's folded wings and behind its thick, ponderous legs. He ignited another light stick to dispel the shadows—and found Lydia Doyle peering back at him.

"She's here."

A small portrait was hidden behind the Great Owl's right leg. Like the tiny owl tucked away among Wisdom's robes, the portrait was placed where it couldn't be seen by anyone who wasn't deliberately searching for it. Percy had hidden her well, right beneath the Court's eyes. Her goddess-like features were rendered in bas-relief, her eyes closed in repose, her lips bearing that same sad smile Batman had come to know so well.

"Where?" Joanna asked excitedly. "Let me see!"

Heedless of the guck, she splashed through the fountain to join Batman, who helped her up onto the fabricated boulder. He stepped aside to let her get a better look as she squeezed between the Owl's scaly legs to get to the newly discovered portrait. He held up the light stick so that the glow fell upon his discovery.

"Oh my God, that's definitely her." Joanna's eyes were wide behind her glasses. "Even after all my research, I never dreamed of finding something like this." She stared at Percy's hidden tribute to his lost love, which he must have carved before he shaped the statue at the university, not long after Lydia's disappearance. "This is so amazing…"

She reached out to touch the portrait, as though to assure herself that she wasn't just seeing things. Her outstretched fingers grazed the polished stone, exploring its graceful contours. Unexpectedly, the portrait slid further back into the marble. She yanked her hand back, gasping in surprise.

"What in the—?"

There was a *click*, followed by a low mechanical rumbling as of concealed gears and counterweights, stirring after a long slumber. The statue began to totter above them.

"Watch out!" Dropping the light stick, Batman sprang forward, seized Joanna, and leapt out from beneath the Great Owl. The force of his leap carried them over the stagnant pool so that they crashed onto the hard marble floor. He rolled into the fall, absorbing the brunt of the impact as he cushioned Joanna with his body. Grunting, he looked past her to see the top of the boulder shear off from the rest of the pedestal, sending the entire monolith toppling toward them.

"Batman!" Batgirl cried, too far away to help.

We didn't get far enough away…

Gripping Joanna tightly, he rolled them out of its path. A tremor shook the Labyrinth as the Great Owl crashed to earth, raising a cloud of dust and pulverized marble. The huge idol shattered into pieces only a few feet away from them. Flying bits of debris pelted his cape as he shielded her from the fragments as best he could. A fist-sized chunk of marble bounced off his shoulder, making him wince and grit his teeth. Armored suit or not, he was going to be black and blue tomorrow.

Yet they had survived.

Rising cautiously, he watched the surrounding walls, ready to respond if they started tumbling as well—but only the Great Owl had been uprooted by whatever long-dormant booby trap Joanna had inadvertently triggered. As the dust and debris began to settle, he looked about for the third member of their party.

"Batgirl?" he called out.

"Over here!" she shouted from the other side of the rubble. Her voice sounded hoarse from the dust. She came into view, clambering over heaps of debris to reach them. "And you two?"

"Alive," Batman said, "and uncrushed." He helped Joanna to her feet. She appeared shaken, but not seriously injured. Even her glasses had survived their narrow escape.

"Oh my God, I'm so sorry," she said. "I had no idea… I just wanted to touch it, to confirm that it was *real*."

"It's not your fault," Batman said. "You couldn't have known. In your world, fine art doesn't come with booby traps."

"Well, except maybe in Gotham," Batgirl quipped. She contemplated the wrecked statue, which was no longer in any shape to adorn a museum. "Boy, Percy really didn't want people messing with his lady."

Batman found that oddly encouraging.

"I wonder what he thought he was protecting?" It occurred to him that the deathtrap had been there the entire time he had been imprisoned in the Labyrinth. Had he known the Great Owl was rigged to collapse, he could have used that to his advantage when he was fighting for his life.

Water under the bridge.

And drugged water, at that.

"Hey, guys," Batgirl called. "You need to see this." She'd made her way over to what had been the base of the statue, where the bottom half of the boulder still remained in place above the center of the pool. The urgency in her voice caught his attention.

"What is it?" he asked, a thrill of anticipation running through him.

"I think we found what Percy wanted to hide."

Batman and Joanna scrambled over to investigate. Inside the bottom half of the rocky pedestal, exposed to the light for the first time in a century, was a bronze sarcophagus fashioned in the shape of a woman: Lydia Doyle, lying supine atop the lid of the casket. Burial cerements draped her form. Her eyes were closed in slumber.

"Oh my," Joanna whispered.

This could be it, he thought.

"Shades of Edgar Allan Poe." Batgirl looked at Batman. "You think this is what it seems to be?"

"Lydia Doyle's tomb," he replied. "Almost certainly. This has always been about Lydia, at least as far as Percy was concerned."

Being careful not to touch it, Batgirl surveyed the sarcophagus, which appeared untouched by the passage of time.

"But how on Earth did Percy manage to hide it here, right under their beaks, as it were?"

"My guess?" Batman said. "He constructed the pedestal off-site, sealed the sarcophagus inside it, then had it installed here in the Labyrinth. He may have bribed or blackmailed some laborers, who—knowing the Court—might have been disposed of after the work was complete. By that time, any squeamishness Percy might have felt likely had given way to cynicism.

"The same for the booby trap," he continued. "If Percy supervised the installation himself, and tied the mechanism in with the hydraulics for the fountain, any special 'modifications' could have gone unnoticed." He shrugged beneath his cloak. "It's not easy, but it's doable. The trick is to divvy up the labor so that nobody can see the whole picture."

He spoke from experience. His very existence as the Dark Knight relied upon the subtle art of commissioning labor and materials from multiple sources, the better to conceal the true nature of his work. If he could establish secret armories throughout Gotham, and equip himself with an ever-growing array of vehicles and gear, then Percy Wright could have been creative enough to hide Lydia's tomb below the Great Owl.

"Right beneath the Court's very noses," Batman said. "He hid Lydia at the heart of the Owls' sanctum as a final ironic act of defiance."

"Not unlike the way he placed a sculpture of Lydia at the door of his own tomb," Joanna observed. "The artist in him was clearly drawn to symbolic acts of revenge."

"I take back what I said before," Batgirl said. "He was even nervier than I gave him credit for."

Batman leaned in to study the sarcophagus. Joanna hung back, keeping her hands to her sides. Batman appreciated her restraint, and approached the casket with caution.

"There's an inscription," Batgirl said. "Running along the edge of the lid—do you see it?"

"Yes." He activated a new light stick to get a better look. It was written in Latin, as befitted Percy's erudition. Squinting at the inscription, Batman took a moment to translate it, then read it aloud. "You will bring conflagration back with you. How great the flames are that you are seeking over these waters, you do not know."

"There's a cheery epitaph." Joanna shuddered, hugging herself. "It sounds familiar."

"It's from Ovid," Batman said. "Cassandra, the doomed prophetess, predicting the Fall of Troy."

"Cassandra," Batgirl echoed. "A seeress, condemned to see the future, consumed by visions of impending disaster. Some stories say it drove her mad."

"And the most beautiful of Troy's daughters," Batman said, "not that it saved her—or her city—from the doom she foretold."

"Cassandra has always been a popular subject for traditional sculptors and painters," Joanna said. "Percy revisited her a few times over the course of his career. One of his earliest works was a bust of Cassandra, gazing off into the future. It took a prize at a student exhibition when he was just starting out. Made his name, in fact."

"A famous beauty. Visions of tomorrow, and a warning of disaster to come," Batman said. "Lydia. Cassandra. As classical allusions go, it's pretty apt."

"So do you think Lydia is inside this... for real?" Joanna asked. "Her actual remains?"

"It seems likely," Batman replied. "This is what we've been looking for all this time, even if we didn't realize it."

And we got here first.

"But Billy Draper said he burned her body."

"We can dismiss that as fiction by now," Batman said. "Lydia may have died by fire—like other victims of the Burning Sickness—but not at the hands of a random stalker. Lydia fell victim to the Court of Owls... and Percy's elixir. The predictions we've been chasing— they were hers."

"That's what Vincent implied," Joanna recalled breathlessly, "but he didn't say anything about wanting to find her body. Just a new-and-improved formula." She gave the casket a speculative look. "Maybe Percy buried the formula with Lydia," she suggested.

"That would certainly be in character. Another ironic jab at the Court."

"That, or there may be another answer," he replied. "What if the final version of elixir is actually *inside* Lydia's body, infused into her tissues… or what's left of them?"

"If that's the case, then the formula isn't written down anywhere, but baked into her flesh and bones." Batgirl considered the possibility. "That's an intriguing theory. Morbid, but intriguing."

"And not without precedent where the Court of Owls is concerned," Batman said. "The very cells of the Talons are suffused with electrum, thanks to chemical treatments devised by geniuses like Percy Wright. It lingers in their bodies no matter how long they're 'dead,' which is why the Court is able to resurrect them as needed. Percy's elixir might still exist in Lydia's remains in much the same way, waiting to be harvested."

"Ugh, that's horrible," Joanna said. "Lydia suffered enough. Why can't they just leave her in peace?"

"If only," Batgirl replied. "But hang on, I'm getting confused here. If Lydia burned up like the other test subjects, doesn't that mean that Percy *didn't* fix his elixir? Or is that not how she died?"

"I suspect not," Batman said. "We'll know more once we discover what secrets this coffin is hiding." Again he considered the inscription. The analogy to Cassandra seemed clear enough, but perhaps they needed to look deeper than that. The myth was an elaborate one. What else might Percy have been alluding to?

"Cassandra warned that Troy would burn to the ground. Percy raved about an inferno awaiting Gotham. What exactly is he trying to tell us here?"

"Let's crack this casket open and find out," Batgirl said eagerly.

"Not so fast," Batman cautioned. "We've already dealt with one booby trap. There could be more."

"Right," Batgirl said, backing off. "I'm just anxious to find out if the formula is really in there."

"Agreed." Batman inspected the narrow seam between the lid and the casket. A metal latch was built into one end of the sarcophagus, artfully embedded in Lydia's bronze tresses. Then he noticed something surprising. "It appears to be entirely airtight."

"To protect the contents from the elements?" Batgirl suggested.

Batman shook his head. "It was already encased in thousands of pounds of marble." Warning bells sounded in his brain. "Percy was a chemist. There had to be a reason he hermetically sealed the casket." He stepped away from the airtight sarcophagus. "Yes, this is a trap of some sort." One last booby trap to deter grave robbers? Or some final trick on Percy's part?

"We can't open it here," Batman said. "We have to do this elsewhere, under controlled conditions." The logistics of transporting the sarcophagus to the Batcave would be daunting, but there was nothing to be done about it. He wasn't about to break the seal on the casket without taking the proper precautions.

"Talk about frustrating," Batgirl said, sighing. "So near and yet so far."

"I know," Joanna said. "After all of this, I'm dying to find out what's really inside this casket."

"Likewise," a new voice said.

Vincent Wright stepped into view at the entrance to the chamber.

36

The whoosh of a blade slicing through the air accompanied Vincent's remark.

Batman deflected the throwing knife with his gauntlet. Behind Vincent, flashlights blazed. He saw a small army of henchmen, and *two* Talons. They had invaded the burial chamber from the darkened maze beyond, armed to the teeth and looking for trouble. An Owl mask hid Vincent's face, but there was no mistaking his sardonic tone and cocky body language.

"Things just got complicated," Batman said in a low voice. He wondered what had brought their foes here. He was certain that he and his companions hadn't been followed during their trek through the sewers.

Reaching into his belt, he flung a handful of smoke-bombs into the midst of the newcomers. Opaque chemical fumes billowed through the chamber, shielding the three of them from view. The fog would do little to slow the Talons, but at least it would make it harder for Vincent's gunmen to get a bead on them. Special filters in Batman's cowl enabled him to keep the enemy in view. Similar lenses, developed by Wayne Industries, afforded Batgirl the same edge.

"Look at the mess you've made of this place," Vincent said, coughing dramatically. Flanked by the Talons, he cautiously picked his way through the smoke and rubble, while his other men stumbled about, afraid to fire their weapons for fear of hitting each other. "As if you didn't do enough damage the last time you graced these venerable chambers," he continued. "Came back to finish the job, did you?"

Had Vincent been among the masked sadists who had enjoyed his ordeal? Volcanic rage threatened to ignite in Batman, and he tamped it down in order to keep his wits about him. This was no time to lose control. Retreat wasn't an option—not if there was a chance that the sarcophagus held the formula. He wasn't about to let it fall into the hands of Vincent and the other Owls—even if that meant taking down *both* Talons.

"Batgirl!" he shouted. "Get Joanna to safety." She had already put what was left of the pedestal between herself, Joanna and the invaders. Vincent's men stumbled through the smoke and rubble. If the women moved quickly, he could cover their retreat as they escaped via the gap in the floor.

"And leave you on your own?" Batgirl protested. "Against the Talons?"

He understood her reluctance. One Talon was bad enough. Two was going to test him to the limit. Then again, he had never expected this to be easy.

"Won't be the first time," he said. "Just do it."

"Forget it," Joanna said forcefully. She picked up a chunk of debris to use as a weapon. "I'm not running anymore. I started this, intentionally or not, and I can't let you keep fighting my battles for me... or let these Owl bastards exploit Lydia again. I owe her that much."

"Don't be foolish," Batman said. Now was not the time. This hunt for Percy's lost elixir had claimed too many lives. "Be smart and get away from here. You'll only get in my way." As he spoke he flung a Batarang at the modern Talon—the one he'd fought before—but the assassin batted it aside with the back of his hand.

His reflexes were *that* fast.

"Go, stay—it doesn't matter anymore." Vincent let the Talons take the lead as they advanced toward the tomb. "*You* don't matter anymore, Joanna, except as a loose end to be disposed of at some point. You're expendable."

"I'll find you wherever you run, college girl," the Talon promised. An empty sheath on his bandolier made clear the source of the knife.

Not if I have anything to say about it, Batman thought, although the window of opportunity was shrinking fast. Firing a Batrope upward, so the grapnel embedded itself in the ceiling, he swung into battle. Launching himself in a broad swing, he collided with the modern Talon, knocking the other man backward. As he did so the second Talon came at Batman from behind, wielding an upraised knife. Vincent fell back, letting the Court's infamous assassins do its dirty work.

"So you're the celebrated Bat-Man of Gotham," the other Talon remarked. His archaic outfit, complete with oiled leather and brass fittings, dated him back to the First World War era. "You've made quite a name for yourself, so I gather, but you've never faced me before."

He brought the knife down toward Batman's back, but an elbow to his gut foiled the attack, causing the Talon to double over in pain. The knife fell short of its target. Before Batman could seize the moment, however, the modern Talon was back in the fight. They traded punches while the vintage Talon recovered.

Batman had only a few moments, tops, before both opponents moved in for the kill. For a brief instant, he flashed back to his life-or-death struggle with another Talon in this very place.

At least this time I'm not starved or drugged.

I can work with that.

His fist collided with the modern Talon's face.

•

"You heard him," Batgirl said to Joanna. "We need to get you out of here."

They crouched behind the truncated pedestal, which provided only limited protection. Batgirl gave the young woman a collapsible gas mask from her arsenal, then tugged on Joanna's arm, but the other woman resisted her.

"No." Joanna shook her head stubbornly. "No more running. I can't spend the rest of my life looking over my shoulder—or blaming myself for whatever happens next. I'm not going anywhere until this is over, one way or another."

Batgirl heard the conviction in Joanna's voice. There was clearly no arguing with her.

"Okay then," she said, accepting the other woman's decision. She couldn't tussle with Joanna *and* take on the foot soldiers—not at the same time. And to be honest, she hated the idea of running out on Batman, even if that was what he wanted. It was always possible that he could manage this fight on his own—just because he was Batman—but he could certainly use some help at the moment. Drawing a compact high-voltage stun gun from a pouch on her belt, she handed it to Joanna.

"Take this, but stay smart and don't take any unnecessary chances. You just make contact and hit the switch. The charge is non-lethal, but it'll hurt like hell," she said. "Batman was right. We don't need you becoming a hostage or a liability."

Joanna nodded. "What's our plan?"

"You guard Lydia's tomb," Batgirl said. "I'm going to take out the small fry... for starters."

As the smoke began to dissipate, drifting along the air currents into side corridors, Vincent's men organized themselves and began fanning out across the burial chamber. Located as it was at the center of the room, the tomb was indefensible in the long term, unless Batgirl could cut down the number of hostiles while there was still a chance to do so. She was a big believer in taking out the bad guys before they knew what hit them.

"Watch yourself," she said, hoping she wasn't making a mistake by leaving Joanna's side—but there didn't seem to be any better options. Pulling some smoke-bombs of her own, she renewed the smoke screen while tossing in a couple of flash-bang grenades for good measure. Blinding bursts of light, accompanied by deafening blares, threw the men off-balance, just the way Batgirl wanted them.

Ready or not, here I come.

Batgirl preferred to approach every fight like a chess match. It was all about keeping track of where all the pieces were, making strategic moves, and taking out your opponents one by one as swiftly and methodically as possible.

Springing from the pedestal, she sprinted across the largest remaining portion of the shattered Great Owl, her insulated boots making little sound as she leapt over gaping fissures caused by the crash. Sweeping the room with a glance, she took inventory of Vincent's pawns and their shifting positions, counting on the smoke to grant her an element of surprise.

She spotted an unwary thug directly below her, hugging the side of the Great Owl's massive trunk. He had one hand against the wreckage to orient himself as he trod cautiously through the swirling fumes. In the other one he gripped a handgun, which he waved back and forth in front of his eyes, trying to fan the smoke away. He peered into the fog, looking everywhere but up.

Big mistake.

Jumping from atop the demolished Owl, she landed feet-first on the unsuspecting minion. The soles of her boots slammed into his upper back, planting his face into the hard marble floor with a satisfying smack. Startled, another pawn turned toward the commotion and was greeted by a hard right hook to his jaw. Lead shot sewn into the knuckles of her gloves added *pow* to her punch, even as she targeted yet another man a few yards away.

While the second hood was still reeling from her punch she pulled a non-edged Batarang from her arsenal and pitched it into the back of the third man's skull, knocking him senseless. A high kick to Glass Jaw's chin dropped him for the duration.

Three pawns in four moves, Batgirl mused. Not a bad start, but the match was far from over. Some trigger-happy idiot opened fire in her direction, endangering his own comrades as well. Bullets chipped away at the toppled statue, barely missing the first goon she'd slammed into the floor, who was stupidly trying to get back on his feet. Batgirl threw out her cape to shield him from the gunfire before decking him with an uppercut. He crumpled to the ground, where he was better off.

"You're welcome," she said. "Now stay down."

A Batarang to the wrist disarmed the shooter, but that didn't stop Vincent Wright from shouting frantically at his men.

"Stop shooting blindly, you fools!" he screeched. "You want to kill me by mistake?" His voice reminded her that while she was trying to clear the pawns from the board, Batman was still pitted against the Court's knights. Between the smoke and the heaping piles of rubble, she couldn't see how he was faring against the Talons, but she was all too aware that her fight was simply a sideshow. The real battle was being fought nearby.

"Over there!" a hoodlum shouted, glimpsing her through the fog. "Get her!"

Not exactly a ninja, he bellowed as he charged at her from behind, his feet stomping across the floor. A second goon answered his call, running toward her. He was a big bruiser, nearly twice her size. Clenched fists and a beet-red face signaled his intentions.

"You should have stayed in your cave, Bat-Bitch!" he bellowed. "I'm going to mess you up!" His words bounced off her like bullets off Superman—she'd heard worse from worse. Instead her eyes zeroed in on the gaping hole in the floor a few feet behind him.

She calculated angles and trajectories. Maybe not chess then, but pool or billiards...

"Got you now!" he yelled. "Say your prayers, you—hey!"

The guy behind her tried to tackle her, but she easily evaded the lunge and, taking hold of his belt and collar turned his own momentum against him. She hurled him straight into the oncoming thug, who was bowled over by the collision. Both men tumbled backward into the hole, splashing into the sewers below. She lobbed another flash-bang into the gap, just because. *Two balls, corner pocket.*

Then she heard more goons shouting and stomping through the smoke. Somebody tripped over a chunk of debris and swore profusely. A baseball bat came swinging at her head, and she had to bend backward like a limbo dancer to avoid a concussion. A knee to the batter's groin distracted him long enough for her straighten up and ram her armored cowl into his face. That was another pawn down, but she frowned anyway.

This was taking too long. Batman needed her help against the Talons.

And so did Joanna.

37

Violence surrounded Joanna. She heard angry shouts and blows and gunshots as she guarded Lydia's tomb, circling the sundered pedestal in a futile attempt to keep it between her and the brutal battles being waged throughout the burial chamber.

Drifting smokescreens obscured her view, adding to her anxiety. Maybe the invaders couldn't see her, but she was also having trouble watching out for them. At least the gas mask kept her from gagging. She gripped the weapon Batgirl had given her, while holding onto a brick-sized marble fragment as well. She couldn't imagine either weapon stopping a Talon, but they were better than nothing. Maybe.

A shotgun didn't save Dennis...

Part of her wished she had listened to Batman and let Batgirl get her out of danger. She had been in danger ever since she'd started probing Lydia's past, and living in fear since that first night she caught a glimpse of the Talon stalking her. This showdown had been coming for a long time. At least it was finally here.

Someone came splashing through the fetid water of the fountain, moving toward her. A flashlight beam cut through the thinning smoke and she made out a figure striding up onto the pedestal. She raised the brick hesitantly.

"Batman?"

"Sorry, no." Vincent Wright emerged from the smoke. An Owl

mask hid his face, but, after her interrogation in the lab, she'd recognize his smarmy voice anywhere. "I'm afraid he's occupied with my associates at the moment, so you'll have to settle for me."

"Stay back!" She moved to put the pedestal between them. He appeared to be unarmed, but she hadn't forgotten how he'd threatened her life before. "I'm not going to let you disturb Lydia."

"Funny you should feel that way," he said, "since you're the one who led us to her, thanks to an ingenious subdermal tracking device we injected you with while you were briefly in our custody. At the time it seemed merely a reasonable precaution, just in case we misplaced you again, but it's paid off more handsomely than I ever imagined."

Tracking device? Joanna didn't remember any such injection. *Must have been when I was drugged.*

"You son of a bitch!" She flung the marble chunk, but her aim was off and Vincent easily dodged it. It splashed down into the puddle. "You're a disgrace to your family name," she growled. "Whatever his sins, Percy at least created lasting works of art. You're just another creepy Gotham psycho!"

"Oh my!" Vincent placed his hand over his heart. "I'd be wounded if I actually cared one whit about your opinion." He snickered behind his mask. "But, ultimately, you're just another silly girl who's in way over her head, no different than the low-class tramp you're defending."

Anger flared inside Joanna, helping to combat the terror. "Lydia brought more grace and beauty to Gotham than any of you greedy, grasping Owls. All you've ever given this city is nightmares!"

"We're not interested in giving," he replied. "Only taking what's rightfully ours—power, wealth, and now the future." He was keeping his distance for the moment, but Joanna knew he wasn't going to be content to keep sparring verbally for long. Keeping her eye on him, she braced for the inevitable attack while waiting anxiously for Batman or Batgirl to intervene.

Maybe if she could just stall Vincent long enough...?

"Grab her," he said.

Footsteps sounded behind her as she realized too late that Vincent had been stalling, as well, distracting her long enough for one of his henchmen to sneak up behind her. Glancing back over her shoulder, she saw a beefy, murderous-looking hoodlum lunging for her. She started to panic, then remembered the stun gun in her hand. Swinging her arm back, she hit the ignition switch and the business end of the weapon collided with an outstretched arm. Electricity popped loudly, sounding like a sudden burst of static.

The high-voltage jolt caught the goon by surprise. He stiffened and tumbled off the base of the pedestal, adding more scum to the fountain. Joanna didn't have time to savor her close call, however, as Vincent darted around the side of the tomb toward her, forcing her to hastily circle around to keep the pedestal between them.

"Uh-uh!" She brandished the weapon menacingly. As she held it over the bronze lid of the sarcophagus, a blue electric charge crackled between the points on the front end. "You try laying hands on me or Lydia, and you're in for the shock of your life... literally!"

An exasperated sound escaped his avian mask. "You're making this far too difficult." He drew a handgun from beneath his tailored jacket. "And it's becoming an untenable waste of time."

She froze at the sight. Memories of her parents, gunned down in the streets so many years ago, came rushing back. Her mouth went dry, so that she could hardly speak.

"You... you had a gun all along?"

"Of course," he replied. "No fancy swords or daggers for me, I'm afraid. Tradition has its place, but I like to think of myself as a thoroughly modern Owl. Besides, those other weapons require far too much training." He aimed the gun at her. "I regret having to resort to such crude tactics, but you've left me little choice." His voice took on a harder edge—one she remembered from the lab in the plasma center. "Now toss away that silly toy."

She wondered why he didn't just shoot her. Perhaps he didn't regard her as quite so expendable after all. Or maybe he just didn't have the balls to pull the trigger.

Could be, she thought.

"Hurry up!" he snapped. "I need to get the formula and get away while the Bats are still occupied!"

Joanna stared down the barrel of the gun. Her own weapon lacked the range of a firearm. The thought of being gunned down in her prime—just like her mother and father—made her afraid, and it made her *angry*. It was as though a bullet had been coming for her all this time, and there was only one thing left to do.

I'm sorry, Lydia, she thought. *For everything.*

Holding the stun gun in front of her, she lunged.

•

Metal claws jabbed the winged emblem on Batman's chest, but failed to penetrate the Kevlar panel beneath the symbol. He brought his right elbow down on the forearm of the modern Talon, cracking it while simultaneously blocking an equally vicious stab at his eyes.

Both defenses were executed flawlessly, yet they didn't stop the *other* Talon from delivering a solid blow to the back of his cowl— one he felt even through the hardened shell. Grunting, he grabbed the older Talon and executed a back-flip that put him behind his foe. The weighted tips of his scalloped cape smacked the hooded killer in the face as he snatched a sword from the scabbard on the Talon's back before landing on his feet.

One less weapon for him, Batman thought. *One more for me.*

He was holding his own, but just barely. No sooner did he repel one strike, then another came at him from another direction. Every time he scored a blow against one opponent, the other was there to keep him from following up. They weren't exactly working as a team—if anything, they seemed to be competing to see which of them landed the most strikes. Unlike the Talons, however, he couldn't heal impossibly fast. He had to tough out every blow, every cut, all while Vincent moved closer to the sarcophagus, Percy's elixir, and Joanna.

This isn't going our way.

He ran the older Talon's own sword through him so that the point emerged from the man's gut. It would have been a fatal blow to a normal adversary. An unnatural ichor, undoubtedly laced with electrum, streamed down the Talon's uniform as he fell to his knees. He was crippled for the moment—but *only* for the moment.

"Deftly done," the man said, choking on what passed for his blood. "You missed your calling, Bat-Man. That was a ploy worthy of a Talon."

"You'll forgive me if I don't take that as a compliment."

He yanked the sword free, imagining that he could already hear the man's organs and muscles and tendons reknitting themselves. Looking past him, he watched the other Talon flex his briefly fractured arm and draw his own sword. Raising it high, he bounded forward, all but trampling his associate in the process.

"Get out of my way, you worthless relic!" the modern Talon snarled. "Let me show you how it's done these days!" That confirmed the rivalry between the two. Joanna had told him there was no love lost there, so he stoked the fires of competition.

"I wouldn't brag if I were you," he taunted. "Last time I checked, my head was still on my shoulders, and you struck out with Claire Nesko—twice. Maybe you should take a few lessons from your senior partner. From what I can tell, he outclasses you in brains and, well... class."

"Shows how much you know." The Talon's furious tone indicated that Batman had hit a nerve. "Those older Talons had it easy back in the day, before you Bats started fighting back. From what I hear, your ancestors were easy pickings!"

Batman's expression darkened, but he didn't take the bait.

Ultimately, this fight wasn't about the crimes committed against Alan Wayne. It wasn't even about the long-dead woman who still graced the fountain in Bruce's mother's garden, or the hell the Court had put him through in this very Labyrinth. He was fighting to protect the future, not avenge the past.

"Times *have* changed," he said. "Bats aren't prey for Owls anymore."

Springing forward with a roar, the Talon swung his sword. Sparks flew as Batman parried the attack with the blade he still held. They dueled across the debris-strewn chamber, the ringing song of steel against steel echoing off the high marble walls, punctuated by the shouts and curses and thuds coming from Batgirl's fracas with Vincent's hired guns.

Batman briefly caught sight of her. She was in constant motion, dispatching the goons with her customary precision and efficiency. Perhaps it was best that she had stuck around after all. He had enough on his hands.

Rapid-fire thrusts, feints, and parries came one after another as Batman took the Talon's measure. He was clearly well-versed in swordplay, but Batman had crossed swords with the likes of Ra's al-Ġūl and survived. He felt confident that, given time, he stood a good chance of besting his opponent.

Problem was, he didn't have time. The other Talon was healing even now. It was only a matter of minutes before he was fighting both of them again.

I need to make this guy angry, Batman thought. *Sloppy.*

"You'll need to do better than this if you want to take my head." Batman drew a Batarang with his free hand and used it in the manner of a parrying dagger, to deflect the Talon's swipes and thrusts while freeing up his sword to stay on the offense. "Or is that just an old nursery rhyme, after all?"

"Ask me again after I've sliced you to pieces!" Mimicking Batman, he pulled a knife from a sheath so that they each wielded two weapons. They circled each other, seeking an opening or advantage. The killer's form and technique were excellent.

Suddenly Batman shifted his tactics and hurled the edged Batarang toward the Talon, just as he had during their first encounter on the rooftops near Claire's apartment. As before, the spinning missile whizzed past the enemy's head. The Talon belted out a laugh.

"You're running out of tricks," he jeered. "Fool me once, shame on you. Fool me twice, shame on me!"

He glanced back to track the weapon's speedy return. That gave Batman the opening he needed. Shifting his grip on the sword hilt, he threw the weapon like a spear, aiming for the Talon's sword-arm. It pierced the wrist and he let out a bellow of pain and fury, losing his grip so that his sword clattered to the floor.

As it did, the Batarang struck its real target: the other "older" Talon, climbing to his feet and clutching his abdomen. It wedged itself in the man's hooded brow. The resurrected Talon reeled unsteadily, grunting in pain, as he wrenched the missile from his skull. Ichor gushed from the head wound, streaming over his antique hood and goggles, blinding him. Outdated expletives spewed from his lips.

Still howling in rage, the modern assassin sheathed his dagger in order to extricate the sword from his wrist, where electrum-laced blood was flowing freely. Batman followed up with a second, razor-edged Batarang that sliced into the Talon's chest and, more importantly, through the bandolier. The assassin's ready supply of throwing knives joined the sword on the floor.

Then he launched a Batrope that snared the Talon, wrapping itself around his legs. Batman swiftly attached the other end of the rope to a grapnel hook and fired it into the ceiling. Yanked off his feet, the Talon abruptly found himself hanging upside-down, high above the ground, swinging back and forth like a pendulum.

"Seriously?" the Talon hissed. He clutched his wrist to staunch the bleeding. "You really think this is going to stop me?"

"It's a start," Batman said. He gave himself a moment to catch his breath. The fight was far from over, he knew, and he seized the bandolier that held the Talon's knives, tossing it into the pit. Clenching his fists, he calculated how much more damage he could inflict while his foes were still disabled—provided he moved quickly enough.

Then a gunshot, followed by a shriek of pain, seized his attention. *Oh, no...*

Turning toward the *bang*, he saw Joanna stagger backwards, clutching her chest, as Vincent looked on, holding a smoking weapon. A stun gun slipped from her fingers.

The harsh report echoed through the cavern as Joanna tumbled backward off the huge pedestal into the fountain, leaving Vincent alone by the tomb.

"Damn it!" the Owl cursed. "You had to push your luck, didn't you?" Still holding the pistol, he approached the sarcophagus. "I told you I was in a hurry!"

"Leave it alone, Vincent!" Batman rushed toward the pedestal. "You don't know what you're doing. It's not safe."

"I beg to differ." He opened fire on Batman as he ripped off his mask, placing it carefully on the edge of the cavity that held the tomb. His face was flushed and sweaty. Exultation rang in his voice. "The future is my inheritance. What was Percy's is now mine!"

Batman held up his cape to shield himself from the bullets. Keeping his head down, he zigged and zagged across the floor of the violated burial chamber in a futile attempt to reach the tomb before Vincent could open it.

As the Owl fumbled with the latch, Batman saw clearly Percy's grand design. As Bruce Wayne, he knew too well what it was like to mourn lost loved ones. Why would Percy place Lydia's tomb here—and plant clues that might lead to it someday being desecrated?

Unless that was his plan all along.

Cassandra.

After the Fall of Troy, Cassandra intentionally left behind a sealed cask bearing a curse for the first Greek who opened it. Thus had the doomed prophetess achieved a measure of revenge, against those who had wronged her.

"Don't do it!" he shouted. "This is just what Percy wanted! That's not treasure…

"It's bait!"

38

MacDougal Lane, Gotham City, 1925

"Time is running out for me, Lydia. My days are numbered."

It was well past midnight and Percy sat alone in his studio, talking to a clay maquette perched atop his sculpting stand. The sculpture captured Lydia posing for what had eventually become Alan Wayne's fountain. He glanced forlornly at the empty platform where she had once posed for this very piece, before he had been forced to rely on old memories and studies. So few years had passed since that halcyon afternoon, yet he felt immeasurably older.

Guilt had aged him.

"Margaret and the other Owls are losing patience with me, growing tired of waiting for their damned elixir." He'd spent those seven years pretending to refine the elixir, which the Court had insisted on testing on yet more human subjects, dredged up from Gotham's poorest neighborhoods. The tests had yielded nothing more than a string of charred corpses—and yet more blood on his hands. The deaths had been attributed to a mysterious new fever— "the Burning Sickness," they called it—but Percy knew the truth. Those people had died to hide his secret from the Court.

That he'd perfected his elixir long ago.

He withdrew a folded piece of paper from his breast pocket. Written on the paper in a fine, legible hand was the formula. He reviewed it one last time, for vanity's sake, and walked over to the fireplace, where a crackling blaze awaited. He crumpled the document into a ball and cast it into the flames, then watched grimly as his greatest scientific achievement burned, fittingly, before his eyes.

"It's the only way, Lydia," he said. "I see that now. The Court must not gain dominion over Gotham's future. They're dreadful enough already." Waiting until he was certain the formula was ashes, he turned away from the fire and looked once more upon his beloved. He envied her graceful repose. He couldn't remember the last time he'd slept well.

"It won't be long now, Lydia. Not after last night."

He had drunk too much the night before, at that damned reception, and the guilt and frustration had gotten the better of him. It had been far too bitter a draught—to be lauded for his accomplishments while carrying so many sins on his conscience. He had rambled drunkenly, alluding to crimes past and yet to be, before being escorted from the scene by his minders. Such a reckless display would not sit well with Margaret and the Court.

"The Talon will be coming for me soon. Oh, they'll make it look as though I died of natural causes, or perhaps in an 'accident' like poor Alan Wayne, but the Court will have their way as they always do. I'll be free of them before long… and they'll think they're rid of me."

A bitter chuckle accompanied his musings.

"But the trap is set, dearest. The clues planted, the breadcrumbs laid out like bait for those with eyes to see. In my lifetime I lacked the courage to defy the Court, fearing for the safety of friends and family, but I have planted the seeds for our revenge, which someday will blossom, long after I am beyond their retribution. As you already are."

He contemplated the maquette's tranquil features, which were hardly those of an avenging fury. "But would you desire vengeance, you who were so full of warmth and compassion? Or would you urge me to show mercy and compassion against those who wronged us, who stole our future? I've pondered this, Lydia, and I've chosen to leave their fate in their hands. As long as you are allowed to rest in peace, no harm will come to the Court or Gotham, but should anyone ever follow my clues, they will find instead... the inferno!"

39

Vincent scorned Batman's warnings.

"Save your breath!" he shouted back. "Scare tactics may work on the thugs and maniacs you're accustomed to, but I'm not so easily manipulated." Gun in hand, he fired to keep his enemy at bay. "As if I'd stop now, with Percy's secrets finally within reach…"

He clicked open the latch, releasing a hiss of air from the sarcophagus. Its bronze lid lifted a few inches, almost as if the sculpted simulacrum of Lydia was taking a breath for the first time in a century. Vincent's eyes gleamed in anticipation.

"Finally! Let's see what we have here."

Dodging Vincent's bullets, Batman wondered for a moment if he'd been wrong about Percy's true intentions. Maybe the tomb wasn't bait after all?

Then a sudden blast of heat and light blew the lid off the sarcophagus. It shot into the air with tremendous force, before crashing back down with a metallic *clang* several yards from its origin. Batman dove out of the way to avoid being crushed.

Marble floor tiles shattered, the sound echoing across the burial chamber. Up on the pedestal, Vincent stumbled backward, his eyebrows and goatee smoking from the blast, his discarded Owl mask clattering to the ground. His usual smug self-assurance had taken damage as well.

"No," he said. "The formula…"

Batman frowned. As impressive as it was, the explosion struck him as relatively inconsequential. Was that the best revenge Percy could manage?

But the blast was only the beginning.

She rose from the tomb, burning bright. Flickering red flames veiled her face and figure, but there was no mistaking her identity. Lydia Doyle—"Miss Gotham"—stood before them, clothed only in fire. The flames blazed hotly, but did not consume her. She lit up the murky burial chamber like a torch, causing shadows to dance erratically across the high marble walls of the maze. Incalescent yellow eyes looked upon the world again as Batman recalled the ominous inscription on the sarcophagus.

You will bring conflagration back with you.

This could only be Percy's doing. Somehow the long-dead genius had combined a variant of his elixir with the serum used to resurrect the Talons and render them indestructible. After a hundred years, the mixture had reanimated Lydia in this fiery new form, which had ignited when oxygen entered her airtight sarcophagus.

It all made sense, in a perversely poetic way.

Lydia *was* the inferno of which Percy had spoken—and the instrument of his long-delayed revenge. Her lambent gaze swept over the battle-scarred chamber. She appeared disoriented at first, likely baffled by her own resurrection and her bizarre new surroundings, but then her eyes registered the shattered remains of the Great Owl, the larger pieces of which were still recognizable.

Her expression darkened. Rage contorted her lovely features, which appeared strangely impervious to the flames rising from her skin. A single word escaped her sizzling lips.

"Owls."

She turned toward Vincent, whose composure evaporated before the heat of her wrath. Instead of the key to the future that he had been searching for, the past had risen up in search of revenge. Perspiration ran down his face. Panic filled his voice.

"Stay away from me! You're supposed to be dead, damn it!"

He emptied his gun into her, but the bullets had no effect. If anything, she appeared to be even more immoveable than the usual Talon. Batman marveled at the way her flesh remained intact beneath the flames, as though it was healing as fast as—or perhaps faster—than it burned. Was she in constant pain, he wondered, or had her nerves been deadened?

He had plenty of questions, but they would have to wait. No longer forced to dodge Vincent's gunfire, he sprinted toward the pedestal.

"Stop her!" the Owl screamed at whomever might be listening. He flung his empty firearm. She cringed instinctively, but batted it away with ease. He stumbled off the pedestal into the fountain, splashing through the filthy water.

"Put her back in her grave—"

She jumped from the sarcophagus with startling speed and grace. Flames trailed behind her like the tail of a comet. Steam billowed, but instead of dousing her fire, the filmy water boiled at her touch as she caught hold of him. Clouds of scalding vapor obscured the view, but Batman could dimly make out Vincent thrashing in Lydia's red-hot embrace. The man had time for one agonized scream before he burst into flames. Vincent lit up like a bonfire, burning to death in a matter of moments.

As had his unlucky test subjects.

Batman grimaced. He had wanted to take Vincent alive, make him face trial for his crimes, but Lydia had dealt out her own fire-and-brimstone brand of retribution. Batman didn't approve, but he couldn't deny that it *was* justice of a sort. The Burning Sickness had claimed a fitting victim for once.

Hopefully the final one.

"The hell!" the modern Talon raged. Still hanging from the ceiling he reacted furiously to Vincent's death. "You killed him, you crazy bitch! You killed a member of the Court!" His metal claws slashed furiously at the rope binding his legs, and he was heedless of the wounds he inflicted on his own flesh. The shredded cable gave way and the assassin plunged downward, crashing to the floor with bone-crunching impact.

Batman braced himself for a rematch. The vintage Talon was recovering, too. His scalp wound no longer bled, although his hood was torn and his goggles smeared with gore. Shaking his head to clear it, he tossed away the goggles and tugged off his hood, revealing the face of a man who had "died" more than a century earlier.

His pallid flesh was corpse-gray, with blue veins visible beneath his skin stretched too tightly over his skull. A monk-like rim of snowy white fuzz ran around his otherwise bald pate. Crooked yellow teeth had never known the benefits of modern dentistry. Gray eyes, streaked with blue traceries, widened at the sight of the burning woman in the fountain. He peered past the flames at the features beneath them.

A look of awe swept over his ghoulish countenance.

"I'll be damned," he said. "We meet again."

Talk about going from the frying pan to the fire, Batman thought. Between the Talons and Lydia's fiery rebirth, it was unclear who posed the greater threat. Was Lydia the enemy of his enemy, or a danger to all concerned? Vengeance, like fire, could blaze out of control, consuming the guilty and the innocent alike.

"Holy crap!" Batgirl leaped down from a heap of busted statuary to stand at his back, staring in shocked amazement at Lydia in all her pyrotechnic glory. "Just when I thought I'd seen everything Gotham could throw at us…"

"Vincent's men?" he asked.

"Running scared, aside from the ones I tossed into the sewers. Guess they didn't bargain on a flaming angel of death toasting their boss." She shot him a worried look. "Joanna?"

Before he could answer, Joanna staggered around the side of the fountain, emerging from the outer fringes of the steam. She winced with every movement, and was slimed from her fall into the water, but she was still very much alive, thanks to the bullet-resistant Kevlar vest beneath her jacket. Batman had fitted her with the vest back at the bunker, dipping into his supplies there. The vest was state of the art, employing the same patented Wayne Industries tech built into his Bat-Suit. Only her glasses were broken.

"Lydia?"

She was transfixed by her flaming double, who threw Vincent's charred and smoldering remains aside. Lydia emerged from the boiling fountain like a volcanic Venus, burning brighter than before. Marble tiles cracked and crumbled beneath the intense heat of her tread. The flames licking her body were edging from red to orange as her temperature increased. She was getting hotter by the moment.

Before he could react, Joanna approached her.

"You don't know me," she said, moving cautiously, "but I know you. I know about you and Percy, how they stole your happiness…"

"Joanna, get away from her!" Batman moved toward them. "Whatever kinship you're feeling for her, it's not safe. We don't know what she's capable of!"

Behind him, the Talons were on the move again. Seeing them, Batgirl unleashed a couple of flash-bangs, and pulled out a Batarang.

"I've got this! Take care of Joanna!"

As he had expected, Lydia's blazing features displayed no sign of understanding or recognition—only indiscriminate rage. Howling in pain and fury she lunged at her descendent, unaware of the blood tie between them. Flaming fingers reached out. No bulletproof vest could save Joanna this time.

"Leave her alone!"

Batman shoved the young woman out of the way, getting between her and Lydia. A canister of flame-retardant foam was in his hand, and he let loose the spray, repelling her for a moment. She blinked and sputtered, swiping angrily at the clinging foam.

"Get Joanna away from here!" he told Batgirl. "I mean it this time!"

"No argument!"

She lobbed a last couple of flash-bangs at the Talons, then darted forward to take control of Joanna. Shaken by her near-incineration, the young woman put up no resistance as they hurried toward the nearest exit. They were preceded by the remainder of Vincent's men, who were dragging their more battered cronies along with them. Batman counted on Batgirl to protect Joanna from any random assailants.

Now he had to buy them time to get clear of the Labyrinth.

The foam had been devised to combat the fiercest blazes, but it failed to extinguish Lydia's perpetual combustion, bubbling and boiling away from her as she came at Batman. He grabbed each of her wrists to keep her at arm's length, and instantly felt the intense heat through his fire-resistant gloves. Hissing and sizzling in frustration, she strained to reach him as he braced his boots against the floor.

Layers of Nomex insulation kept him from being incinerated, but his palms already felt like they were bare against the flames. He had to fight the urge to let go of her wrists—it was like gripping hot glass or metal. He wasn't going to be able to hold her back for long.

"Lydia! Listen to me! I'm not your enemy!"

Their faces and bodies only a few feet apart, they continued to grapple. Her crazed, vengeful expression bore no resemblance to the serene and elegant countenance that graced her many likenesses throughout the city. He barely recognized her as the same woman who peacefully adorned his mother's favorite garden, back at the Manor. Could he still get through to that woman, or had she been burned away entirely, leaving only an inferno in her place?

"Think!" he said. "Remember who you were! You're Lydia

Doyle. You brought beauty to Gotham. You loved and were loved!"

His words seemed as ineffective as the foam. She spat in his face, the hot saliva blistering his exposed chin. Her flames had gone entirely orange now, infiltrated with traces of yellow. Raw hatred fueled the fire in her eyes. Crackling flames filled her mouth, distorting her speech.

"Talon!" she roared. "TALON!"

"No!" Batman's menacing appearance was working against him. He couldn't blame her for mistaking him for some new and exotic assassin. His burnt chin stung like hell. His hands were screaming at him to let go. "Listen to me. I'm not a Talon. I'm not with the Court of Owls. I want to help you!"

He feared he was wasting his breath, but then her flaming brow wrinkled in confusion. She stopped pushing against him as her bewildered gaze dropped to the emblem on his chest. She gasped, as though she recognized it. She raised her eyes to meet his.

"The Bat?"

Startled by her query, it took him a moment to grasp how she could possibly know who he was. Then it hit him.

The elixir. Her visions of the future.

"That's right," he said, opening a bit of space between them. "You've seen me before, haven't you? In your visions. You know who I am."

"The Bat," she said, nodding. "The enemy of the Owls."

Her expression softened, revealing the face of the girl in the garden. He let go of her wrists and none too soon. If and when he survived this night, his hands were going to require first-aid and plenty of ice. The yellow in her flames faded back into the orange, but the cooling was negligible. He stepped away from her, to get some relief from the heat. Even from several feet away, it was like standing too near a bonfire.

"You can trust me," he said. "You know that."

"How sweet," the modern Talon said. "And here I was hoping

you'd take each other out, to save me the trouble."

He pulled himself up from the floor. His fellow assassin also advanced on them, drawing his second sword from its scabbard. His cadaverous gray expression showed no emotion.

"Never count on fate to do your work for you," he chided the younger assassin. "Life is seldom so generous."

"Spare me the words of wisdom, old man."

As soon as Lydia spied the Talons, her rage ignited once more, sending tendrils of yellow running across her form. She shoved past Batman, grazing him with her flames, as she charged at the unmasked assassin, her contemporary from days gone by.

"TALON!" she screeched.

Her blazing feet left scorched tracks across the floor. Marble couldn't burn, but extreme heat caused it to crack and even crumble. In theory, she could actually destroy the Labyrinth, if she got hot enough.

When she got hot enough?

The younger assassin gave Batman no time to ponder. Leaving his antique counterpart to face Lydia's wrath on his own, he pounced on the Dark Knight, slashing at the hero with his eponymous metal claws. Batman caught his right arm in a lock. The Talon drew back his left fist for a knock-out blow.

"Don't think that ancient skank is going to save you," he growled. "I'm finishing you, if it's the last thing I do!"

"Are you insane?" Batman caught the Talon's fist in his palm, sending a shock of pain through his hand. He retaliated with a right hook that sent the Talon reeling to the floor. "Don't you see what's happening? This is Percy Wright's revenge on the Court… and Gotham! We've got a living inferno to bring under control."

"Doesn't settle the score between us," the Talon said. "A member of the Court is dead because of your interference. Vincent Wright burned because you kept me from protecting him." He kicked out at Batman's leg with steel-toed boots, knocking the Dark Knight onto his back, then pounced with his claws extended. "It's my duty to avenge him!"

There was no point in arguing with a fanatic. The sharpened points of the Talon's claws came at his face, but he deflected them with his gauntlet before throwing his opponent off. Leaping to his feet, Batman raked the metal fins on his glove across the Talon's face, drawing blood and cracking one of his goggles, then grunted in satisfaction. He didn't have time for this fight, but that didn't mean he couldn't enjoy getting in his licks.

"That's for all the people you helped burn."

"More than worth it," the Talon shot back. "You should have seen them go up in flames. It was a wonder to behold!"

•

Several yards away, across the rubble, the older Talon defended himself with his sword. Even a flaming angel of death, it appeared, instinctively avoided having a limb lopped off, but she remained intent on revenge.

Blazing like a funeral pyre she ducked and dodged, trying to get past the sword to burn him to a crisp. The Talon's blade was a blur of motion, and she glared at him with unquenched fury. More and more yellow appeared in her flames, with hints of blue.

"You!" Her voice crackled like fire. "You were there, before!"

"So I was," he said gravely. "Fancy meeting you again, Miss Doyle, so far past our own day and age. It's not a reunion I ever anticipated, but here we are." He chuckled, as though amused by such an unlikely twist of fate. "Funny that."

"You will burn, Talon!" Lydia vowed. "Burn in Hell!"

"That may well be," he replied, "but not just yet."

"Run!" Batman shouted across the space that separated them. "Get out of here before she destroys you, too." Indeed, a strategic retreat seemed his best option.

The Talon shook his head. He felt strangely calm.

"My doing. My responsibility," he said ruefully. "My penance, perhaps."

Without warning he charged forward, spearing Lydia in the stomach with his sword and driving her back into a high marble wall that had seen better days. She was pinned like a preserved insect mounted to a slice of cork. The blade sank hilt-deep into her burning flesh as he held her fast with no thought of his own safety. She wrapped her arms around him, pulling him closer, as her infernal fury engulfed him.

Without uttering a sound, he died.

•

The younger Talon spared only a glance for his dying predecessor. He lashed out at Batman, delivering a backhanded swipe to the side of his head. The blow staggered him, giving the Talon a chance to slip behind him and toss him to the ground. He grabbed Batman's cowl from behind and rammed his face into the rubble.

Cowl or no cowl, the impact dazed Batman, but he still managed to kick back at the Talon's right knee, throwing him off-balance for a moment. He rolled over onto his back, the better to defend himself against his foe, who drove his good knee into Batman's gut and seized Batman's throat to hold him down. Only the reinforced steel gorget built into the neckpiece kept his throat and larynx from being crushed by the preternaturally powerful grip.

"No more sparring," the killer vowed. "No more stalemates. This ends tonight!"

Couldn't agree more.

Across the chamber, the elder Talon was charcoal. His carbonized remains fell away from his angel of death, who remained pinned to the wall by his sword, which was glowing red-hot as though newly forged. She thrashed violently, howling like a demon as she took hold of the hilt and struggled to free herself.

The wall behind her cracked and flaked as the outer layers heated up faster than its interior, causing random fragments to fall away. Powdered stone rained down on Lydia as she painfully pulled the molten sword from her midriff, then stumbled away from the crumbling wall. She spotted Batman wrestling with his opponent, who had one fist around Batman's throat and the other one poised to slash downward. Lydia lurched toward them, shouting over the crackling of her own flames.

"All Talons must burn!"

The threat distracted the Talon, who glanced in her direction. The lapse in attention cost him as Batman delivered a punch to the man's jaw. It knocked him backward and away, enabling Batman to regain his feet and kick the Talon squarely in the chest. The blow propelled the Talon across the floor and away from Lydia, so that she found Batman blocking her approach to their common enemy.

"Leave him to me!" he said to her. "I'll see that he faces justice."

"Fire is justice," she responded. "The inferno is justice!"

There was a sound behind him, and he turned his back on her. The enraged assassin was moving again, closing in—presumably for the kill. Batman was almost impressed by the Talon's work ethic. The assassin wanted to defeat his foe more than he wanted to escape death by fire.

"Give it up, you brainwashed lunatic," Batman growled. "I'm trying to save you!"

"I don't need a Bat to protect me," the man replied. "The Court of Owls demands that I rip you to shreds." His own anger burning almost as hot as Lydia's, the Talon swung a clawed hand wildly. Batman easily dodged the intemperate attack, let the Talon's momentum carry the killer past him, then grabbed him by the shoulders and flung him across the room into a wall.

The same wall to which Lydia had been nailed only moments before. The crumbling wall that trembled noticeably at the collision, just as Batman had anticipated. The Talon bounced off the towering stone slab onto the floor, landing in a heap amidst the fresh debris.

Wait for it, Batman thought.

The Talon clambered to his feet.

There it is.

Batman fired his grapnel gun directly at his foe, who was lined up perfectly. The titanium grappling hook, designed to drill into steel and concrete buildings, pierced the Talon entirely before embedding itself in the wall behind him. The assassin glanced down at the taut cable stretching between him and Batman, pain mixed with bewilderment.

"What do you think you're doing?"

"Bringing the house down," Batman said. Wrapping the cable around his fists, he tugged with all his strength. He was no Superman, but the compromised structure had already taken a beating. Gritting his teeth, he pulled on the cable until the weakened wall gave way—and toppled down on top of the Talon, burying him alive.

Heal all you want, Batman thought. *You're still trapped.*

It was just him and Lydia now. He turned slowly to face her.

Even with the Talons dead or buried, Miss Gotham was blazing hotter with every passing moment, like a chain reaction building in intensity. Her eyes were blue as a welder's torch. Heat poured off her as if from a blast furnace, forcing Batman to keep his distance and shield himself with his cape. The bright light outshone all else, reflecting off what remained of the polished marble walls. Even with the filtered lenses in his cowl, it hurt his eyes to gaze upon her directly.

"You have to cool down!" he shouted over the crackling flames. "Can you do that?"

She shook her head. "I see only fire." Her voice crackled like a bonfire. "I bring only the inferno."

Just as Percy predicted. There was no way her fire could keep building at this rate without reaching some sort of explosive peak. *She's going critical.*

"Leave me!" She gestured toward the gaping hole in the floor. "The future needs you. Gotham needs the Bat…"

Batman refused to accept that the future was set in stone.

"Let me help you," he pleaded. "Maybe we can find a cure, some way to reverse what was done to you."

His mind chased after solutions. If he could get Lydia back into her sarcophagus, deprive her flames, of oxygen, that could serve as a stopgap until he could have her placed in cryogenic suspension. Victor Fries's singular experiments in bio-thermodynamics might help, or perhaps STAR Labs could be brought in to consult.

"No." Her eyes shifted from blue to blinding white as she peered into eternity. "I see Percy, waiting for me. Our future together is…"

Despite the increasingly unbearable heat, a chill ran down Batman's spine. Were her words just romantic delusion, or was she seeing beyond her own destruction?

"Leave!"

With that command she stalked toward him, the heat of her driving him back through the shattered remains of the Great Owl, toward the gap in the floor he had used for his escape months ago. White flames enveloped her, forcing him to avert his eyes. The burial chamber became an oven… no, a crematorium. His fireproof suit and cape began to smoke.

The Talon remained buried beneath the collapsed wall.

Was there a way to save him?

"I see you, Percy!" she exulted. "Our future is now." She flared up like an incendiary charge, her face and figure lost behind an expanding ball of white-hot fire that rushed at Batman, making his decision for him. He dove through the gap to escape an inferno foreseen a century ago.

●

Harbor House was in flames. The Court of Owl's property was built over the ruins of the Labyrinth, which was collapsing beneath it. Brick walls and sturdy timbers crashed into the depths.

Batman, Batgirl, and Joanna watched from a rooftop a safe distance away as the Gotham City Fire Department valiantly fought to contain the fire. From what Batman could tell, the fire-fighters were bringing it under control, although Harbor House was past saving—as were those left behind in the Labyrinth.

"I keep thinking there must be something else I could have done," Batman said as he watched the diminishing flames light up the night. His shoulders slumped beneath his cape. His hands were bandaged beneath his gloves. "There had to have been some way to save her."

"Lydia died more than a century ago," Batgirl said. She stood beside him as they contemplated the dying inferno—the culmination of the prediction they had been chasing for days and nights now. A portion of her cape was draped over Joanna to combat the chill night air. "Her fate was decided long before you or I were born. Her future was never in your hands."

Despite her efforts, Batman found little solace. "I can't accept that."

"You saved Joanna," she reminded him. "You foiled the Owls. You traced the Burning Sickness to that plasma center, shutting that down. No more innocent people are going to be used as test subjects, and with Vincent Wright gone, chances are the 'outbreaks' have been stamped out for good." She looked over at him. "Take the win, Batman."

He found it difficult to let go, thinking back to that first night in Professor Morse's office. So many people, both innocent and guilty, had been consumed by a fire that should have been extinguished long ago.

"If only I had put the pieces together sooner," he persisted.

"You can't see the future," Batgirl said. "None of us can, thank goodness."

Despite Percy's best efforts, Batman thought. The century-long quest for his elixir had yielded nothing but violence and tragedy. As with Cassandra, the lure of prophecy had doomed everyone it touched.

"I think you're right about that," he replied.

"Wouldn't be the first time," she said. "I may go by 'Oracle' some days, but actual precognition? That's a gift I wouldn't wish on my worst enemy."

A thunderous crash reached them as the last of Harbor House tumbled into the ground, sending up a new pillar of flames. Batman doubted that anything remained of the Labyrinth or those who had perished there. Even the bronze replica of Cassandra had surely melted to slag by now. The long-lost formula was gone, if it had ever truly existed.

Which was probably just as well.

40

"Oh, thank God, I was afraid I was never going to see you again!"

"You and me both!"

Reunited at last back at their apartment in the University District, Joanna and Claire hugged each other fiercely. Batman and Nightwing looked on as the roommates rejoiced in their mutual survival.

"I'm so sorry," Joanna said to her friend, tears welling up in her eyes. "I never meant to get you involved in any of this. I swear to God, I had no idea how dangerous it was."

"It's okay," Claire assured her. "I mean, it was utterly terrifying, but it's over now." She glanced over at Batman. "It *is* over, right?"

"I expect so," he said. "With Vincent Wright gone and his search for the elixir proven to be a costly wild goose chase, the Court of Owls has little incentive to pursue a matter that's already drawn too much unwanted attention. This was Wright's pet project and obsession."

The Grandmaster would have received a full report from Vincent's men on what had transpired in the Labyrinth. The Owls knew now that Percy's elusive formula had been bait for a deathtrap—one that had cost them Wright and two Talons. Through his underworld contacts, Batman would spread the word that all trace of the formula had been destroyed. That should make the Court as ready to close the books as he was.

Just in case, though, Bruce Wayne would quietly acquire the girls' apartment and gift it to them. Then he and Nightwing would outfit the place with a top-of-the-line security system.

"What about your thesis?" Nightwing asked, cradling a bandaged arm. He was still recovering from the injuries he'd sustained protecting Claire from the Talon, but had assured Batman that he'd be back in fighting form soon. "Are you still going forward with it?"

"Not a chance." She shook her head. "I'm not going to push my luck there, let alone risk provoking the Owls any further. Too many people have been hurt already." She dabbed at her eyes. "Let Percy and Lydia rest in peace. And Dennis."

Claire looked appalled. "But all of your work...?"

"It's fine," Joanna said. "I got the answers I was looking for. More than I bargained for, really. I just want to put this all behind me now. There's plenty of beautiful and inspiring art out there that's *not* linked to crimes and conspiracies. I think I want to study those instead."

"Good idea," Batman said. "Let sleeping Owls lie."

They were his problem, not hers.

•

"...today, the unseen was everything, the unknown the only real fact of life."

Bruce sipped a cup of herbal tea as he relaxed in the garden on the Wayne estate, leafing through an illustrated edition of *The Wind in the Willows*. It was a cool, clear afternoon, so he was perfectly comfortable in a sweater and slacks. He could have been training or studying down in the cave, prepping for wherever his mission took him next, but instead he had made time to enjoy his mother's favorite garden for the first time in decades.

Lydia Doyle, preserved in an idyllic moment of time as she reclined by the water's edge, kept him company.

"Penny for your thoughts, sir?" Alfred joined him in the garden, bearing a tray of cucumber sandwiches, which he set down on the marble bench. Bruce lifted his eyes from the book.

"Nothing in particular, Alfred, which is… refreshing."

"I can imagine," the butler said, lingering. "I must say it does my heart good to see you at ease here." He looked over the scene wistfully. "Brings back memories of simpler times, if you don't mind me saying so."

Bruce nodded. "I'd misplaced those memories, until recently." He regarded the sculpture of Lydia gracing the center of Percy's fountain. "Not that the past was ever truly as simple as we like to imagine it."

"Too true, Master Bruce." His gaze followed the younger man's. "I hope your newfound knowledge of Miss Doyle's tragic history will not sully your own cherished memories of this spot."

"I don't think so," Bruce replied. "I was afraid of that at first—that the Court of Owls had contaminated the past beyond redemption, tainting it irrevocably—but I've come to realize that is too narrow and defeatist a view. If this case has taught me anything, it's that the history of Gotham isn't just the history of the Owls and their victims. It's also the history of men and women fighting back against the Court, no matter the cost, and finding love and beauty in their lives, regardless of how dark the encroaching shadows might seem at times."

"A comforting sentiment, sir." Alfred took Bruce's empty tea cup from him. "One likes to think that Miss Doyle would agree."

"Look at her, Alfred," Bruce said. "That sculpture alone, which we owe to both Percy and Lydia, is proof that Gotham's past holds more than just crime and bloodshed. Peace and grace can also be found there, and endure for generations to come, long after the sins of the past are dead and buried."

"And Gotham's future, sir?"

"That's up to us to carve out, as best as we can, in hopes of achieving something good and lasting."

"As did your own parents, if I may be so bold," Alfred said. "In any event, I'll leave you to your reading… and your memories."

"Thank you, Alfred."

The butler departed, leaving Bruce alone with "Miss Gotham." A passing cloud dimmed the light illuminating the statue, casting it in a more melancholy hue. Bruce's face took on Batman's grimly resolute profile as his memory superimposed Lydia's blazing final moments on the lovely visage of the fountain sculpture. He meant what he had said to Alfred, about finding hope in the art and elegance Lydia and Percy had bestowed. Yet he hadn't forgotten their tragic fate—or the unfinished business before him.

You'll outlast the Court of Owls, Lydia. You have my promise.

•

"Report," the Grandmaster said.

An emergency meeting of the Court had been convened in the wake of Vincent Wright's disastrous return to the Labyrinth. To guarantee their privacy, the meeting was being held in a forgotten bomb shelter that had been gathering dust since the end of the Cold War, on a night when Bruce Wayne was known to be hosting a charity benefit on the other side of town.

As was custom, the bunker had been swept—twice—for any concealed electronic surveillance devices. Only the highest-ranking members of the Court were in attendance, which suited the Grandmaster just fine.

"Efforts are already underway to ensure that none of Vincent Wright's illicit activities can be traced back to us," a masked man said. "His estate and properties will be transferred through a number of proxies and cut-outs, and will end up in our hands. As instructed, we have divested ourselves of any interest in his pharmaceutical enterprises, which are currently under investigation by the authorities. Our contacts in law-enforcement will see to it that our name stays out of the reports."

"Good," the Grandmaster said. "Proceed along those lines, with the utmost discretion."

In truth, there was a silver lining here. Vincent Wright had been taken off the playing field and could no longer challenge her control of the Court. It was probably just as well that his family's obsessive search for Percy Wright's lost elixir could finally be terminated. That quixotic quest had consumed enough of the Court's time and resources over the last century. It was time to move on to new challenges and opportunities.

Percy's elixir would have been a valuable asset, to be sure, but the Court of Owls had managed to reign over Gotham for centuries without it. They could do the same in the future. As long as their secrets were safe, Gotham was theirs and always would be.

Regardless of the Batman.

ACKNOWLEDGMENTS

Batman has his Bat-Family and other allies watching his back. He would not be able to protect Gotham without the aid of Alfred, Commissioner Gordon, Batgirl, and so many other invaluable team players. In the same way, this book would not have been possible without the generous support and assistance of my own allies. Many thanks are due to:

My editor, Steve Saffel, and the rest of the team at Titan Books, for waiting patiently for this book while I moved—twice—from one home to another. Special thanks to Nick Landau, Vivian Cheung, Sam Matthews, and Natasha MacKenzie.

Scott Snyder and Greg Capullo for creating the Court of Owls in the first place and giving me such great material to work with. Josh Anderson, Amy Weingartner, and everyone at Warner Bros. and DC Comics for providing me with plenty of encouragement and inspiration.

My agent, Russ Galen, for deftly handling the business end of things.

And, as ever, Karen and our cat Sophie for giving me plenty of support on the home front, while patiently listening to me babble on about Batman for days and weeks on end.

ABOUT THE AUTHOR

GREG COX is the *New York Times* bestselling author of numerous books and short stories, including the official movie novelizations of *The Dark Knight Rises*, *Man of Steel*, *Godzilla*, *War for the Planet of the Apes*, *Ghost Rider*, *Daredevil*, and the first three *Underworld* movies. He has also written books and stories based on such popular series as *Alias*, *Buffy the Vampire Slayer*, *CSI: Crime Scene Investigation*, *Farscape*, *The 4400*, *The Green Hornet*, *The Librarians*, *Roswell*, *Star Trek*, *Warehouse 13*, *Xena: Warrior Princess*, and *Zorro*.

He has received three Scribe Awards from the International Association of Media Tie-In Writers as well as the Grandmaster Award for Life Achievement. He lives in Lancaster, Pennsylvania.

Visit him at: www.gregcox-author.com.

Beware the Court of Owls that watches all the time.
Ruling Gotham from a shadowed perch, behind granite and lime.
They watch you at your hearth, they watch you at your bed.
Speak not a whispered word of them, or they'll send the Talon for your head!